YOU ARE THE JOURNEY

A NOVEL

A. R. RÊVE

A.R. RÊVE STUDIO

You Are The Journey is a work of fiction. Names, characters, places, and incidents are the products of the author's imagination or are used fictitiously. Any resemblance to actual events, locales, or persons, living or dead, is entirely coincidental.

No part of this book may be reproduced, stored in a retrieval system, or transmitted in any form or by any means, electronic, mechanical, photocopying, recording, or otherwise, without express written permission of the publisher.

Published by A.R. Rêve Studio
areve.studio@gmail.com

To everyone who's ever felt lost

PART 1

NEW YORK

1

"SOPH, WAKE UP... SOPHIE!"

"What? Are you serious? My head is pounding..."

"Well, I may not be serious, but the time certainly is."

The girl with red hair, tied up in a bun, stood over the bed, holding a phone.

"Seriously? It's noon already?"

"I'm afraid so."

"Mum, the tablet ran out of battery," a child's voice called from another room.

"What's Mia doing here? Oh, damn, is it Monday today?"

"Relax, it's Sunday. Kevin brought her a day early, the idiot."

"Emily, keep it down. She can hear you..."

Emily collapsed onto the bed, landing on her friend's feet, emitting a quiet groan.

"What did we drink last night? I need to know if I should head straight to the hospital."

"It was tequila. Why did we think that was a good idea after everything?"

"My head hurts so much, I can't even remember what year it is."

Sophie propped herself up on her elbows, her head in her hands, her hair tangling between her fingers. "This mess can't wait. Okay, Em, I have to go."

"So you'll spend the day freshening up, and I'll entertain the little one."

"Sorry, I need to prepare for that interview."

"I'm pretty sure you're overthinking it…"

"I need to know everything inside out."

"Well, Iron Lady, go conquer the world."

Sophie moved closer to Emily, giving her a light peck on the blushing cheek. Emily pulled her into a hug, then back onto the bed.

"Wait! Traditional bets... Sophie Lind bets that…"

"He won't call."

"And I bet he will."

"I won't answer, and you'll be the one buying lunch."

"Now get outta here, you cheeky bugger."

Sophie extricated herself from Emily's embrace and the pile of blankets, not without receiving a playful smack from Emily.

In the living room, Sophie found Emily's daughter sitting on the couch, intently poking at a tablet. She kissed the top of the girl's head.

"Did you have fun with daddy, Mia?"

"Yes, but he wouldn't buy me a pony."

"Maybe he's planning a birthday surprise for you?"

"Soph, don't start!" came Emily's chiding voice from the bedroom.

"Let's be a bit gentler with mom today, okay?"

"Okay." Mia bumped her fist against Sophie's.

"How about Six Flags next weekend?" Mia nodded in response, her eyes still glued to the tablet.

"Love you, baby!"

"Love you too," Mia mumbled.

Stepping onto the road, Sophie barely raised her hand before a taxi pulled up. She slumped into the back seat, clutching her bag and low-heeled shoes, her head throbbing relentlessly. Despite her efforts to hide it, excitement for tomorrow seeped through her clenched lips.

"Home. I mean, 415 W 24th, thanks."

2

ALTHOUGH THE SUN HAD NOT YET RISEN OVER THE HORIZON, crowds of people in sportswear were already running in Battery Park City. The breeze of a late summer morning was filled with freshness. Two young men jogged side by side, deep in conversation.

"At two-tenths, how is that even possible?"

"It's cryptocurrency. It took a dive - probably involved bribing some heavyweight."

"What's your next move?"

"Now's the best time to buy."

Approaching with a light jog, a young woman caught their attention. She wore a wide belt around her waist, from which a leash extended to a spaniel trotting beside her. The dog, with its well-groomed coat, adorable black eyes, and charming face, mirrored its owner's appeal. The woman, a petite blonde with a slender build, glanced at Nick and offered a shy smile as she passed.

"Dude, she's been eyeing you for a week."

"I've noticed, but I'm not interested."

"I see. You're not...?"

"No," Nick grinned, his dimples deepening.

"Maybe that's why you've stuck by me for a year."

"I run with you because we sync up well — same pace, same schedule. And after a year, I've learned enough about cryptocurrency to hold a conversation and trade on my own."

"Reach out when you're done with the books."

"Sure," Nick said, checking his black Hanowa watch. "And if you're into her, why not ask her out?"

"Nah, that's a no-go. She was all about you. It'd be like enduring a disappointing season of your favorite show — a total letdown."

"Your call. I've got to head out early today."

They shook hands and parted ways. Slowing his pace as he approached his building, Nick entered his apartment, drenched in sweat. He kicked off his sneakers with practiced ease and headed straight to the bathroom, leaving a trail of damp clothing in his wake. Fifteen minutes later, he emerged, toweling off his hair, water droplets tracing paths down his skin. He moved to his dresser, where his phone lay, and pressed the voicemail button. A sharp, deep voice filled the room.

"Nick, I'm running late. Grab the usual for me."

"As always, Dad," Nick responded aloud.

3

AT SIX IN THE MORNING, WITH THE SUNLIGHT ALREADY CASTING ITS glow, Sophie begrudgingly opened an eye. She was grateful for the day's early light; waking up in darkness was never her preference. Today held significant weight, an interview she couldn't afford to falter in. Understanding the importance, she was poised to give it her all.

In her bathroom, she wiped away the mirror's condensation to reveal a lineup of cosmetics and skincare products. Each bottle promised a solution — hair mousse, lotion, conditioner, face mask, and an array of creams. When her gaze landed on a tiny bottle labeled 'anti-aging,' she scoffed, placing it back on the shelf.

"It's not that dire," she told her reflection, her spirits buoyed by the day's prospects. Yet, the reality of nearing thirty cast a shadow over her morning enthusiasm. With a resigned smile, she reached for her skincare arsenal.

Sophie didn't rely heavily on cosmetics; her natural allure was merely enhanced by her confidence, excellent posture, and innate charm. Beneath her poised exterior burned a fierce curiosity and a relentless drive. Though her choices might seem erratic at times, her focus was singular — keep moving forward and find satisfaction in her achievements, even if fleeting. Her work capacity was immense, often achieving in a month what took others half a year. She never stopped to ponder her exhaustion or question the correctness of her path.

Sophie's world was one of ceaseless effort, fueled by passion and new connections while navigating the obligatory family gatherings with dread. Only a few close to her — her sister, a childhood friend Emily, and little Mia, whom she doted on like a daughter — truly fulfilled her emotional needs.

Strapping on her watch, Sophie checked the time, finding herself perfectly on schedule. The concept of tardiness was foreign to her. With the interview at 9:00, she had enough time for her ritualistic morning coffee. She preferred it black, no milk, no sugar. A cherished tradition she wouldn't compromise.

Arriving at Art & Culture New York at 8:45, Sophie exited the taxi with grace. She had no need to rush. Her punctuality, a trait she took pride in, often left her with time to spare — a concept that irritated some but suited her just fine. She took a moment to admire the building's signage. Art & Culture New York was a leader in the art market, known not just for logistics and legal matters but also for investing in cultural ventures. Yet, beyond their services, this organization held a special place in the hearts of the tight-knit art enthusiast community. They dedicated a significant portion of their resources to nurturing and supporting local creative communities. Sophie sighed, momentarily feeling a twinge of envy; this was precisely what she had once aspired to create. And it seemed like she had all the tools to start. So, when had everything changed? Why had she stopped pursuing her dreams?

Entering the building, Sophie approached the reception, offering a warm smile to the receptionist. She waited patiently to be addressed first.

"Good morning! How can I help you?" The receptionist, with her hair neatly arranged and sporting the company's signature neck scarf, spoke politely and softly, trying her best not to scrutinize Sophie from head to toe. She briefly glanced at her computer but, realizing it might be considered rude, quickly became flustered.

"Sophie Lind. I have an interview scheduled with Mr. Kinkade."

The receptionist checked the information on her computer. "This is your final interview, right?"

"Yes, I've already been to your HR department."

"Please, have a seat. I'll call for you."

Sophie sat in the chair, resting one hand on the armrest. She fought the urge to open her laptop, a constant companion, and check her schedule for the day. Her workload was always invariably heavy.

"Miss Lind, please follow me."

Walking down the hall, Sophie smiled and started a casual conversation.

"Any advice for me?"

Her companion slightly flinched, as if she were abruptly pulled out of her train of thought. "I wish you luck, Miss Lind," she mumbled shyly.

Sophie felt irritated. The girls working here took corporate etiquette too seriously, making them appear intimidated. "I won't stay here long anyway; fortunately, I never planned to," Sophie thought. They reached the elevator. There was silence, seemingly by mutual consent. Twenty floors later, they found themselves in a spacious office with panoramic window walls. The view was quite nice. It overlooked the Hudson River and the Hoboken Waterfront with a small clock tower of the old Lackawanna Railroad Terminal.

"Sophie Lind, sir. For the position of Senior Manager in the Logistics Department."

"Thank you, Zoe. Please, have a seat, Miss Lind."

The office held three men, each embodying a different presence. One sat in a chair positioned nearly at the center of the room, facing the window, while another chair on the opposite side was reserved for the interviewee. Although Sophie could only see his back, the authoritative timbre of his voice left no doubt about his decision-making authority.

Another man occupied a couch against the wall, lounging comfortably with one leg crossed over the other. His relaxed posture and the way his gaze leisurely traveled from Sophie's head to toe made it clear he was unburdened by urgent tasks. The third man stood near the window, his back to the room. He wore a navy blue suit of impeccable tailoring, highlighting his broad shoulders and trim figure. His right hand casually slipped into his pocket, revealing the crisp white cuff of his shirt and a cufflink engraved with the initials "N.D." He remained motionless, appearing reluctant to face the others.

Sophie approached and seated herself, her demeanor calm and composed. Her cream-colored pencil skirt naturally encouraged her knees together, leaving her only to elegantly angle her legs to the side.

"Pleasure to meet you, Mr. Kinkade," her velvety voice sounded.

"Likewise," he glanced down, then looked at the man on the couch, "Don't mind them, Miss Lind. These are my guests. Well," he gestured, locking his hands at his stomach, the slightly rounded figure creating a special place for such a gesture, "What brought you to us?"

"The name Art & Culture New York and the opportunities it presented."

"So, you're ambitious," he said, his tone tinged with a hint of contempt. He reached for a piece of paper in front of him, left by his assistant, and quickly scanned it.

Sophie maintained her composure, having learned long ago not to take others' arrogance personally. Here, she wasn't the boss, but she was an excellent actress. She played the role and genuinely believed in it. She didn't even need to lie because people heard what they wanted to hear.

"Graduate of Goldsmiths. And where are you from?" the man didn't take his eyes off the paper.

"From London."

"That's interesting; your accent is barely noticeable. What prompted you to make the journey across the ocean?"

"Aspiring to be a cross-cultural specialist."

"A commendable path you've chosen, although not the easiest. Tell me, why did you opt for the logistics direction?"

"I have prior experience at Sotheby's in their logistics department. My knowledge of cost reduction strategies and attention to detail qualify me for this role."

"Don't get me wrong, you don't strike me as someone aiming for the position you want to take. Perhaps you'd be a better fit in the PR department. But alright, I'm willing..."

His words were cut short by an interruption. Sophie sensed a presence behind her. In the next moment, she saw a hand with a cufflink reaching decisively across the table towards her interviewer. Mr. Kinkade's face briefly lit up with friendliness. He shook hands with the young man, giving a slight nod.

"Take care, Nick. Give it some thought."

A man named Nick, whose last name began with 'D,' silently made his way to the door. For a fleeting moment, Sophie caught a glimpse of his profile before he exited. She redirected her focus to her hands, sensing her concentration waver. Fortunately, the interview didn't drag on much longer. The remaining discussion revolved around formal details. Mr. Kinkade, her future boss, coldly bid her farewell. As the door clicked shut behind Sophie, a new voice echoed through the room.

"Seriously? It sounds like you're just trying to give HR something to do. They'll be too distracted by her to focus on logistics..." It seemed like this remark came from the man on the couch.

"Bill, not everyone is as captivated by female beauty as you. Pick your jaw up, you old lech. Moreover, this country has progressed; we're now aware of something called sexism," retorted Kinkade.

"Have it your way."

Sophie smiled. The job was hers. The HR department offered her to start tomorrow. Exiting the building, she settled in the nearest coffee shop. Opening her laptop, she immediately logged into Zoom and pressed the call button.

"Bethany, what's on the agenda for today?" Slipping on her headphones, she said, "The next month will be hectic, so please keep me updated if you're feeling overwhelmed."

4

SOPHIE'S FAVORITE HAUNT WAS THIS COZY, DIMLY LIT BAR, ITS WELL-worn furniture echoing the charm of an old American pub. The soft lighting intentionally concealed the wear and tear of the furnishings, but Sophie adored it for the authentic people who frequented the place. It wasn't a typical upscale bar where you needed to dress up or pretend to be someone you're not.

Located in Greenwich Village, just a couple of blocks south of Washington Square Park, this hidden gem wasn't widely known. It mainly attracted blues enthusiasts because a live blues band performed on weekends, and during the week, the bar was pleasantly quiet.

Sophie and her companion sat at the bar, each with a martini glass in hand. The bartender, treating them like old friends, engaged in occasional conversations. At a glance, the two women seemed similar in height, build, and even their choice of clothing colors. Yet, upon closer scrutiny, their differences became more apparent.

"So, any amusing tales from the new job? I'm all ears for a juicy story or two."

"It's kind of hard to call it a job, really. My guys in advertising manage to cram more work into a day than these folks do in a week. But the department employees seem to be bowled over by my enthusiasm to grasp all the nitty-gritty," Sophie chuckled. "I've even had a couple of dates thanks to it. It's been a crazy busy month."

"Do you regret taking it on?" Natalie asked.

"No, not at all. It's better to get the full picture from the inside. I know very little about the rules that govern the local market. Besides, I've got just one shot at getting into that project I embarked on all this for."

"Sorry," Natalie leaned in, covering Sophie's wrist with her hand, "But that guy at the table by the wall has been giving you the intense stare, and he's not being subtle about it."

"Maybe he's seen me here before."

"Dark brown hair, the look of a person who's seen infinity, doesn't ring a bell?"

Sophie laughed, catching the bartender's attention.

"No, he's practically stealing my seat!" Natalie persisted, "But honestly, darling, I really need to dash. The martini is calling my name. I hope ten minutes will be enough," she added with a sigh as she dismounted from the high barstool.

Even to an onlooker, the stark contrast between the two was unmistakable. Natalie, a couple of years older than Sophie, dressed with less flair and moved with a certain awkwardness, using broad gestures. Yet, her eyes radiated an inner composure. She exuded a sense of contentment with her identity, and her intense gaze seemed to convey, 'You're enough just as you are.'

In under a minute, the man described by Natalie approached Sophie. She dipped her head and smiled slightly, only turning toward him once she heard his voice.

"Excuse me, but I feel like we've met."

A tall man in dark jeans and an unzipped burgundy sweater stood before Sophie, his presence commanding yet casual. On initial inspection, he seemed to be in his early thirties, but determining the age of such individuals at a glance was always a challenge due to their contradictory appearance. He possessed a well-built physique, clearly maintaining good physical shape and well-groomed skin that reflected a healthy lifestyle. Attractive features and a lack of wrinkles suggested youth, yet his choice of high-quality clothing without ostentatious logos and the confident demeanor of someone not inclined toward idle chatter hinted at an age beyond thirty.

"I don't think so," Sophie replied in a friendly tone, yet with a hint of cold politeness.

"My memory doesn't usually fail me. I'm Nick," he extended his hand. Sophie shook it lightly.

"I don't recall meeting you, Nick. I'm Sophie Lind."

"Well then, nice to meet you, Sophie," he smiled, revealing a row of perfectly white teeth, the kind only Americans seem to have.

"Likewise. I've been coming here for a while, but haven't seen you before. This place doesn't get random visitors."

"I've been coming here for a while too. I think it's the dim atmosphere. They only light up the bar and the tables slightly, enough to see your companion and of course, the bartender."

He slightly raised his hand above the bar counter, catching the bartender's attention. He turned away from Sophie to place an order. For a moment, she recognized that profile.

"You have an exceptional memory, Nick. We're not acquainted, but we've seen each other once before," Sophie said. "Your last name starts with D."

Nick frowned slightly, quickly overcoming his confusion. "Strange way we met, Sophie."

"But there was no 'meeting' per se. You were standing by the window. The sleeve of your jacket was raised, showing your cufflinks. Then you said goodbye to Mr. Kinkade and left. That was about a month ago."

"But you couldn't have been there. Bill and I came in, then there was some intern...," he mumbled the last word. His eyes widened in

15

surprise; it seemed that people rarely surprised him. He stared at Sophie, who was sitting in front of him.

"Intern? That was me," Sophie said, her smile tinged with amusement.

"I apologize. You don't look like an intern at all."

"Well, looks can be deceiving, Mr…?" she intoned questioningly.

"Davidson." He smiled at her.

"Well, Mr. Davidson, my knowledge about you is growing remarkably fast."

"I would have never…"

At that moment, Natalie approached the bar, interrupting Nick in mid-sentence. "I hope you haven't just arrived because I've been waiting in the loo for ages," Natalie said, plopping back into her seat.

"I apologize. Let me get you some drinks," Nick gracefully made another gesture with his hand, as if he did it multiple times a day.

"That's very kind of you!" Natalie replied.

"Nat, it's time for us to go," Sophie looked at her, feeling a bit awkward.

"Oh, yes, I'm sorry. She always does this when someone tries to take her number, but now we indeed have to leave." Natalie shrugged, looking apologetically at Nick.

"It was nice to meet you, fully," Sophie smiled with a radiant smile. For a moment, Nick felt as though she was busy with her own life and didn't care about someone with absurd memories. She just wanted to get back to her business. It stung him a little, as he wasn't used to such reactions from women.

"Have a pleasant evening!" Nick managed to say before his new acquaintances were already heading towards the exit.

Nick's gaze lingered on Sophie's sparkling hair until she vanished through the entrance. Suddenly, he felt the urge to do something to catch her attention, something to distract her from her life and make her look at him. This unfamiliar, compelling desire baffled him. He stood by the bar counter, feeling an electric current pulse through his veins.

"Do you know him?" Natalie asked once they stepped outside.

"Not really. Saw him fleetingly at Art & Culture. No idea who he is."

"And already dreaming about having sex with him?"

"What? Natalie," Sophie rolled her eyes as if she knew what would follow.

"Well, he fits your type. Cold, polite, and emotionally detached during the conversation. Those are right up your alley. Behind this Downton Abbey mask could be hiding anything. And for the time being, it's an adventure for you."

"Out of all the sisters in the world, I had to get the psychotherapist, didn't I?"

"Practicing psychotherapist. I can prescribe you some pills, so you'd be more compliant with the guys you like."

"What do you mean 'compliant'? He didn't even ask for my number."

"Ah, I see, you were expecting it. Well, maybe he would have asked if you hadn't bolted from the spot like a wounded deer."

"Stop it! Firstly, we're late. Secondly, you know I'm not interested in any strangers."

"Oh, dear. It doesn't quite work like that," Natalie said, shaking her head with a knowing smile.

She didn't argue further with her little sister since she was right about one thing. They were indeed running late.

5

NICK FOUND SOLACE IN A SECLUDED BAR, HIS GO-TO REFUGE ON FREE evenings, assured of solitude amidst the crowd. He was sure he wouldn't encounter anyone he knew here. The other visitors didn't interest him; he never observed them or made acquaintances in this place. It was his time to be alone with himself.

After ordering whiskey, he comfortably settled at a distant table with his laptop. Immersed in his sole purpose for being there, Nick didn't notice how much time had passed. Lost in thought, he absentmindedly glanced around the room. Suddenly, a fleeting glimpse caught his attention behind the bar counter — a woman's hair, catching the dim light, captured his gaze. The bar's poor lighting made him strain his eyes to see. In the center of the bar counter, sat a girl with long locks that slightly bounced whenever she laughed. For a moment, he thought he heard the sound of her laughter, even though it seemed impossible with the distance that separated them.

Nick continued to look at her until she turned around. Her gaze wandered around the room, not focusing on anything. She turned back to her companion. In those brief seconds, time seemed to stretch, marking changes that would last a lifetime. This feeling stays forever, akin to a lightning strike — an immense surge of electricity running through the veins, shattering the familiar perception of the world. Nick took a deep breath. He didn't feel his body or hear the surrounding sounds. If someone were to ask him later what was happening around him, he wouldn't be able to recall. At that moment, his entire world was focused on this person — an absolute stranger. The only thing he knew was that she was a woman. She turned around again, and this time, a strong sense of familiarity washed over him. But he couldn't remember where he might have seen her before. Her companion got up and left. Nick felt both agitation and concern. Surprisingly, these feelings combined with his resolute actions. He stood up and headed towards her. His insides tightened.

"Excuse me, I think we've met before."

Instead of words, her smile responded, brightening the dimly lit room as she regarded him with eyes wide in recognition.

"Of course! Where have you been all this time?"

"But I can't recall where we met!"

She laughed. Nick tried to find the right words to convince her to stay. It was crucial that she stayed, but he stumbled... and woke up in the darkness of his bedroom.

He looked at the clock. Five in the morning. He didn't need to get up so early at the end of the week, but sleep eluded him. Before heading to the office, he contemplated a detour to Art & Culture. As he entered the building, he was immediately greeted by a receptionist. Her eyes sparkled at the sight of him, a reaction Nick never appreciated. He found that such an intense glimmer in women's eyes clouded his ability to see their true selves.

"Good morning, Mr. Davidson. How can I help you?"

"Good morning," he briefly glanced at her and then looked away, "Could you please remind me which floor your HR department is on?"

"The fifteenth floor, Mr. Davidson."

"Thank you!"

Nick walked over to the elevator. He didn't encounter anyone he knew, and to his surprise, he felt relieved. Arriving at his destination, he intentionally bypassed the department head's office and stopped at the desk with the sign 'Junior Assistant. Anne Young.'

"Good morning!" he smiled. "I'm sorry to interrupt your work."

"Good morning!" The girl with chubby cheeks looked up at Nick. "It's okay, I haven't started yet."

"Anne, can I ask you for a favor? I need some information about your employee, Sophie Lind, working in your logistics department."

"She was with us, but she quit yesterday. She didn't provide any specific reasons for leaving though."

"That's odd," Nick frowned. "Could you share her contact number with me?"

"Sorry, I'm not allowed to disclose personal information about our employees, even former ones."

"And if I ask you on behalf of Mr. Kinkade?" Nick approached her desk.

"I'm sorry, sir. Company policy prohibits me from disclosing our employees' data."

With a sigh of understanding, Nick leaned in, hoping for empathy. "How about if I invite you for a coffee during lunchtime, you won't be at your workplace."

"I'm sorry," the girl smiled sweetly, raising her eyebrows, "I could lose my job."

"Sure, I understand."

Nick bid farewell politely and left. A whirlwind of thoughts clouded his mind, yet a clear path forward eluded him. He decided to head to his office and have breakfast at the café on the first floor, as he had done for several years.

Upon reaching the twenty-fifth floor, he strolled down the hallway, and at its center, the Puzzle Publisher's logo glinted. His office was situated here, along with the editor-in-chief's, financial director's, and general manager's offices. Nick stepped into his office, realizing his assistant had yet to arrive. He opened his laptop, promptly delving into his tasks, and time slipped away unnoticed until noon when a female voice from the intercom jolted him back to reality.

"Mr. Davidson, Mr. Greg Davidson is on the line."

"Connect us."

"Nick," a sharp, deep voice sounded, "Yesterday, my lawyer prepared all the documents. You can proceed."

"Thank you, dad."

"Schedule a meeting with Paul, discuss all the details. He won't cause any problems."

"Alright."

Silence hung in the air. Nick didn't know what else to discuss if all work-related matters were settled.

"See you on Sunday, son."

"See you Sunday!"

His father hung up. Nick sighed. He didn't want to dwell on the question that had been bothering him for a while. So, he closed his eyes and laced his hands behind his head. After turning his swivel chair 180 degrees, he reopened his eyes, facing a model of a building's firewall across the street. Lost in thought, he vividly conjured the girl from the bar, painstakingly recreating her image from memory. In a typical state, this might appear obsessive, but not now. Instead, Nick couldn't imagine how he had lived without this incredible sense of engagement. It made the world so vibrant and colorful, so... complete.

He pressed the intercom again.

"Lindsay, schedule a meeting with Paul Stowell for next week. Check his availability."

"Sure, Mr. Davidson. Where would you like to have the meeting?"

"In our office."

6

THE DOORMAN GRACIOUSLY OPENED THE DOORS, NODDING courteously. Sophie approached the hostess and inquired about the person she was meeting. Guided by the hostess, Sophie was led to a table where a slightly overweight middle-aged man sat, his receding hairline prominent. He tried to compensate for his less-than-charming appearance with extravagant manners, a condescending tone, and selecting opulent restaurants for his meetings. Upon seeing Sophie, his face broke into an overly confident smile, as if the presence of beautiful women entitled him to their company.

"Good evening, Sophie!" he stood, greeting her warmly.

"Good evening, Mr. Stowell," she replied, extending her hand.

"I've ordered an aperitif. Would you like one?"

"Neither of us needs it, believe me," she quipped, injecting humor into the conversation.

"Go ahead, order your usual. We have a business dinner on Monday; treat yourself."

"Or maybe we should be tougher on ourselves," Sophie mused silently.

After placing their orders, Sophie steered the conversation. She knew it could easily veer off course otherwise. The arrival of the aperitif signaled a need for caution.

"I'm genuinely impressed with your idea and would love to be part of this project," she began.

Paul, attempting to seem more integral than he was, masked the fact that the idea wasn't his. Sophie didn't know much, so he had the opportunity to appear more significant in her eyes.

"Well, the concept of a free port isn't new."

"But branding it, rather than just offering tax exemptions, is innovative."

"Our free port focuses on art - paintings, sculptures, antiques. Our clients value not just tax savings but also the security of their investments. What we need is..."

"A strong PR campaign," Sophie interjected.

"Exactly, and clients who trust us."

"That's why I'm here, Mr. Stowell."

"Please, call me Paul," he replied, sipping his vodka martini.

"Paul, I've built an extensive network in the art industry. People who would find such services invaluable. I wonder..." She paused, glancing at his hands. "What are your long-term plans for the company? It seems like you aim to expand beyond just a free port."

Paul cut her off, "I appreciate your ambition, Sophie, but let's focus on our immediate objectives. You and your friends from Sotheby's should know that our streamlined documentation process will simplify the experience for our clients."

"Understood. Can we discuss my role?"

"Please, go ahead."

"I aim to lead the PR for the initial campaign and any future ones, should you expand."

"You've got quite an appetite."

"I'm just getting started," she replied, her smile sharp with sarcasm.

Their conversation shifted to the specifics of the deal. Sophie noted Paul's evasion on certain details, but she wasn't deterred. She was perfect for this project. She tried to hide her disappointment over his unwillingness to share more about the future of the company. Despite his guarded stance, she saw through his intent to leverage her connections.

As dinner concluded, Paul offered Sophie a ride home since his driver was waiting. Along the way, they spoke of work, and with feigned indifference, Paul leaned back and said: "I admire your persistence. I believe the only worthwhile relationships are with a woman like you."

"Oh, here we go... As if you're interested in a relationship," Sophie inwardly rolled her eyes. Aware of how sensitive men like Paul could be to rejection, she tactfully navigated the conversation.

"How about having dinner at the end of the week?" he said, giving her a pointed look.

"I'd be delighted, Mr... Paul. It'll be a perfect time to finalize some agreements."

Fortunately for Sophie, they were already arriving at her place. She exited the car gracefully, eager to escape despite her outward calm.

7

A FEW DAYS LATER, PAUL RECEIVED A CALL FROM NICK DAVIDSON'S assistant, arranging a meeting at the Puzzle Publisher's office. Although prepared, Paul felt a distinct lack of enthusiasm for this encounter. Upon seeing Nick, he was confronted with the very sentiment he loathed: disdain for another person. The mere acknowledgment of hate was distasteful to him. Despite a fifteen-year age gap, both hailing from the same ethnic background and city, Paul and Nick might as well have been from different worlds.

Admitting to being outclassed was hard enough, but realizing he could never emulate Nick's success was unbearable for Paul. Success seemed to be an innate trait in Nick, something Paul knew he couldn't cultivate within himself. Nick was indifferent to others' opinions of him. He was dedicated to his work, which he clearly loved, guided by an unfailing intuition. He treated everyone as equals and always secured the best position for himself. In contrast, Paul was deeply concerned about his image. His life revolved around proving his worth to himself and others, consuming almost all his energy. This included climbing the corporate ladder, engaging in shallow relationships, fearing subordinates, and anything else that would bolster his image as a mediocre, predictable upstart. Yet, despite his shortcomings, Paul's adeptness in project management was undeniable, a skill that had him seated across from Nick.

A table set for two awaited Paul. Nick gestured for him to sit.

"No rest for the weary, Mr. Stowell? Can't even grab a bite in peace," Nick quipped, reaching for a napkin.

"I'm more than happy to join you," Paul replied, his unease palpable as he reached for some water.

"I'll be upfront; our meetings will be infrequent, no more than once a month, and they'll be with me, not my father, as you've deduced."

"As you wish, Mr. Davidson."

"I'll remain hands-off unless necessary. I just need the project to function smoothly. You're capable of that."

"Thank you!" Paul momentarily brightened at the compliment. "We've already made significant progress. The foreman informed me we're close to finishing the construction. I've also secured someone for our first clients and to lead the PR campaign…"

"And who is this person?"

"A remarkable woman," Paul recalled Sophie with an involuntary smile, "She runs her own advertising agency, highly regarded. She's well-connected, especially with Sotheby's. She's resourceful, undeterred by the finer legalities of our operations. She's seeking a modest share but insists on being the lead PR agent for the initial free port and any that follow."

"Sotheby's, huh? That's ambitious."

"You'd be impressed," Paul's enthusiasm was evident, "She's quite striking…"

Paul was poised to continue, but Nick, familiar with his penchant for digression, would typically cut him off. However, this time, his intuition urged silence.

"What did you say her name was?"

"Sophie Lind. We met through a mutual contact from BBDO."

"Interesting coincidence," Nick mused, leaning back, "It seems, Mr. Stowell, our plans may need adjusting."

8

THE DAY SOPHIE LIND HAD AGREED TO DINE WITH PAUL STOWELL had arrived, a Friday she approached with the detachment of a business necessity. Yet, from the moment she awoke, something felt amiss.

By noon, her phone chimed with an unexpected message from Paul, its contents leaving her confused. The tone was uncharacteristically formal, almost apologetic.

"Miss Lind, I regret to inform you that tonight's dinner must be canceled. Furthermore, adjustments to our agreement are necessary due to the emergence of another candidate for your role. To put it plainly, I offer you to share responsibility with him," Paul's voice wavered slightly, "He's a former colleague of mine, Nick Davidson, a reputable figure in the publishing industry. I encourage you to meet and discuss the possibility of collaboration."

"The guy from the bar?" Sophie, clearly confused, spoke louder than intended.

She was unsure of her next steps. According to Stowell's message, she was expected to meet with Nick that evening instead of him. Sophie raised an eyebrow in bewilderment. To her, all of this felt like a strange coincidence. She wasn't fond of surprises, although she felt relieved to escape the advances from this clueless Paul.

However, her expectations went unmet, and no meeting was scheduled for her that day. As evening approached, she received an email from Nick, inviting her to breakfast the following morning.

Resolved to maintain her poise, Sophie met the new day with a composed stride into the café located within the Puzzle Publisher's building, a spot Nick frequented each morning. There was no hostess present. Before she had a chance to look around, a man dressed in a dark blue suit and a tie, secured with a classic silver clip, approached her. She walked calmly towards him.

"Good morning!" He greeted her with a genial smile.

"Good morning, Mr…?"

"Davidson."

"How could I forget?"

"Well, life persistently brings us together, Miss Lind."

Seated, Sophie noted Nick's coffee, already half-enjoyed.

"Do you want anything?" he inquired.

"Just coffee, black," she replied, prompting Nick to order with a familiar gesture that didn't escape Sophie's notice.

"So, it seems we're to work together…" Nick began, only for Sophie to interject with evident surprise.

"Imagine my surprise!"

"Equally surprising for me. You're in logistics, right?" Nick queried, his amusement clear.

"And how did you end up here? Is the paper out of the country?"

A grin spread across Nick's face. He hadn't expected such pushback; her sarcasm was surprisingly charming. Sophie stared back at him.

"Well, I've heard rumors that you left without explanations. Did you find out everything you needed to?"

"I didn't steal the intermediary database, if that's what you're insinuating."

"I'm not insinuating anything. I'm being straightforward. Like it or not, we're going to have to work together."

"Excuse me, may I speak frankly? I don't know where you came from, but clearly, you lack any real experience in this field. Why don't you stick to what you actually know how to do?"

They exchanged glances. Feeling uncomfortable under his gaze, Sophie started to reach towards her earlobe but then pulled back and crossed her arms. He couldn't help but smile to himself, finding her habit endearing.

"You strike me as intelligent, Miss Lind. Together, we can achieve mutual benefits."

"And you give the impression of a guy who's swiping left — not particularly interested in getting to know women, finding them too impersonal."

Nick let out a loud "whoa."

"I assure you, you'll take back those words."

"I doubt it. Nevertheless, thank you for the breakfast. Since Mr. Stowell insists on our collaboration, I suggest we share the responsibility," she said as she stood up. Just then, the waitress approached with a cup in her hands. Sophie turned to her, "I'm sure your coffee is excellent. Goodbye, Mr. Davidson."

Sophie left the café without a backward glance. Nick watched her go, then reached for Sophie's cup. Taking a sip, he shook his head, smiling. It had been a long time since a conversation with a stranger stirred so many emotions in him.

9

A WEEK HAD FLOWN BY SINCE THE CAFE INCIDENT, NOW ALL BUT forgotten as Sophie buried herself in her daily routine. Now, her workload had seemingly doubled overnight, leaving her in dire need of assistance. The thought of hiring an assistant crossed her mind, but she was more inclined to share her burden with someone competent. Despite her reluctance to admit it, especially to Nick, she often found herself pondering his silence.

Opting for formality, Sophie composed a brief, to-the-point email, to which he replied within the hour, matching her tone. She attempted to logically piece together the bizarre series of events that had intertwined their paths over the past few months. However, her attempt at clarity only unearthed a tangled mix of irritation and an unexpected joy. She didn't like that someone was interfering with her work plans, yet deep down, she found a faint sense of relief. The thought of never encountering the stranger from the bar again stirred an unexpected sadness within her.

She tore her gaze away from the computer screen, straightened her back, and tilted her neck from side to side, trying to shake off these thoughts. Sophie forbade herself from dwelling on such thoughts, aware they only spelled further trouble.

Soon after, another email arrived from Nick, pulling her back from her reflections.

"Good day, Miss Lind. Once again, I hope I caught you in good spirits. We have a team-building event this Saturday. Find the address and time attached. Hopefully, you can join us."

Sophie mused that a co-working session might have been more practical than team-building. She couldn't contain the irony in her voice. The address indicated that the team-building event would take place on a pier in Hoboken. The time caught her off guard: five in the morning. Surely, that had to be a mistake. Not that she didn't enjoy spending time outdoors and engaging in sports, but getting up in the middle of the night to travel to New Jersey was too much.

She was about to write a reply to decline the invitation, but then the scene from the cafe flashed in her memory. Nibbling her lip, Sophie considered it wise to curb her impatience. After all, she wanted to be a part of this project.

This fervent desire fueled her determination, compelling her to rise two hours before the sun. Pride swelled within her with each step she took toward the pier. As usual, she had some spare time when she arrived at the designated location. Just a bit short of reaching the pier, Sophie stopped to take in the view. It was breathtaking. Manhattan at this time of day was incredibly beautiful. A light purple haze enshrouded the island. Here and there, lights could be seen in the buildings, but they were so few that two bright stars in the sky captured all the attention. Their light gradually faded with the approaching dawn.

"Wow," Sophie whispered in awe, her lips parting in a silent gasp.

She had always been sensitive to the visual expressions of nature. What she also enjoyed was the contrast she felt when standing at the heart of bustling Manhattan, and then seeing it from a distance, as if in the palm of her hand. For reasons she couldn't understand, standing there on the pier, the beauty of the view struck her with the fresh wonder of a first-time encounter.

Sophie glanced at the uneven row of yachts of various colors and sizes, and there she noticed a male figure on a small pleasure yacht with a white sail. As she approached, she heard Nick's voice.

"A love for early mornings and punctuality? That's a rare find in this world," Nick said, standing by the starboard side, where a silver engraving with the name Elaine sparkled.

"And if I were late, would you have set sail without me?" Sophie looked around with a smile.

"Of course! There's no other way at sea..."

"Well, then punctuality is my curse," she approached the side, and Nick reached out his hand to help her aboard.

"Have you ever sailed before?"

"A couple of times."

"Then it'll be the three of us navigating today — you, me, and that ever-present irony of yours."

Sophie lowered her head, biting her lips, which curved into a smile. This made her face come alive and expressive, showing that her beauty wasn't always cold.

"And where is everyone else?"

"Apparently, no one else loves early mornings except us."

"I must admit I'm not a big fan of waking up before sunrise. But this..." Her gaze focused ahead. "This is breathtaking!"

"Wait until you see the sunrise."

Nick noticed a subtle glisten in her eyes, as though tears had welled up in them. He didn't immediately realize that it was just an optical illusion caused by the dim light of dawn. Feeling his gaze had lingered a moment too long, Nick discreetly turned away, gesturing towards the port side.

Nick had everything prepared for departure even before Sophie arrived, and just a couple of minutes later, they set sail. Sophie sat on the yacht's edge, close to where Nick stood. She watched his calm and focused movements. It seemed like he rarely expressed any emotions. She pondered how often his calm demeanor was mistaken for indifference.

"Do you live in Hoboken?" Her voice sounded casual.

"I live over there," Nick pointed to Battery Park City separated from them by the Hudson. "And this beauty lives here."

"It's truly beautiful. Is it yours?"

"A family heirloom... but it turns out that I sail more often than any other member of our family."

Their conversation paused as the sun broke through the skyline. Nick followed Sophie's gaze. Suddenly, doubt engulfed him. He had achieved his goal: the girl from the bar was now beside him, physically unable to leave the space they shared. But what now? In this moment of clarity, he saw the folly of his initial deception. It was foolish to impose a professional relationship when all he thought about was her. What life was she living? Did she enjoy that life? And who made her life worth living?

"What's next?" Sophie said good-naturedly, shrugging her shoulders.

"How about we start with that breakfast we never finished last time?" Nick suggested with a smile.

They sat on the deck, holding backpacking mugs with tea. For breakfast, they had freshly baked panini sandwiches. Sophie wondered how early Nick woke up to prepare all this. She smirked, glancing at him. Despite the strong wind, which tangled her hair and made eating a bit challenging, she enjoyed it.

"I can't imagine how you can handle this yacht alone," she looked around at the boat.

"It's possible, but it comes with experience. My father taught me. Once, when I was sixteen, I decided I could sail alone. I invited friends, but none of them knew how to manage it, of course."

"So, judging by the fact that we are sitting here, everything ended well."

"Yes, there's a small dent on the starboard side from my attempt to moor. And I almost drowned a friend when I turned... he should have held on tighter."

Sophie burst into laughter.

"You have a contagious laugh," he said.

"And you're excellent at telling stories!"

"Careful, that's already half the secret to a happy family life!"

Sophie laughed again.

"It seems we started our previous meeting on the wrong foot," he reached out his hand, "I'm Nick Davidson, I work in publishing, and I respect you as a professional. I'm glad we met!"

Sophie met his gaze intently as they shook hands, a trace of regret flickering in her eyes.

"I'm Sophie Lind, involved in advertising. I can be overly emotional at times, but overall, I'm not a bad person. And I'm glad to meet you too, Nick."

"Do you love what you do?" He asked.

Sophie pondered for a moment, lowering her gaze.

"Yes, I like it, mostly because of the team I've built. I enjoy working with them. But I'm still waiting for that moment when I will be truly inspired by this work, but so far, it hasn't happened. That's why I'm looking for new projects, like this free port."

"I know that feeling of searching," he nodded, lost in thought. "By the way, you're doing great. Everything you do for this project is simply impeccable."

It was nice for Sophie to hear those words, and they sounded sincere. She was surprised that she didn't feel any sense of rivalry between them. Perhaps, together, they really could become an excellent team. "Thanks!"

"And how long ago did you start this business?"

"Right after graduating. I got my master's degree and completed an internship at Sotheby's."

"You switched from art to marketing? I haven't heard people do that often..."

"I wanted to change a lot in my life. I moved to New York, but that didn't feel like enough, so I changed my field and started an advertising agency."

"You're brave," Nick sighed.

"My sister had been living here for several years already. You saw her at the bar. Without much thought, my childhood best friend and I decided to follow her."

"Interesting..." Nick paused, choosing his words, "It looks like you choose projects directly related to art, unconsciously trying to be closer to what you truly love."

"It does seem that way," Sophie murmured, her gaze drifting to the horizon, lost in thought.

Sophie didn't notice how quickly time flew by. It was already noon. She enjoyed the view and the sea breeze, even though the days were getting colder, and the wind sent shivers down her spine. She watched as Nick effortlessly handled the ropes alone. At one point, the wind lifted his t-shirt, revealing his lower abs. Sophie instinctively averted her gaze, yet the brief glimpse lingered in her mind, teasing her senses. At least now she could gaze within the bounds of decency. "Damn!" she thought in passing. After spending the day with him, she couldn't ignore the fact that he was incredibly charming. And now, with the added detail of his abs, she found herself stealing glances at his hands too. Why hadn't she noticed before how strong they were? "Okay, he's very attractive." She tightly closed her eyes, trying to convince herself to stop thinking about it. At times, the deluge of her own thoughts was intimidating, overwhelming her mind to the point where focusing on anything else became a struggle. However, she skillfully managed her reactions, body language, and facial expressions, creating a striking contrast between her turbulent inner thoughts and her outward composure. And then there was the nagging feeling of loneliness, which scared her even more.

As the day was coming to an end, they were heading back to the dock. Out of curiosity, Sophie followed Nick's instructions and tightened a couple of ropes. She got so engrossed that she didn't even notice how the cold wind gave her goosebumps.

"You're freezing. I'll get you a sweatshirt," Nick said.

He returned holding a crimson Harvard sweatshirt. "It's the only thing lying around in the cabin."

"Harvard? You know, these things would look cooler if only graduates wore them."

The fabric was soft, worn from use, yet it carried a comforting warmth that felt like an embrace. Sophie put on the sweatshirt, and it had a new scent for her. A combination of spicy cologne with woody notes and the smell of the body, which we remember but can never describe. A sudden gust of wind rocked the boat, causing her to lose her footing and sway dangerously close to the edge. Nick managed to grab both of her hands and pulled her closer.

"Careful..." he said softly as they found themselves closer than they anticipated.

They stood there, looking at each other as if frozen in uncertainty. Nick heard a silence he hadn't experienced in a long time. All the surrounding sounds ceased at once, leaving only their breathing in a vacuum. He listened, matching the rhythm of their breaths. Wind tangled Sophie's hair, and a few locks fell onto her face. She took advantage of the moment to close her eyes. She longed to close her eyes for just a moment. Nick gently brushed the hair away from her face, then looked at her slightly parted lips before pulling back.

When they finally reached the shore, Nick offered to drive Sophie home. She didn't object, eager to get home and soak in a hot bath to process the events of the day. When saying goodbye, Sophie hesitated for a moment before getting out of the car.

"Do you organize such team-building events often?" Fire sparkled in her eyes.

"Every second Tuesday," Nick shrugged.

"Thanks for the day!"

"I'll send you a couple of new ideas for the project, okay?"

She smiled and nodded back before getting out of the car.

10

THE FOLLOWING MORNING, SOPHIE FOUND NICK'S EMAIL WAITING in her inbox, filled with ideas he mentioned before. They were good. So good that she began to doubt what she was doing in this project. Days went by, and Sophie got to know the new team members who were gradually forming. They communicated a lot with Nick, exchanging business emails, calls, and online meetings.

Gradually, Nick found himself adrift in the whirlpool of his tasks. The workload kept increasing, while time dwindled. His schedule didn't allow him to take on a new project. He was supposed to hire a project manager who would report to him once a month. Instead, he found himself staying late, conducting strategic sessions that were as much about the project as they were about stealing moments with Sophie. He admired her vision and her approach to work. He no longer cared what he was doing, as long as it was with her. With each passing day, it became harder for him to figure out how he would tell her the whole truth.

As the week waned, Sophie felt she needed rest more than ever. She decided to take a day off once in a very long time when a call from her friend Emily reminded her that today was the promised Sunday when she was supposed to take Mia to the amusement park. What could she do? She had to keep her word.

Upon parking near Emily's house, Sophie's exhaustion cascaded into a deep, weary sigh, her forehead finding momentary solace against the coolness of the steering wheel. A cell phone chimed with the sound of a text message. Her gaze, heavy and unfocused, drifted to the glowing screen. A message from Nick Davidson: "How about grabbing some coffee?" With a weary chuckle, she mused that her upcoming message might just top her chart of most amusing rejections ever penned.

"Sorry, I promised to take a kid to Six Flags, not mine."

Suddenly, the car door swung open, ushering in a burst of sunlight and a whirlwind of energy in the form of a little girl, her mop of red hair a stark contrast to the day's earlier gloom. Across the yard, Emily's silhouette lingered by the closing door, her lips forming a silent "THANK YOU." Sophie took another deep breath and ruffled Mia's hair.

"Time to buckle up, princess," her voice imbued with a resolve to make the day as magical as possible for her young companion.

By noon, the amusement park buzzed with the vibrant energy of excited voices and laughter, its paths swarming with families and children eager for adventure. Lines for each attraction stretched at least ten meters long. Any lingering doubts Sophie may have had evaporated the moment she caught sight of the sheer joy radiating from Mia's wide, sparkling eyes.

"Now where to next?" Sophie asked, lowering herself to crouch in front of the child.

"For cotton candy!" In an instant, Mia's eyes transformed into the most adorable Disney version of herself.

"You are just adorable! Let's go and get you the most beautiful pink cotton candy."

They headed towards the central entrance, where the food truck with candies stood. Joining the queue at the end, Sophie looked ahead and furrowed her brows in surprise. Approaching through the throng of people at the entrance, like a familiar face in a sea of strangers, was Nick.

"Well, what a surprise!" She laughed, still in disbelief.

"Any normal person would have asked in response to your message what you're doing here, but I wanted to see it in person," he said, lightly touching his lips to Sophie's cheek.

"I don't know you," came a voice from below.

"Nick, meet Mia. The sweetest girl and the most passionate fan of cotton candy."

Nick crouched down, bringing himself to Mia's eye level.

"Hi, I'm Nick."

"Hi," she shyly peeked from behind Sophie's leg.

"Nice to meet you, Mia!"

"Is he your friend?" The girl looked up at Sophie.

"He's my colleague at work."

"Then why did you kiss him?"

Nick chuckled. "I like her!"

"Yes, she's a very special girl. Don't be fooled by her shyness," Sophie said, lifting the girl into her arms, "Because sometimes adults do that when they greet each other. And what happens to those who ask too many questions?"

"They know a lot..."

"I meant they won't get any cotton candy."

"But you told me that asking questions is good!"

"You're right, sunshine!" Sophie kissed the girl's cheek.

Their turn came, and Sophie handed Mia the money with a theatrical hand gesture, like a playwright before an actor's line. For a fleeting moment, Nick lost himself in the scene before him, the relentless midday sun and the press of the crowd fading into insignificance. Sophie settled Mia in the shade with her massive cotton candy while she and Nick waited to get coffee.

"Well, they have coffee here too."

"Yes, and it seems you want to share my fate today?"

"Why do you think so?"

"Just a little longer, and she'll like you, and won't let you go," Sophie nodded toward Mia. "I received your email. You've got some excellent work there; I honestly didn't expect it. The ideas are fantastic, and I'm sure it will work."

"They're not entirely mine, but thank you!" Nick pressed his lips tightly, taking two paper coffee cups, and handing one to Sophie. "I think this is what you need right now, Sophie. You look exhausted."

"It's been a busy week. Not the first time."

They looked at each other. Sophie felt like resting her head on Nick's chest and falling asleep.

"I understand. Instead of getting some rest, you're here. And what do Mia's parents do while you take care of their child?"

"We're not related. She's my best friend's daughter," Sophie explained, her voice softened, "We've been friends since second grade; she's like family. Mia's father left them when she was two years old. Now he sees her a couple of times a month." Sophie's facial expression indicated her disapproval.

"Your friend is lucky to have you. And Mia too."

Nick absorbed every detail Sophie shared about the people in her life, noting the slight droop in her shoulders and the fatigue shadowing her eyes. In that moment, his heart ached to lift the weariness from her, to infuse her with ease and comfort.

With the last wisps of cotton candy dissolved, Mia's excitement bubbled over as she tugged at Sophie's hand, eager to explore the next wonder the park held.

"Are you hungry?" Nick suddenly asked.

Sophie's gaze wandered for an answer. It settled on a tray brimming with ripe mangoes. "I see fruits over there," she pointed in its direction.

"Are you a vegan?" Nick raised an eyebrow questioningly.

"No, I just love fresh fruits, especially mangoes. I could eat them every day."

"That's better," he grinned, "Right now, it seems like you don't eat, sleep, just work."

"It's not that bad. Besides, don't most people live like this here?"

"No," Nick shook his head, "New York is unique in its diversity. I can show you many examples of people living completely different lives here."

Sophie looked in the opposite direction, listening to Nick's words.

"Anyway, I need this right now," she said.

"Whatever you say," he looked around, taking a deep breath as if he suddenly felt an impossible weight on his shoulders, "My younger brother and I used to love this place in our childhood."

"You have a sibling too. How sweet... What does your brother do now?"

"He died in a car accident seven years ago," those words still sent an icy shiver down Nick's spine.

"I'm so sorry," she looked at him.

Initially, her gaze seemed unreadable, but it soon became clear that she was trying to understand his feelings and emotions, rather than adopting a pre-made mask of fake sympathy.

"So, work is not everything, right?" he responded to her gaze.

Sophie nodded, her heart heavy with sadness. Suddenly, she felt lost, not knowing what to do and where to go with so much sadness inside.

"I can't truly understand this because I don't know what it's like."

"It's sudden, this shock. But what truly catches you off guard is what follows: an unbearable, vast sea of pain. You never anticipate discovering such an abyss of sorrow within yourself."

Compelled by an unspoken urge, Sophie closed the distance between them, resting her chin on his shoulder in a silent offer of solace, their shared silence a stark contrast to the park's jubilance.

"You're deeply empathetic, aren't you?" he asked.

"I don't know. Sometimes I feel like I don't know a thing about myself."

"From the outside, you make quite a different impression."

"Yes, I've heard that."

He inhaled the scent of her hair, feeling her fragile back with his hands. It seemed like he should share her emotions, and yet he felt relieved. As if he made it just in time for the last flight.

Soon, Mia became completely exhausted, falling asleep as they walked. Nick picked her up in his arms, and as they made their way to the car, the little girl dozed off. He gently placed her in the child's seat and stopped next to Sophie with the car doors open.

"Thank you," she looked into his eyes.

"You're welcome," he replied, "You know it's only because we're colleagues."

"I know."

"I'd love to invite you to dinner, but I think you should get some rest."

"You know, I think I could manage one dinner, but you're right, better next time," Sophie said, offering him a smile as she made her way to the driver's seat.

The next morning, a knock at Sophie's apartment door broke the quiet. A courier stood outside, a basket of mangoes in hand, addressed to Sophie Lind. She accepted the delivery to discover a note nestled among the fruit: 'You're always beautiful, even when tired.'

As Sophie sliced into a mango, its rich, sweet scent filled the morning air. Hesitant, she pondered over her response in the messaging app. Finally, she typed: "Too sweet. Thank you."

11

DAWN BROKE WITH AN UNWELCOME GUEST: A CRIPPLING HEADACHE that pulled Sophie from the depths of sleep into a harsh, unwelcoming wakefulness. She managed to make her way to the bathroom, looking in the mirror. It reflected a stranger — a ghostly pale girl with eyes reddened by fatigue and fever. Feeling cold, she checked her temperature. "One hundred point four. Perfect timing," she thought ironically.

With a determined yet faltering spirit, Sophie tried to tether herself to work, only to concede defeat as her body demanded rest. She informed everyone necessary about her illness, allowing her to lie back in bed with a clear conscience. The last person on that list was Nick.

"Falling sick. I'm counting on you for a few tasks," she messaged him.

The day blurred into a monotonous cycle of sleep punctuated by the ritualistic brewing of countless cups of lemon tea, her supposed elixir. As usual, that was her entire recovery plan. Towards the evening, Sophie sought comfort in the familiar laughter of the 'Friends' series, cocooned in a blanket before the TV's flickering glow. She felt her fever intensify, wrapping her in a sweltering embrace.

Interrupted by the doorbell's insistent chime, Sophie slid off the couch, grimacing from discomfort. Opening the door, Sophie saw Nick on the doorstep, holding a Whole Foods bag.

"Want to get infected to avoid work? This spot is already taken," Sophie weakly smiled, adjusting her silk robe. She was wearing cream-colored shorts and a lace top. She opened the door to let Nick in.

"I'm sure it's not a virus but rather your exhaustion," he said, kissing her before frowning. "It looks like you have a high fever. Did you check your temperature?"

"Only in the morning. I think it's bad."

"I'll make you some tea, and you check your temperature," he pointed at the bag, "Ginger's on the menu tonight. Non-negotiable."

Sophie sat on the couch, taking the thermometer. A few minutes later, seeing the result, she rolled her eyes. Nick sat next to her, handing her a steaming cup of tea, and took the thermometer from her.

"One hundred two point two… That's not good," he looked at Sophie attentively.

There was something reassuring about Nick's unspoken confidence, a silent assertion that he knew best at that moment, and Sophie found herself inexplicably comforted by it. He glanced at the TV screen.

"This is excellent medicine!"

"I love this show. My sister used to watch it in the evenings when it first came out. I was little back then and didn't quite understand what they were talking about. But now, it's associated with the feeling of home comfort and warmth," she wrapped herself in the blanket, "And what did you watch in your childhood?"

"I loved Steve Irwin's show about dangerous animals. Where strong men climbed into crocodile mouths, tamed venomous snakes, and other monsters."

"You'd fit that role."

"Well, I do pretty much the same thing every day at work."

Sophie laughed. Her voice was slightly hoarse, but it made it sound even more special.

"Tell me about your job."

"Well, the publishing house was passed down to me as an inheritance. My grandfather, who founded the publishing house, believed that promoting national culture was just as important as saving lives in hospitals. My father, despite his promise to continue the legacy, never really took to it. So, when I graduated from Harvard, he was more than happy to pass the baton to me. To my own surprise, I fell in love with it."

"Well, a happy ending does exist after all."

"I don't believe in anything calculated."

"We share that similarity. Thank you for being here," Sophie added after a brief pause.

"I had to make sure you were okay. Everything will be fine; you just need some rest," he moved closer to her, hugging her.

Sophie rested her head on Nick's chest, finding a tranquility she hadn't realized she was seeking. He kissed her forehead gently.

"Headache?"

She groaned in response.

"You need to sleep. I'll stay here if you want."

"Stay," she said and closed her eyes.

Darkness had settled in. Sophie awoke, finding comfort in her pillow, with a sliver of light from the kitchen slicing through the gloom. She looked around, remembering that Nick was at her place. There on the floor, against the couch's edge, sat Nick. Lost in an e-book, glasses perched on his nose gave him a studious look. Nick didn't immediately notice that Sophie woke up, engrossed in his reading. He sometimes had to work late to finish his usual workload throughout the day since reading what they published wasn't part of his direct duties. But it was his desire that had turned into a habit over the years. Additionally, the chief editor of the publishing house had become a good friend of his. They could have long discussions on contemporary literature, which became a sort of outlet for him in a job that only required entrepreneurial skills.

"What are you reading?" Her voice was soft, threading through the quiet room, reaching for Nick.

"Uh... it's a new book," he looked up at the sound of her voice, "We published it last month. The author contemplates what a person truly experiences when falling in love for the first time."

"Interesting... I think it's not easy to describe such intense feelings."

"I was drawn to the idea, and I can't help but agree with it. None of us are prepared to experience first love. It's such a powerful and overwhelming feeling. It catches us off guard and has a force we can't control. Equally strong, we experience tragic events. We can't control those shades of emotions either."

Sophie listened to him, feeling his words drawing her into a trance. Nick turned to her, tucking a strand of her hair behind her ear.

"I can't stand being alone when I'm sick. Even when it happens, I think back to childhood memories," she paused, "My sister and I loved building pillow forts. They were real castles made of pillows and blankets for us. We could even fall asleep there, and our parents wouldn't wake us up. Once, our mom brought a carved lamp with an electric candle in it, and it flickered, illuminating the space inside our castle with dancing shadows. We still have it with Natalie, and it's kept in our summer house in Scarborough. We go there every summer. Sometimes, I miss those days so unbearably."

"Do you have a large family?"

"It's Natalie, our mom, and stepfather."

"What about your biological father?"

"He left when I was two, and Nat was seven. He never showed up again," her voice trembled slightly, "I have only faint memories of him. Charlie, despite often being away for work, truly became a good father to us. We always spent Sundays together."

Nick glanced down at his hands, momentarily lost in his own memories, a rare peek behind his usual composure.

"When we were kids, my younger brother used to tell me the most embarrassing and shameful stories about himself when I was sick, just to make me laugh. Once, my mom overheard our conversation," Nick lowered his head, smiling, "One day, when I got sick again, my mom and my brother went to church for the Sunday service. As they were leaving with all the other visitors, Chris accidentally stepped on the hem of a lady's skirt. It was summertime, and the skirt was light, so it immediately slipped off. The lady was horrified and tried to pull it back up, but as soon as she did, her garter belt with stockings came undone. She couldn't go any further. Mom thought he did it on purpose to have something funny to tell me. Oh, how she scolded him…"

"What a priceless story!" Sophie laughed, "Thanks for sharing."

"Well, you might be surprised, but I don't just swipe left," he smiled, making a swipe gesture with his right thumb.

"I clearly went too far back then, sorry."

"It's the fever talking, and maybe hallucinations have already started," Nick placed his hand on Sophie's forehead, and she immediately brushed it away.

They gazed at each other. As sleep beckoned Sophie again, her words gently broke the silence:

"I regret that we work together," she said, but the response was already distant.

"Me too," Nick answered quietly. He ran his hand over his face, feeling completely lost.

Sophie's apartment was a study in spacious elegance, with clearly defined living and sleeping areas that were bathed in light, a surprising find in this neighborhood. She had opted for simplicity in her décor, avoiding the clutter of excessive furniture and the small, dust-collecting knick-knacks that tend to accumulate over time. At first glance, the space seemed minimalist, but a closer look revealed layers of personal touches.

Nick's attention was drawn to a string of Polaroid pictures suspended above the dressing table. These images appeared to be gateways to Sophie's private world, showcasing moments reserved for those closest to her. There were family gatherings, candid shots with her sister, and intimate snapshots with a friend, beside which was a photo of the same friend cradling a newborn. Nick deduced these were moments with Emily and Mia. In every frame, Sophie radiated happiness; her eyes shone, and her smile was magnetic. It struck Nick that maybe this was the essence of it all. Surrounding oneself with those who uplift and affirm us not only boosts our confidence but also anchors us in a sense of belonging and security. Sophie's curated collection of memories spoke volumes about her philosophy of life: to cherish and hold close to those who matter, keeping her circle intimate and meaningful, and clear of unnecessary people.

12

SOPHIE WOKE UP AS IF FROM A FALL, STARTLED AND DISORIENTED. It seemed only seconds since she had dozed off on the couch, Nick nearby. Now, she was in her bed alone, and a faint voice from the morning show came from below. Sophie shuffled to the kitchen, muscles protesting mildly, but her fever seemed to have receded. The rich aroma of coffee filled the apartment. Natalie was there, tinkering with the coffee maker.

"Morning, dear! How do you feel?" Natalie's voice was warm with concern.

"Like I've been steamrolled. And where is...?"

"Nick took off as soon as I got here. Said he had to get to work, now that I'm here to look after you."

Sophie leaned in for a hug, and Natalie instinctively checked her forehead.

"The fever's broken, it seems. Brought you some no-fuss remedies."

"Thanks, Nat. The smell of your coffee is driving me crazy, but I'm sticking to ginger tea today."

Natalie's eyebrows danced with curiosity. "So, spill. What happened?"

"What's there to tell? He showed up last night with a survival kit for my cold and stayed over. I don't remember anything, though, as I was sleeping off a high fever."

"You're dodging. Something else went on?"

"What could happen? He's not a pervert."

Natalie sighed, "It's not all black and white with you two, is it?"

"Understatement of the year."

"Listen, Sof, did I ever steer you wrong with your guys? Tell you someone was right when they weren't?"

"Nope…"

"This time, I'm saying it. You two click."

"Hearing that from a psychotherapist is the pinnacle of my life. But, we work together. I can't gamble that."

"You're overthinking this. It's just another project of yours; you won't end up on the streets. How often does someone right come along?"

"What's your angle? Want me running through the field of daisies after him?"

"He'll ask you out. Just say yes, not for me, but because it feels right."

"Alright, I promise," Sophie sighed, resting her head on Natalie's shoulder, slightly less miserable than before.

After another restful day, Sophie was back to her usual self. Preparing for an upcoming meeting, she was interrupted by the doorbell. This time, a courier greeted her, presenting a lush bouquet of peonies, their soft hues reminiscent of cotton candy. As she arranged the flowers in a vase, a small card caught her eye. 'Dinner tonight?' it proposed. A smile tugged at her lips; she found herself leaning into the idea of saying yes. She picked up her phone, the cursor blinking back at her in an empty message box. She hesitated. A tangible resistance surfaced, its roots unclear even to herself. It was a reminder of the strange certainty we claim over convictions whose origins we barely grasp. Finally, she typed, "Tonight at 8. Don't be late."

The day stretched out, yet every instance Sophie found her mind drifting to the evening plans with Nick, her fatigue seemed to dissolve. Her agenda was packed, but she had one final work meeting to attend. It took her to Sotheby's, located in Lenox Hill. Throughout her years in New York, Sophie had cultivated a network within the American branch of the prestigious company. It was the regional marketing director who became her go-to for any inquiries, their relationship was marked by professionalism and camaraderie. He was well-informed about the project that currently occupied her efforts.

They ascended to the second floor, finding themselves in a designated area for employees equipped with a coffee machine and cozy seating.

"How's everything on your end?" her acquaintance asked.

"Pretty good, Tom. Actually, it's going rather well. I do have a few questions for you, hope you don't mind the direct approach."

"I had a hunch you weren't here just to catch up over coffee," he replied with a playful smirk. "Fire away."

Their conversation was productive, with Sophie receiving the clarifications she sought. As their meeting wound down, Tom queried, "How large is your team for this free port project?"

"It's fairly small, so the workload is intense. Technically, I could manage most of it solo... However, they've brought in someone else for my role, Nick Davidson. It seems likely one of us might be on the way out."

"Nick Davidson?" Tom's eyebrow arched, his expression turning incredulously amused. "Sophie, you do realize he owns the free port, right? There's no way you two are vying for the same job. It's just not feasible," he chuckled lightly.

Caught off guard, Sophie's reaction was a blend of surprise and embarrassment, her mouth slightly agape. For a moment, she was at a loss for words, striving to maintain her dignity.

"Oh, of course! I must have confused him with someone else. You know how it is in a new team, names can be tricky."

They exchanged farewells, and Sophie exited the building, her mind engulfed by swirling thoughts that monopolized her focus. She found herself unable to hail a taxi, paralyzed by the uncertainty of her destination. Then, her phone vibrated with a new message.

"Where should I pick you up?" it read, from Nick.

Sophie glanced at the message preview without fully opening it, then promptly locked her phone screen. A mix of frustration and self-reproach washed over her. Amidst the whirlwind of peculiar events, she hadn't even bothered to google his name. Now, in every sense, it was too late.

13

A FEW DAYS PASSED, AND SOPHIE RECEIVED A PACKAGE FROM PAUL Stowell, including the documents for her to sign and a note requesting a phone call upon their receipt. Promptly, Sophie reached for her phone and dialed his number.

"Good afternoon, Sophie! Have the documents reached you safely?" Paul's voice came through the line.

"Yes, good afternoon, Paul. I've got them right here," she confirmed.

"We're eager for you to take on this project as the sole contractor, managing the entire client base. All that's left is for you to sign off and return the paperwork to my office," Paul explained.

Hesitating, Sophie responded, "Paul, I'm not sure I'm the person you need for this project," her voice wavering slightly with the admission, betraying her internal conflict.

"Frankly, Sophie, I can't imagine anyone more suited for the role," Paul countered.

"Thank you for your confidence in me, but I need a bit of time to think it over. May I get back to you tomorrow?" she asked, seeking a reprieve.

"Of course, take the time you need," Paul agreed.

After exchanging goodbyes and ending the call, Sophie found herself rooted to the spot, enveloped in a wave of solitude. The desire to isolate herself, to avoid any interaction, was overpowering. Yet, she remembered her promise to Natalie to spend an evening together just a week prior.

Sophie wrapped up her work and headed to their usual spot, the bar with its comfortably dim lighting. She had tried to back out of their meeting, however, Natalie insisted on coming, eager to learn about the events that had unfolded. Although part of Sophie longed for support, she was all too aware of the type her sister typically provided. Arriving early, Sophie indulged in a Negroni, finishing it just as Natalie made her entrance, shaking off the rain.

"Can you believe this rain? And here you are, starting without me," Natalie remarked, ordering a vodka martini for herself.

"It was a tough day!"

"So, what's been going on?" Natalie pressed, settling in beside her sister.

"Where do I even start?" Sophie pondered aloud.

"For once, try starting with how you feel, not like you usually do," Natalie prodded.

"And what's 'usual' for me?" Sophie countered.

"You know, getting angry at yourself. Haven't I always told you that's not good for you?" Natalie chided gently.

"Look, I was hoping to find my sister here, not my psychotherapist," Sophie retorted with a half-smile.

"And your sister sees you're troubled," Natalie responded softly. "So, talk to me. What's going on?"

"Don't overplay it, okay? I tried following your advice. Next time, I'll pass."

Sophie took a deep breath.

"What exactly did this guy do wrong? First, he rescued you from that creep's advances. Second, he gave you a leg up in a project everyone's dying to be a part of. Third, he organized romantic dates to genuinely get to know you, instead of hurrying to take you to bed," Natalie said, casually brushing away a non-existent eyelash from her eye. "Yes, feeling manipulated is unpleasant because it suggests control, and you're accustomed to going head-to-head with men. But this guy's intentions weren't to harm. It seems he genuinely has feelings for you. I get his reasoning; a simple 'let's grab coffee' wouldn't have cut it with you."

"It would," Sophie protested.

"Yeah, we both know the truth."

"It's not about manipulation. He lied," Sophie said quietly.

After Sophie spoke, hope sparked in Natalie's eyes.

"Dear, this doesn't necessarily mean he'll act like our..."

"It means he'll keep lying. We're finished talking about this," Sophie interjected, taking a sip of her second Negroni.

"Suit yourself, it's your life."

"Precisely, and I intend to live it my way."

Natalie looked away, recognizing that pressing Sophie further was pointless; she never gave up. As a practicing psychotherapist, Natalie understood that others might have succumbed to clinical depression under similar circumstances. Yet, her sister remained resilient.

They lingered a bit longer, and then Natalie mentioned needing to get up early the next day. When they stepped outside, the rain had stopped, leaving behind deep puddles. As they prepared to part ways, Sophie paused, turning to look at Natalie.

"Nat..." Sophie began, her voice trembling slightly, "I'm so tired."

Natalie stood frozen, surprised to hear such words from Sophie. She stepped closer, trying to find answers in her eyes.

"What can't you handle?" she asked softly.

"All of it," Sophie said, her gaze shifting away as tears started rolling down her cheeks. "Doing the right things, saying the right things, trusting... the right people."

Natalie hugged her, feeling a knot of concern in her chest. Sophie was the one person who could evoke such emotions in her.

"Sophie," she said gently, holding her sister tight, "Maybe it's time to stop fighting."

"What do you mean?"

"You've shut so many doors. Now, try trusting your feelings for once."

"I don't feel anything," Sophie replied.

"That will change," Natalie assured her, suddenly brightening. "I have a great idea! How about a pajama party at my place tonight? You could stay over."

Sophie nodded, still motionless. Natalie's worries about waking up early vanished, realizing how much her sister needed her right now.

The next morning, Natalie was jolted awake by the grating sound of her alarm clock. She gently covered Sophie with a blanket and quietly closed the bedroom door, careful not to disturb her rest. An hour later, as she was about to leave the apartment, her phone rang with an incoming call from an unknown number.

"Hello," she answered, glancing at her shabby leather wristwatch; it was 9 a.m.

"Natalie? It's Nick Davidson. Please, hear me out."

"Nick. How…" She was about to inquire how he got her number, but then she realized it didn't really matter.

"Sophie isn't answering my calls," he said, his voice laced with distress.

"Well, no wonder!" she interrupted him in her typical manner, commenting on every sentence as if it were playing in her mind.

"I need to talk to her. To explain everything," he implored. Natalie exhaled sharply.

"Let me give you a little test. What do you think Sophie would be least likely to forgive?"

"A lie. She sees it as a betrayal."

"Correct. You're catching on."

"Natalie, please. Sophie means more to me than any other woman ever had," he pleaded.

"She's going to be furious with me," she paused, "So, you better make this worth my while. You have one hour to get here. And pick up her favorite croissants and coffee on your way."

"I owe you one."

"Just remember, if you screw this up, we're done talking," she said carelessly.

"I'll do everything I can," he promised.

"Good luck, Romeo."

After hanging up, Natalie sent him her address and stepped outside, her mind awash with curiosity about how the day would unfold.

Sophie woke up half an hour later, relieved that her sister had already left for work, which meant no rush for the bathroom. At precisely ten o'clock, the doorbell rang. Still clad in shorts and a crop top borrowed from Natalie, Sophie opened the door to find Nick standing there, holding a coffee and a bag from her favorite bakery. Without a word, she slammed the door shut.

"Sophie, please. I'm not leaving," Nick's voice filtered through the door, tinged with determination.

Biting her lip, Sophie reluctantly opened the door again.

"What are you doing here? How did you get my sister's address?" she demanded, her eyes narrowing suspiciously.

Nick exhaled, his gaze meeting hers, filled with remorse.

"Alright. What do you want?" Sophie's tone was icy.

"First of all, I brought you these. And I also need to explain everything," he said, offering the bag with croissants and the coffee. Without hesitation, Sophie snatched them from his hands.

"We can keep up this charade indefinitely. I'll accept the coffee, but I won't listen to you," she declared, her voice unyielding.

"Sophie, please. Just let me explain, and I promise I'll leave you alone afterward."

She opened the door wider, allowing him to enter, then nudged it closed with her foot. She observed him as he made his way down the hall, noting his weary appearance as if he hadn't slept for nights. His hair was unkempt and slightly tangled.

"I'm listening," she stated, taking a sip of coffee.

"I lied about us competing for the same position," he began.

"Imagine my shock," she dryly commented.

"I appointed Paul Stowell as the COO for this project. After I met you, he mentioned hiring someone I knew immediately. I asked him to go along with my plan."

"Why? Is taking a phone number out of fashion? What's wrong with you?" Despite her words, Sophie's tone remained distant.

"I did it...," he faltered, struggling to articulate his reasoning, "to get closer to you. It seemed like work was the only thing you'd make time for."

Reflecting on her sister's earlier remarks, Sophie felt a pang of realization. She contemplated how others viewed her behavior as odd and withdrawn. Had her surroundings changed her, or was it her own choices? Crossing her arms, she longed for solitude.

Nick noticed not anger or resentment in her, but sadness and introspection she tried to mask. He sensed her craving for solitude and recognized his own actions more clearly. He had sought her affection by any means, fearing rejection. Lies, manipulation, hypocrisy – he had employed them all. He could easily justify his actions — after all, he genuinely liked her, and anyone could understand his reasoning. History is full of far worse deeds done in the name of love. Yet, no justification could erase the underlying fear that had driven him to manipulate Sophie.

"I've regretted dragging you into this from the beginning. You were the right choice for the job," Nick said, their eyes locking, "I've ruined everything. I've lost your trust."

"Nick," Sophie spoke softly, her voice tinged with distance, "I believe you're a decent person, even if your actions suggest otherwise. But I'm not waiting for an apology. I don't... need it. Besides, the whole story still sounds vague."

"I took on Paul for the project because I wasn't prepared to deal with it myself. I lacked the time and the moral fortitude. But then you revitalized it. I spent nights trying to match your pace," he said, briefly smiling at the memory. "Remember those drafts I sent you, claiming the ideas weren't mine? The truth is, this project was my mother's brainchild."

Sophie's expression sharpened, and she frowned slightly.

"She conceived it from the ground up but never got the chance to initiate it. In that car accident, it wasn't just my younger brother who passed away. They were together."

A metallic taste filled Sophie's mouth. Though she rarely saw herself as empathetic, Nick's revelations resonated with her, stirring a familiar ache. A shiver coursed through her.

"I've been wrestling with this project for years. My dad outright refused to engage with it, but I felt compelled by what I believed would be my mother's wishes. Yet, every approach seemed flawed. Then I met you, and suddenly, you were all I could think about." His eyes dropped. "I want you to know... you don't need to feel the same way. You're not obligated to meet my expectations. You owe me nothing. You're just beautiful in every way."

With those words, he moved toward the door, giving Sophie space to process her thoughts.

"Wait!"

He paused, turning back at her call. She stood before him, her gaze searching his. Feeling her hand gently touch his cheek followed by the soft press of her lips against his, the world quieted once more. In that moment, everything else faded away — the noise, the people, the trivial concerns. She kissed him tenderly, seeking an answer to an unasked question, then slowly drew back.

14

THEY FOUND THEMSELVES IN A QUAINT CAFE THAT SERVED breakfast well into the afternoon. Choosing a table by the window, they settled into their seats, exchanging silent glances.

"I'm truly sorry about your loss," Sophie began, a pensive look crossing her face. "I say this because it's what's expected, but honestly, I can't even begin to imagine what going through such a tragedy feels like."

"It's strange. I've received countless condolences, and people claiming to understand my pain. Yet, you're the first person whose empathy feels genuine," he paused, reflecting. "Thank you for listening."

Sophie responded with a soft "Uh-huh," still processing his story. "What about your dad? How's he coping?"

"He's... managing, thankfully. But this loss has transformed him. He lost his warmth... and became reclusive. It was as if I had lost my entire family in one fell swoop. Communication broke down, and we barely saw each other. It took years before we could resume our Sunday brunch tradition."

"That sounds incredibly tough," Sophie murmured, her eyes briefly closing.

"There's more I need to share. After they passed, I made an incredibly foolish decision."

She looked at him curiously, sensing his unease.

"I married someone I didn't love."

"You were married?" Sophie echoed, her surprise evident in her tone.

"I'd be interested to know about your secrets too," Nick replied with a light chuckle.

"They're securely hidden," Sophie replied, narrowing her eyes playfully. "How long were you married?"

"Only a year. Divorce was my initiative. We got together during our last year of university. She was sweet and caring — exactly what I thought I needed as my world was falling apart. But as time passed, I watched her lose herself in our marriage. Any plans she made always involved me, which, while normal for some married couples, started to feel suffocating for our relationship."

"It's challenging to be with someone who drowns you in their affection."

"I wanted her to continue growing, to live her own life. But things only deteriorated. Divorcing was hard, but five years on, I know it was the right choice for us both. She's made progress too; she didn't block my birthday message this year."

Sophie grimaced slightly, turning her gaze. "Wow, that's quite something. Is that the whole truth? Just so you know, croissants won't always be your get-out-of-jail-free card," she said, a faint smile playing on her lips.

"I wasn't under the impression I could buy my way out of this. Frankly, I didn't expect you to even listen."

"Well, you did show up at my sister's, catching me in my sleepwear. Not exactly a compelling argument on its own. Listening to someone is easy; it's trusting them again that's hard," Sophie said, her gaze drifting to a girl getting into a taxi outside the window.

They fell silent again, gazing at each other.

"Did you burn those documents they sent over yesterday?" Nick asked.

Sophie maintained a stoic expression. "Absolutely, I torched them," she replied, her voice dripping with sarcasm.

"Sign them instead."

"No," she countered firmly, shaking her head.

"Sophie."

"Nick."

"I do want you on board with this project."

"I just don't see it being wise. What exactly are you asking me to choose here?"

"There's no choice involved. My involvement is going to be minimal moving forward. I practically don't have enough hours in the day. Even if they decided to let you go, it wouldn't cross my desk," he said, spreading his hands in a gesture of surrender, a smile playing on his lips.

Sophie's lips pressed together as she weighed her options, her mind a tangle of thoughts.

"Fine, I'll do it. Under one condition: formally, you won't be my boss," she finally conceded.

"It's a deal."

"Okay then. I had planned to call Paul this morning to reject the offer. I even threw away the contract," she admitted, feeling slightly embarrassed by her admission.

"Come by my office tomorrow," he suggested, suppressing a smile, "And that'll be the end of our working relationship."

15

THE DAY WAS SLOWLY WINDING DOWN. SOPHIE HAD MADE A promise to drop by Nick's office to finalize the paperwork as soon as she wrapped up her own commitments. Yet, a series of unexpected hurdles cropped up, causing her to delay her departure time and again. Her most recent message to him was sent at eight in the evening, well past regular business hours, offering to make up for the delay by bringing coffee.

At last, having called a taxi, Sophie stopped at her preferred coffee shop, convinced they served the best cappuccinos around. The office lay merely ten blocks away. She watched the new barista carefully preparing the cappuccinos, her impatience growing. Once the barista finished, she began to place the cups into a holder.

"No need for that, I'm not going far," Sophie assured her.

The barista glanced towards the door, observing the darkening sky. "Looks like rain is on the way. Are you sure?"

"Yes, I'd better hurry then," Sophie responded with irritation.

She grabbed the drinks and stepped outside. The rain began as a light drizzle, which would not have been a major issue if not for the gusting wind. Her once carefully styled hair quickly became a tangled mess. Sophie made her way, accelerating as the rain grew heavier.

The drizzle had escalated to a downpour, with the wind making it tough to proceed. Her phone rang, displaying Nick's name.

"Are you okay? It's turned into a real hurricane out there!"

"If I can heroically survive the next few blocks, you might have to start a fire in your office — I'm soaked to the bone."

When Sophie arrived at Puzzle Publisher, her shoes were squished with water. The automatic doors swung open, revealing a lone security guard in the lobby who stared at her, surprised.

"I'm here to see Nick Davidson," she explained.

"The workday's over, ma'am."

"I'm aware, but he's expecting me."

"One moment, please," he said, somewhat flustered, and picked up the landline to make a call.

As she waited, Sophie removed her shoes, letting the water drain out. Her hair was drenched, and she suspected her makeup had not fared any better. Dressed in a flesh-toned pencil skirt and a white blouse, her outfit had transformed from morning's professional to unintendedly revealing due to the fabric clinging to her body, highlighting her undergarments. She attempted to dry the hem of her skirt, but it clung stubbornly to her figure. Catching her reflection in a wall mirror, she couldn't help but think, 'Just great!'

"Excuse me, ma'am! Mr. Davidson is ready for you now," the guard called out.

"That's fantastic," she replied, maintaining her composure as she made her way to the elevator.

As she rode the elevator up to the office, Sophie tried to guess how Nick would react to seeing her. Her expectations were spot on. The moment the elevator doors slid open, there he was, waiting for her. His expression was one of shock, and after a brief, courteous pause, he met her eyes. Stepping out, she offered the cupholder forward.

"Your drenched coffee," she said with a smile.

"Good heavens, you're soaked," he observed, allowing her past while his gaze lingered a moment too long on her thighs and the outline of her undergarments.

Nick set the coffee cups down and grabbed his jacket from the back of a chair. Approaching Sophie, who sat on the edge of the table, he gently placed the jacket over her shoulders. It was comically large on her, her small frame nearly swallowed by its bulk.

"You're shivering," he noted, his fingers brushing her elbow inadvertently.

Sophie didn't respond, locking eyes with Nick while his hand lingered on her arm. Suddenly, they were kissing — fervently, as if this kiss was all they had.

"It's very sweet of you to offer me your jacket, but there's something else I'd prefer right now."

"Is that so?" Their lips were still just inches apart. He took the jacket off, as well as her soaked blouse. His hands tighten around her breasts in a wet bra. Sophie undid the clasp behind her back. She held his hands, feeling her nipples become more sensitive in the wet clothes. She breathed out, tilting her head back and feeling the tension rising.

"You are so beautiful," he whispered.

Nick began kissing her dimple on the neck gently while his fingers unzipped her skirt. He pulled her to his side and deftly turned her back before taking the skirt off. He was torn by an intense longing; he yearned to savor the moment slowly, yet he also desired to feel himself inside her. He slapped her and the wet fabric of the skirt made a loud sound. Sophie caught her breath, her fingers instinctively gripping the edge of the table.

Taking off her skirt, he crouched to the level of her thighs. Her butt was taut, and together with the skinny legs, it reminded the shape of the heart. He kissed it on one side and squeezed the other. Nick moved her panties aside, biting his lips. The girl from the bar was standing in front of him, almost naked and his fingers were moving inside her.

Nick took his shirt off in a moment, while Sophie was unzipping his pants. Her heart was pounding; her muscles were so tensed she fought the urge to tighten her thighs. Nick glanced back to the sofa in the corner, looking for the most comfortable spot. He pulled her closer, kissing firmly until their tongues intertwined. His fingers rhythmically explored her body.

Sophie found herself mesmerized by the intensity of his passion, each confident gesture weaving a spell of allure and desire around her. Sophie couldn't recall the last instance she had experienced such intense desire from a man, especially on their first night. Nick led her slowly to the couch. He sat down, pulling her arms. It was only tiny panties remaining on her, which he quickly pulled back, fixing on her thigh. He looked her in the eyes, tucking a strand of her hair behind her ear unhurriedly. Sophie felt him inside, moving gently and slowly. She took a deep breath.

"What do you like?" he said quietly, his fingers touching her chin, "Tell me…"

As she met his gaze, the thought flickered through her mind: 'No wonder his ex had been crazy about him.' But this fleeting insight was quickly eclipsed by a more immediate sensation, a growing heaviness in her lower stomach. He was already deep inside her.

"Right now?" Her chest heaved with deep, ragged breaths.

"I want to know everything about you," Nick kissed her, biting her lower lip. His hands were tightened around her hips, making her move faster.

"You're so deep…" her palms pushed against his chest.

"Do you like it this way?"

"Yes," The groan made her voice snap as he pulled her hair.

Nick's chest rose and fell with deep breaths; he could feel her muscles tightening inside. It was getting harder to control himself. His palm arched her back gently as he started kissing her nipples one by one, biting them softly. His gaze lingered on her parted lips and the strands of her wet hair. Sophie felt his fingers on her lips. Swiftly caught on, she began licking them. But he took his hand off and pointed it down. He started by touching her clitoris gently, steadily accelerating the rhythm. The next moment he got into her with his fourth finger, moving it toward himself.

"God… What are you…" She jumped a little with unexpected sensations, clutching his collarbone.

He watched her reaction, moving inside her faster. Sophie could feel the pleasure smashing into her, like waves. Long distances at first, but gradually they shrank, engulfing her entirely until the world as she knew it faded away. Time and space lost all meaning, leaving her scarcely able to recall her own surroundings.

"How about we do this together?" He whispered, listening to her groans grow louder.

Sophie put her arms around his neck and pulled his hair. She no longer controlled the strength of her movements. A blaze ignited within her, its flames stoked with every rapid breath he took. With her eyes closed, the physical boundaries melted away, leaving behind an intense energy that filled the space around them — a fervent sphere of heat that seemed to encompass everything. With her muscles tightened once again, Sophie opened her mouth, grabbing the air. Tension yielded to infinite pleasure. Nick drew her in closer, his eyes shut as he savored the moment. The steady beat of a heart thrummed between them, indistinguishable in its owner — his or hers, he couldn't tell. Their bodies stopped moving gradually. The agony slowly faded, giving way to a delightful tension that lingered in the muscles.

Their foreheads met, and at that moment, they both paused, catching their breath. Nick gently kissed the edge of her lips. Sophie looked at his lips, slowly tracing them with her fingers, barely touching them. Her hands trembled slightly.

"Why did we wait so long for this?" She said quietly. Nick smiled in response.

"We needed to draft a contract and sort out all the details," he smirked.

Sophie settled beside him, her movements fluid and languid, leaving her wondering if she could even stand at that moment.

"Shall we go to my place? I'll warm you up by the fireplace with a glass of wine," his breath was still slightly uneven.

Sophie nodded, looking at him with a tired gaze. With no alternatives besides Nick's jacket, she reluctantly slipped back into her damp clothes.

They drove in silence, occasionally stealing glances at each other. Nick reached for her hand, raised it to his lips, and planted a slow, deliberate kiss on the back, before gently grazing a patch of her skin with a playful nip of his teeth. Sophie melted with pleasure in the passenger seat.

"I think asking how many women you've been with is definitely not a good idea."

"Why not? You can ask," Nick said, smiling as he kept his eyes on the road.

"I guess I'll stick to my original plan," she smirked. "But you don't strike me as a womanizer."

"Have you met many of them?" Nick glanced at her.

"Enough to know I have nothing in common with such people."

"Then maybe I should ask you the same question…"

"How many women have I been with? No need," she shook her head, barely suppressing a smile.

Nick laughed in response. "Well, I'll ask you a different question then," he paused, turning on the blinker, "How do you feel about sex in general? How important is it to you? Do you believe sex is exclusive to relationships, or not?"

"That's more than one question. Well, okay, for me... sex is important. But it's definitely exclusive to relationships," she looked back at Nick.

"So, does this mean we're in a relationship now that we've had sex?"

"I don't know. It was quite spontaneous."

"I'm asking because people have different attitudes toward it. I mean, regarding first-time sex and what comes after."

"If you're asking about that, it would be great if you called me tomorrow," she said, laughter in her voice, "And I'm not joking."

"I understand. It doesn't sound like a joke. But I'm curious about your expectations."

"I don't like making plans for the future, and I don't have any expectations for them either," she looked ahead, avoiding his gaze.

"I see. And in the real world, are you waiting for me to call, invite you on a date, or send flowers? Or should I give you some space?"

"Nick, you're making me uncomfortable," she said, watching the barrier of the underground parking rise.

"Why? If you're important to me, and I want to express that, how should I know the best way to make you hear it?"

Sophie paused, a pang hitting her inside as she exhaled slowly, a lump forming in her throat. She hadn't expected such words at this moment. By now, the car was parked. Nick looked at her, awaiting any response. In his mind, he noted that falling in love makes people more attentive and anxious than usual, with time slowing down and heartbeats quickening.

"You're important to me too, so please, let's not rush," she whispered, meeting his gaze. Her lips slightly parted, but he sensed she was holding her breath.

Nick nodded, softly repeating "Let's not rush," then got out of the car. Walking around to her side, he opened the door for her.

"Lady," he extended his hand.

It was late at night when they lay in bed. Sophie finally found a comfortable position on Nick's chest, ensuring her neck wouldn't become stiff. As thoughts of the coming day stirred anxiety within her, she exhaled, deciding to focus solely on the present. Nick's fingers gently combed through her hair.

"Are you okay?"

"Yes. It usually takes me a long time to fall asleep, with different thoughts swirling in my mind."

"Me too," he admitted, pulling her closer. "I've always envied those who fall asleep within minutes," he paused. "Being with you, I realize it's very easy for me to be myself. I've only just recognized that now."

"That's a very precious feeling," she murmured, opening her eyes. "I know because I struggle with it."

Her voice always softened when she spoke of something difficult. Nick wished to ease her discomfort, knowing such peace couldn't be achieved in a single night.

"You're charming," he whispered, kissing the top of her head. "You just haven't realized it yet."

16

SOPHIE SWIFTLY SLIPPED INTO A BLACK TOP THAT PAIRED IMPECCABLY with her white, trapezoid-shaped skirt. In a rush, she dug through the depths of her jewelry box, fingers searching for a gold necklace. Tardiness was something she could never abide, even for casual meetings with her dearest. Today marked a long-awaited evening out with her best friend Emily and her sister.

Sophie's destination, a local, somewhat fancy bar favored by Emily, was a mere ten-minute walk from her home. Situated in Chelsea, the bar was known for its exceptional gin cocktails, though Sophie found it rather noisy. Upon entering, she immediately spotted Emily and Natalie at their table. She caught a man's exacting glance as she walked by. She could have sworn that, even after she passed, he continued to stare at her from behind.

"Sorry, I'm a bit late!" she apologized, kissing Emily and Natalie before taking her seat at the table and setting her silver fabric clutch in front of her.

"Well, well, it looks like someone's been preoccupied with her new beau! We're all ears, Sophie," Natalie teased, her hands clasped in anticipation.

"Even my daughter's met him, yet I'm the last to know," Emily chimed in with a playful pout.

Refusing to dive into the details, Sophie's hesitance led Emily to speculate, "This is either going exceptionally well or terribly wrong…"

Natalie, never one to shy away from prying, leaned in with a smirk, "Sophie, come on! Is he a disappointment in bed? Lacking in enthusiasm or something else…?" She raised her eyebrows suggestively.

"Was it all rushed? Did you feel anything?" Emily quickly added, joining the teasing.

"Actually, it was the best sex I've ever had," Sophie admitted, her eyes downcast.

"Oh my," Emily grabbed Natalie's wrist, "She's blushing!"

"Yes, blushing indeed," Natalie observed, capturing Sophie's evasive gaze. "Seems we've stumbled upon something serious here, little one."

"I don't know. I mean… I really like him. I've been clinging to you guys for that sense of family warmth and support I've been missing lately. But with Nick, it's different. I feel that warmth with him, even though it's only been a month. Strange, isn't it?"

Natalie smiled; everything was just as she had expected. Then, turning her gaze to Emily, she noticed an unusual despondency and confusion in her eyes.

"Let's not dwell on this for now… I'm off to greet Teddy," Sophie declared, nodding toward the bartender. "He's the only one I trust with my martini."

As Sophie departed, Natalie observed, "See that guy in the red tie? Looks like he's going to follow her."

"I wouldn't bet against it. Tonight, Sophie's covering my drinks," Emily laughed.

"Are you going to be alone the entire weekend?"

"Yeah."

"So, you could potentially relax and not worry about heading home tonight?"

"Perhaps," Emily hesitated, her gaze dropping — an unusual behavior for her. Natalie, who had known Emily since childhood, could always sense when something was amiss. Her professional instincts told her not to press; alcohol would likely loosen Emily's tongue soon enough.

"You seem off today, Em."

"It's just..." Emily started, hesitantly. It was always impossible to hide anything from Natalie; she paused, finding the courage to meet her gaze. "Why is it so hard to find what you're searching for?"

"That's just it," Natalie said, taking Emily's hand reassuringly. "Sophie wasn't looking; in fact, she was denying what was happening. It's puzzling how they even crossed paths. By all psychological theories, they should've missed each other. Yet, they met, and life keeps weaving them together," she mused. "Either I'm a terrible therapist, or miracles do exist."

"Why do you think so?" Emily looked up, intrigued.

"Well, Sophie tends to choose emotionally unavailable men, like her ex, Dean. Cold and indifferent, ready to leave at any moment. She views her relationships with men through the same lens as her relationship with her father."

"It's amusing how different you two are. How do you see your relationship with your father?"

"It's different. We talk. I'm not a child anymore, Em."

Emily merely nodded, lost in thought and unable to articulate her own turmoil.

"My advice? Stop searching," Natalie suggested. "Both you and Sophie might benefit from trying out each other's approach to life, even just as an experiment."

"What kind of experiment are you suggesting?" Sophie's voice rang.

"The one where you realize the importance of family," Natalie glanced at her sister, "And you take care of yourself, Em."

"Em has always dreamed of having a family and children. She has her adorable Mia, and I've always wanted to indulge my desires shamelessly," Sophie lifted her martini glass in a toast.

The clinking of glasses resonated around the table.

"And what about you, Nat?" Sophie turned to her sister with a meaningful look. "What are your aspirations?"

"I aim to earn a Ph.D., publish my book, and become a member of the American Psychological Association," Natalie replied matter-of-factly.

Sophie smirked, addressing Emily, "She tells me I'm too focused on my career…"

"No, she's right," Emily's voice softened as she spoke, "That's how it should be. Otherwise, you'll wake up one morning and not recognize yourself," she covered her face with her hands.

Concern etched on Sophie's face as she leaned in to embrace her friend, "Em, what's wrong?"

"It's nothing, really," Emily reassured, her voice tinged with emotion. "But tomorrow, you'll wake up, and go about your day, no matter how chaotic it is. It's what you wanted, and you're achieving your goals. In the evening, you'll go out," she gestured towards Natalie. "Let me tell you about my days. You probably know, but not in detail. I wake up, barely having time to compose myself, and I need to get Mia ready for school. Then, it's a rush to drop her off. I have just five hours of free time, which I spend on household chores, errands, or paperwork. After school, it's all about Mia — homework, playdates, activities. And on weekends, I hardly have those five hours to myself. Except for rare occasions, like today, when I can have a drink and spend the night with a stranger, not even knowing why I'm doing it. Everyone says it's supposed to be fun."

Natalie listened with calm understanding, aware that Emily had harbored these feelings for a long while, and now it was time for them to surface. Emily, a devoted mother, never voiced complaints about her daughter. Yet, Natalie sensed the unspoken question: Did she have regrets? She knew Emily feared even contemplating such a thought. Surrounded by peers grappling with similar parental doubts, Emily might have found her own choices more bearable. However, her reality was different, immersed in a world where ambition and personal growth took precedence. These confessions stemmed not from envy but from a deep-seated fear. What decisions had she made, and how should she navigate her life going forward?

"Emily, you do know you're exaggerating, don't you? Mia is the most wonderful miracle there is. Yes, Kevin turned out to be a disappointment. But it's too soon to conclude. Everything will fall into place, just wait and see. Deep down, you wouldn't have it any other way. You made all the right choices," Sophie said with a reassuring squeeze of her friend's shoulders.

Natalie found no words necessary to add. Her silent nod conveyed a supportive affirmation, understanding the delicate balance between expressing concern and offering hope.

Their night out passed uneventfully. As they left the bar, Sophie felt an urge for a quiet walk along the Hudson River Greenway, finding sleep elusive with Emily's words reverberating in her thoughts, stirring a desire to confide in someone. After a brief moment of hesitation, she made her way towards Battery Park City.

Standing before Nick's apartment building, she typed: "If you lived on the first floor, I'd throw pebbles at your window."

Within a minute, a response came: "Come on up."

Sophie ascended to the top floor of the residential building. As the elevator doors parted, Nick was already there waiting. With a smile, she approached him, and they shared a kiss that felt overdue, despite it being less than twenty-four hours since they last met.

"You smell like a martini," Nick said with a tender gaze.

"I wouldn't mind another," she replied as they moved towards the entrance.

"I didn't expect you'd come over. Thought you'd stay at the bar till morning."

"I usually head back around this time."

"A bit early, isn't it? How old did you say you are?" he teased with a grin.

"I'm 19, and I have a fake ID," she tried to sound as serious as possible.

"Wow, I never imagined I'd still be having such adventures," he laughed, fetching a bottle of martini from the bar.

Sophie was greeted by a cozy scene. The fireplace in the hall was alive with a comforting crackle. Beside the couch, on the coffee table, lay a book and a glass of whiskey atop a leather coaster. Irresistibly drawn, she leaped onto the couch, nestling comfortably. Flipping open the book cover, she discovered 'Islands in the Stream' by Hemingway. A sense of peace and quietude offered a soothing contrast to the bar's clamor.

Nick handed her a glass with a few olives settled at the bottom. He sat beside her, gently lifting her legs onto his lap.

"Tell me, what if..." Sophie began, taking a thoughtful sip.

"What if?" Nick prompted, his fingers tracing her bare legs.

"What if you had a child with your ex-wife, but you still ended up divorcing? Would you regret having that child?" She fixed her eyes on him.

"Oh, the questions you ask late at night... Where do these thoughts come from?"

"Just answer me."

"I don't think so. Hypothetical questions like these are tricky. People aim to fulfill a dream scenario in their lives, but reality often has other plans. It wouldn't be fair to blame a child for the way things turn out."

Sophie nodded, letting out a sigh. Emily's revelations about her struggles with Mia lingered in her mind, stirring a mix of pity and a sense of her own ignorance.

"Emily opened up today about how challenging it is for her to raise Mia by herself. She's never mentioned it before. But today, her words hinted at regret."

"It's understandable she's overwhelmed. But I'm sure her opening up doesn't come out of nowhere. There's always a reason behind someone's behavior and the change of perspective."

"You're probably right. Maybe I haven't been as attentive to her lately and missed the signs."

Nick gently took Sophie's hand.

"Don't be too hard on yourself. Some experiences, like divorce, are difficult to comprehend without going through them firsthand. It's a heart-wrenching process for both. One recovers faster, while it inflicts deeper wounds on the other. I hope you never have to endure something like that."

His words were imbued with sincerity. Such a rare finding in love, where often, every word is filtered through self-interest, calibrated to provoke a certain response. Sophie had grown accustomed to men tailoring their words to manipulate her actions, but with Nick, it was different. He was authentically himself, allowing her to be the same.

"I don't think she regrets it. She's just exhausted and confused," Nick added.

Sophie squeezed his hand.

"Has anyone ever told you how charming you are?" she smiled softly, looking into his eyes, "Sincere, perceptive, smart, and sexy."

"Martini seems to bring out a peculiar side of you. What happened to the reserved lady I met a month ago?"

"She's here, just a bit more relaxed thanks to the martini."

"I detect a touch of English tradition. There are many other ways to unwind, and I'd be happy to explore them with you."

Suppressing a smile, Sophie bit her lower lip as his fingers traced a path from her wrist to her elbow, stirring goosebumps on her skin. Leaning in, she kissed him, fighting the urge to take things further immediately. She thought finishing her glass would ensure the night was memorable. However, Nick was the first to pull away.

"Next Friday, my father is hosting a traditional charity event. Will you be my date?"

Sophie paused, her smile slowly emerging.

"Are you sure you want to introduce me to your father, friends, and more?"

"Should I have doubts?"

"I don't know. Maybe."

"The simple answer is yes, I do want to. And I'd appreciate not dying of boredom there without you."

Sophie took a moment, not so much considering his invitation as trying to read his intentions.

"Alright. I'll be your plus one."

"Thank you," he kissed her hand.

Nick reflected on how all the women who had been in his home expected an invitation to stay, while he was usually eager for them to leave. And now, the girl sitting before him truly didn't care whether she stayed or left. Yet, for the first time, he found himself wanting her to stay as long as possible.

17

SOPHIE AWOKE TO THE SOUND OF THE FRONT DOOR CLOSING. Even nestled in the remote corner of the apartment, her keen sense of hearing didn't fail her. Half-asleep, she groped for her phone on the floor next to the bed. It was early still, suggesting Nick had left for his morning run.

Lying on her back, she let her gaze wander around the room, now gently illuminated by the first rays of sunrise. The details of the interior, previously unnoticed, caught her attention. She found herself admiring the room's tranquil palette of grays and whites, highlighted by accents of black and dark brown wood. The bed, low to the ground with a tall, elegant headboard that merged into polished strips of dark wood, caught her eye. Instead of traditional bedside tables, a large floor lamp stood sentinel by the window, its warm light adding to the room's coziness. The eastern wall was dominated by a large window, bare of curtains or drapes, and a sliding mirror door on the opposite side concealed the walk-in closet and bathroom.

With what she guessed was an hour to herself, Sophie peeked into the bathroom. The sight of a large, immaculate white bathtub promised a magnificent time. Stretching languidly, she emitted a soft sigh of contentment. Across from her, a large round mirror hung, reflecting her naked form. She observed herself, not scrutinizing individual parts for their beauty or flaws. Sophie believed such self-examination should be left behind in adolescence.

After her bath, Sophie noticed Nick's white robe hanging on the door. Wrapping herself in it, she stepped out into the kitchen, feeling an unusual desire to prepare breakfast for two. While peering into the fridge, she heard the guest bathroom door open and Nick emerged, clad only in a towel. She peeked around the fridge door at him.

"I want to make us breakfast. Are you okay with eating at home?"

Nick walked over and kissed her, his breath still heavy from his run. "Sure. You're cooking? Does that mean we had a good night?"

"Yes, and I discovered an amazing bathtub where I soaked for an hour."

"Ah, that explains it," he said, pulling her close for another kiss. "Good morning."

"Morning," she replied with a soft smile.

"Next time, we can take a bath together."

"So, that's its purpose," she joked, raising an eyebrow.

"You won't believe it, but those who've stayed over never made it to the bath."

"Any interesting stories?"

"Do you really want to know? It might stick in your mind afterward."

She couldn't help but agree and turned her attention to making toast while Nick brewed coffee.

"Do you always have coffee in the morning?" she inquired.

"Since my freshman year. Can't shake the habit."

"Should you?"

He pondered playfully, then changed the subject. "Were you mad at Natalie when she told me where you were that morning?"

"No, she always thinks she knows what's best for me," Sophie sighed.

"Maybe she just cares about you. How much older is she?"

"Five years older."

"That's quite a bit," Nick remarked.

Sophie nodded, her thoughts drifting. "Ever feel like people's care doesn't feel like care at all?"

"All the time. My dad always knew what was 'best' for me. That was his initial approach to dealing with me, and fundamentally, it never changed. My ex-wife was a care 'expert' — dinner ready every night, shirts ironed perfectly," Nick said, shaking his head.

Sophie was listening to him when images of the bar scene flickered through her mind unexpectedly. She thought of Emily, a heaviness settling over her. Nick noticed her change in expression.

"Thinking of another story?"

"I might visit Emily today," she said, lost in thought.

Nick nodded, letting her decide whether to share more.

Sophie pulled up to Emily's house and headed straight for the building's entrance. Pressing the doorbell, she waited, the tension mounting within her. The sound of the door unlocking echoed, and juggling a bag from the children's bakery along with hot beverages, she managed to open the door. As she walked down the hallway on the ground floor, Emily showed up.

"Sophie?" Emily appeared both tired and surprised.

"Were you expecting someone else?"

"The mother of one of Mia's classmates picked them up for their dance class. I thought they would have been back by now. Come in," she said, stepping inside first. "Why are you here so early?"

"I brought your favorite caramel latte and macarons for Mia. Honestly, I was hoping we could talk."

Emily smiled slightly, kissed Sophie on the cheek, and took the bag and the drinks from her.

"Black, as always," Emily observed, looking at her cup.

"As always," Sophie responded, settling onto a high stool by the kitchen counter. "Um, you scared me with what you said last night."

"I know, but I was telling the truth."

"Why didn't you say anything sooner? I could have…"

"What could you have done, Sophie?" Emily's gaze was indifferent as she interrupted.

"First off, I would have listened," Sophie retorted, a note of indignation in her voice. "Emily, after nineteen years of friendship, do you believe we couldn't have figured something out together?"

"There's no magical solution, Soph. You already do so much. You take Mia on weekends whenever possible, showering her with love and attention. What's next? Offering me money for a nanny?" Emily's frustration was evident; she wasn't seeking sympathy.

"Why do you have to say it like that?" Sophie said quietly.

"I'm not downplaying your support. I'm simply exhausted from ignoring the reality. I don't fit in here. I belong with parents who, like me, are deeply involved in their kids' lives and scrambling for decent-paying jobs. You're fortunate enough not to understand that struggle. I'm out of my depth with your business affairs, the art industry, and all that. You probably wish for a friend who can easily join you in the upscale shops you frequent, with whom you don't have to hide what you can afford," Emily shook her head.

"I never thought we'd reach this point."

"Neither did I. But here we are. I can't keep pretending that everything is alright. It's costing me too much, both financially and emotionally. Yes, I was eager for a fresh start and moved to New York with you. But now, I see it was a mistake."

"Are you serious…?" Sophie was taken aback, her words trailing off.

"We're going back to London, to my family. I've even started looking at flight tickets."

"When were you planning on telling me?"

"I guess when I had the tickets in hand."

"Em, I can't believe this."

"Sophie, you need to live your life and find joy in it. You've earned that. You shouldn't have to exhaust yourself trying to fix mine."

"But I want to help!"

"The best help you can offer now is to drive Mia and me to the airport. And to come visit us in London."

This declaration stunned Sophie. She paused, reflecting on how long she had neglected her friend's inner state, absorbed with her own life.

"I'm sorry it turned out this way..." Sophie gazed into the distance, her voice heavy with regret.

"Me too. I had hoped moving here would mean Mia seeing her father more often. Yet, he's still split between two cities, seeing her only once a month. And then," Emily paused, looking out the window, "this city suits people like you. I lack the strength, time, and so much more to thrive here. Leaving doesn't sadden me. I'll miss you and Natalie, of course, but the exhaustion is overwhelming, Soph."

The girls shared a look. Emily felt a weight lift with her confession, whereas Sophie was visibly perplexed. For Sophie, saying goodbye to loved ones, whom she considered family, was deeply painful. Her strong network of close relationships made navigating life's other challenges seem more manageable.

Sophie lingered until Mia returned. After some quality time with her, she sensed it was time to leave. Crouching down to Mia's level, she asked, "What should you say about the macarons?"

"Bring more next time!" Mia exclaimed, throwing her arms around Sophie's neck with joy.

"My girl! Love you, sweetheart," Sophie said, planting a kiss on Mia's forehead.

Leaving, Sophie caught Emily's look. For a moment, it seemed to flicker with regret. Indeed, Emily did feel a twinge of regret, but she wouldn't concede that the ensuing relief swiftly eclipsed it. They had grown past the days of being schoolgirls sharing a desk. Sometimes, sentiments needed to be set aside, Emily decided, as she closed the door on her best friend.

18

SOPHIE THREW HERSELF INTO WORK, HER USUAL REMEDY FOR LIFE'S challenges, but this time it failed to offer solace. She hadn't spoken to Emily since their last meeting, aware that her friend's departure was imminent, scheduled for Saturday. With a glance at her electronic calendar and two days to go, she couldn't shake the feeling that it was a mistake. 'Never give up!' had always been her guiding principle, yet she recognized it had little bearing on her friend's pivotal life choices.

Feeling angry and further irritated by her own emotions, Sophie found herself withdrawing from those around her. She had not seen Nick since the weekend and only responded to her sister's messages with reluctance, focusing her attention solely on her team. Her dedication this week was so pronounced that her project manager, reporting directly to her, suggested Sophie take a step back and trust her to handle things.

While staring at her calendar, a red mark caught her eye — the charity event hosted by Nick's father, scheduled for the next day. Though she hadn't forgotten, preparing for it now seemed a necessary distraction. Under different circumstances, she might have found reasons to avoid it. Sophie knew what awaited her there. She was someone who could confront the truth, both within herself and when speaking to others. Nick was successful, wealthy, and now, importantly, divorced and free. Yet, she was acutely aware of how his social circle might perceive her: an outsider with an obscure past, a recent immigrant to the country, seemingly appearing from nowhere. With a sigh, she acknowledged it was time to weave Shamballa against curses.

Sophie decided to attend, unsure of any other way to divert her mind from her best friend's departure. But to do so, she recognized that she needed to address her anger and suppressed feelings. It was then that a solution came to her. She dialed her favorite spa hotel and secured a room for the evening. This spot was her sanctuary — a seemingly ordinary boutique hotel with top-tier skincare services that transformed entirely once they knew you needed to dazzle for an event. They would arrange for a stylist, makeup artist, and hairdresser; it was an oasis of pampering in the city's relentless bustle.

Without hesitation, Sophie headed to the hotel and approached the reception, where the familiar face of the plump receptionist brightened in recognition.

"Good afternoon, Sophie. Happy to see you!"

"Likewise," Sophie returned the smile. "Actually, I'm not in the best spirits. My best friend just declared she doesn't need me anymore, and tomorrow, I have this crucial event where I must look perfect, lest my boyfriend decides he feels the same," she quipped with a broader smile, leaning on the counter.

Her dramatics were an exaggeration, but her state of mind dictated a complete indifference to the world around her. She found the reaction of the girl behind the counter amusing upon the unexpected and unwanted revelation. The truth, as always, was unwelcome.

"Don't worry, we've got you covered!"

"Thanks," Sophie replied, accepting her key card. With just her laptop bag and the quintessential items of femininity in tow, she entered her room and collapsed onto the bed. The agenda was clear: indulge in the luxury of self-care, a privilege she relished as a successful, child-free woman. Massages, body wraps, sauna visits — every small delight was at her disposal.

Immersed in the hot tub, a skincare mask applied by a kindly attendant on her face, Sophie didn't even inquire about the concoction's contents. Cradling a glass of her favored champagne, she began to unwind. The knots of anger and frustration slowly untangled. As she stared blankly ahead, trying to piece together her feelings, a serene yet indifferent calm enveloped her, stemming not from peace but from a profound apathy. Memories surfaced — her tenth birthday, a house bustling with guests and a cake, yet marred by the absence of the one person she yearned for. Hidden in the kitchen, tears streaming, she was discovered by Natalie. But confiding in her sister brought no solace, only the dismissive words: "You're just a silly little girl."

Sophie's reverie was cut short by her phone ringing. Glancing at the screen, she saw Nick's name displayed.

"Hey. How are you?"

"I'm not sure how to answer that. I'm at a spa hotel," her voice was soft.

"When is Emily leaving?"

"Saturday."

"Do you want me to come over?"

"No."

"Okay. Where should I pick you up tomorrow?"

"From here. I'll send you the address."

"Alright."

"Nick?"

"Yes?"

"I don't feel anything. Is that normal?"

"I know. Just give yourself some time."

"It never helps."

He sighed.

"It does, eventually. It always takes longer than we think."

After saying goodbye, Sophie smiled weakly. She appreciated everything about their relationship so far. Nick was respectful of her space; he didn't push for conversations, try to force intimacy, or bombard her with questions under the guise of concern — a tactic others often use to mask their own insecurities and pretensions. She didn't need to defend her feelings or justify herself with him, avoiding those exhausting explanations. Nick shared her worldview, and Sophie was beginning to appreciate the value of their connection.

The following day, Sophie awoke naturally and promptly called the reception to request breakfast in her room. Although she wasn't in a hurry, she was aware that a team with a crucial task would soon arrive to transform her into a princess.

As the stylist presented various dresses on an iPad, they decided on a red gown with elegant round necklines at both the front and back. Crafted from satin, the fabric elegantly enveloped her form, fitting snugly without being too tight. Drapery at each neckline added a touch of modesty. The dress fell to her ankles, gracefully concealing her legs, embodying sophistication without being ostentatious.

"Thank you," Sophie expressed her genuine appreciation, adding with a light-hearted smile, "Though I feel more like a hoodie kind of person right now."

"I understand," the stylist responded with professionalism.

Once all the beauty treatments were complete, Sophie looked at her reflection and was thoroughly pleased with the outcome. Red, her power color, was now represented in the crimson hue of her dress, complemented by slightly darker lipstick. The makeup was understated, and her hair was stylishly tied back in a chignon, adding an elegant touch. This look mirrored her inner spirit; she felt calm and assured. Despite her underlying sense of detachment, she found something to anchor her for the evening.

As Sophie emerged onto the street, Nick was by the car, absorbed in a phone call, his back to her. The driver waited patiently behind the wheel. Sophie paused a few steps away, in no rush, anticipating his reaction to her transformation. Her patience paid off. While still on the phone, Nick turned towards the hotel and caught sight of Sophie. He momentarily fell silent. After a brief pause, he wrapped up the call and pocketed his phone, shaking his head with a smile.

Approaching her, Nick kissed her hand.

"You look breathtaking."

"It took a whole army of stylists to achieve this," she replied with a grin, playfully adjusting Nick's bowtie.

"Shall we escape the country?"

"Was that the plan?"

"Yes."

"I'd rather prefer to get to know people in your circle."

"I'd personally prefer the first option," he quipped, holding the car door open for her.

During the ride, Sophie stole glances at Nick's suit. It was a classic black tuxedo, tailored narrower at the waist and the collar. A bowtie, matching the suit's color, sat elegantly around his neck. It was her first time seeing him in such attire, and it was undeniable that he looked as though he was meant to wear it.

"The tuxedo suits you very well," she said, covering his hand with hers.

"I'm not sure; I usually feel more at ease in a polo."

"I was tempted to wear a hoodie tonight."

"You'd look equally stunning," he replied, his gaze momentarily dropping to her legs, "but this color is particularly flattering on you."

Sophie's smile was radiant as she leaned in for a gentle kiss on the corner of his lips, careful not to leave a mark of her lipstick.

In less than twenty minutes, they arrived and were ascending in the elevator.

"Do you mind if I occasionally step away to socialize with the guests?"

"I can handle myself," she assured him with a backward glance.

He nodded. "My dad mentioned my aunt was quite invested in the musicians being the highlight," he shared with a grin, "But it seems they've already made their impression."

As the elevator doors opened, Sophie was taken aback by the expansiveness of the hallway before them. It was vast, almost as if the entire area comprised a single room. Directly opposite the entrance, a white grand piano demanded attention. The space was tastefully divided with artful flower arrangements, creating distinct zones while the dark parquet flooring seemed to swallow the sound of their steps.

The evening's host was unmistakable. A tall, older man with broad shoulders and a resolute gaze stood near the elevator, deep in conversation with an elegant woman. He periodically swept his gaze across the hall. Upon Nick and Sophie's arrival, he briefly acknowledged them with a glance before returning his focus to his companion. Sophie sensed the curious eyes of guests upon her, those already mingling with champagne in hand in the cozy nooks of the room.

"Father," Nick said succinctly. The man turned at the sound of his voice.

"Nick," they greeted each other with a handshake.

"Good evening, Lucy," Nick added with a nod to the woman, before turning his attention to his father, "I'm pleased to introduce you Sophie."

"It's a pleasure to meet you, Mr. Davidson," Sophie extended her greetings with a slow, deliberate courtesy.

"Please, call me Greg. The pleasure is mine. My son has spoken quite a bit about you recently."

Greg's words were cordial, hinting at concern, yet his gaze seemed distant as if part of him were elsewhere. Sophie, sensing an awkward pause looming, was about to speak when they were interrupted by a crisp, feminine voice. A petite woman in a straight-cut dark olive dress approached briskly.

"Greg, the host has confirmed we can start on time. After all my calls today..." her voice was sharp, requiring attention to catch every word.

"Linda, Nick and Sophie are here," Greg interjected, barely acknowledging her flurry of words, and gestured towards his son and Sophie.

"Nick..." Linda's voice trailed off as she noticed Sophie, "You didn't say you'd be bringing a guest. It's lovely to meet you, Sophie."

"This is my sister, Linda," Greg introduced, briefly meeting Sophie's gaze before looking away and clearing his throat.

"A pleasure to meet you, Linda," Sophie replied, her smile subtle.

"I recall Nick saying he'd bring someone, but he didn't mention you'd resemble Grace Kelly," Linda observed, one eyebrow raised.

"It must be the lighting," Sophie quipped, scanning the gathering.

"Let's catch up later," Nick suggested, wrapping an arm around Sophie, indicating it was time to move on.

Sophie nodded, following Nick to a table where a waiter was meticulously arranging champagne glasses. Nick selected two, offering one to Sophie.

"To an evening of awkward conversations!"

"To the evening," Sophie agreed, taking a sip and appreciating the champagne's refined taste. "Don't act surprised. You seem to have grown up around these kinds of gatherings. Is this your family place?"

"It used to be," Nick revealed. "The normal living spaces are on the west side of the floor. This area is specifically redesigned for events."

A couple approached them. The man, dressed in a bespoke suit, appeared familiar with Nick and made a beeline towards them. His interest in Sophie was undisguised, while the woman with him seemed slightly out of place, her gaze frequently shifting downwards before darting around when she looked up. Her floor-length dress was a muted gray, fitting well but not seeming to boost her confidence.

"Brother!" the man greeted Nick enthusiastically.

"Hey, Dan. Sophie, meet Daniel, my cousin."

"And this is Sophie," he said, drawing attention to her, "And my girlfriend, Rachel."

"Pleased to meet you," Sophie greeted them with a smile.

Daniel offered a glass to his girlfriend, but she responded with a bewildered look.

"Excuse me," Rachel said, giving Dan a questioning look.

"Past the piano, then left straight down the hallway," he directed her quickly.

"I'll join you," Sophie offered, wanting not just to accompany her new acquaintance but also to explore the penthouse.

"See you soon," Nick said with a wink, to which Sophie responded with a playful smile.

As the girls left, Dan turned to Nick, his energy palpable in his lively gestures and expressive demeanor.

"Wow! She doesn't exactly seem ready to take a bullet for you. Did she actually come with you, or did you two meet on the elevator?" Dan asked, amusement in his eyes as he took a sip of his champagne.

"Can you not, cousin?" Nick retorted, a touch of irritation in his voice. "She's here with me."

Nick caught Dan's reference to his ex-wife, who used to pray for him day and night. At gatherings like this, she'd barely acknowledge anyone else, sticking closely to Nick.

"And what's got your girlfriend so troubled?"

"I'm not sure. She didn't seem too thrilled about coming tonight."

Meanwhile, in the restroom, Sophie stood before a large mirror, pretending to adjust her hair while Rachel struggled with the zipper of her dress.

"Could you help me with this?" Rachel asked, looking at Sophie with a hint of desperation.

"Of course," Sophie responded, attempting to zip the dress. However, it snagged. "Wait a minute, it's stuck."

"I'm just not myself today. Do you, by any chance, have Adderall or something stronger?"

Sophie shook her head, her focus on Rachel. "It depends on what you find helpful. Maybe some champagne could ease the tension?"

"I actually don't drink," Rachel admitted.

Sophie let out a surprised sigh.

"Then perhaps it's best to skip the drink and just get through the evening."

Exiting the restroom, Sophie accidentally collided with a waiter donning a white collar, nearly upsetting a tray of appetizers. She caught a fleeting glimpse into the bustling kitchen as the door swung shut, noting an unexpectedly high number of people inside.

Venturing back into the hall, Sophie encountered an even more unexpected figure: Mr. Kinkade. Their eyes met, and with no room to retreat, Sophie confidently approached him.

"Well, well, well... You continue to surprise me with each meeting," Kinkade remarked, his chin tilted slightly upward.

"Mr. Kinkade! What a pleasant surprise. I hope you're not harboring any grudges against me."

"Edward. Had you revealed your identity earlier, I could have spared you the interview process."

"The thing is..." Sophie realized that Edward Kinkade, her former boss of just a month, was unaware of her presence at this charity event.

She felt compelled to clarify the misunderstanding, as he seemed to view her as deceitful.

However, their conversation was cut short by an interruption. An elderly man with gray hair and a congenial air approached, giving Kinkade a friendly pat on the shoulder.

"Edward! I was searching for my old friend, and here you are, captivating the ladies in the quieter corners of the hall."

"Arthur! It's good to see you," they exchanged handshakes.

Arthur's gaze turned to Sophie, expecting an introduction. Kinkade hesitated, seemingly forgetting her name.

"Sophie Lind," she introduced herself, making eye contact with the newcomer.

"Sophie, you're a delight to all the men here! Arthur Harrison."

"It's a pleasure, Mr. Harrison," she replied with a smile, acknowledging his compliment.

"Miss Lind is involved in..." Kinkade trailed off, visibly perturbed by the situation.

"Advertising agency GT," Sophie interjected.

"Ah, we once reached out to your firm," Arthur recalled with a frown.

"I remember all our collaborations."

"Spotlight Construction Holdings, but that was several years back..."

"Your project manager was Lewis."

"Remarkable memory! I was impressed then; your agency was relatively new but handled the project professionally. Bravo!"

"It's wonderful to meet you in person, Mr. Harrison," Sophie said, glancing subtly at Kinkade. She was about to revisit their conversation when Nick's voice interrupted.

"Edward, Arthur," he greeted, joining their group and shaking hands.

Wrapping an arm around Sophie, he added, "I didn't want to leave Sophie by herself, but it seems my concern was unnecessary," his smile reflecting his satisfaction.

"Who else could such a lady accompany!" Arthur chuckled.

Sophie caught Edward Kinkade's puzzled look.

"The first time Sophie and I met was in Edward's office, but our acquaintance truly began by chance at a bar," Nick explained.

"The mysterious ways of fate!" Arthur exclaimed, his arms raised in a gesture of wonder.

"I see," Edward drew out the word, "That's truly remarkable!"

"Excuse us! I must whisk Sophie away," Nick said, taking her hand.

Sophie quickly turned to address Kinkade. "Mr. Kinkade, please, let me make it up to you. We can have lunch whenever you're free," her eyes conveyed earnest hope.

"Get my number from Nick," Kinkade responded, his demeanor softening at her sincere gesture.

Stepping aside, Sophie sighed and averted her gaze.

"You didn't mention he'd be here!"

"I didn't think I needed to," Nick replied, his eyes searching Sophie's face, trying to recall the connection between her and Kinkade. Seeing her wide-eyed stare gave him a moment to piece it together. "Oh, that..." he finally acknowledged.

"Yes, exactly. I don't want to leave things unresolved. It seems I've misled him, leaving him confused."

"And if he hadn't been here today, would you have just left things as they were?" Nick teased, struggling to suppress a smile, his lips twitching.

"No," Sophie asserted, her expression serious as she briefly looked away before meeting his gaze again. "I would've asked you how to contact him... Okay, I admit I forgot about it!"

Nick's laughter broke through, his eyes softening with fondness.

"Don't worry, Edward is a close friend of the family. He won't harbor any ill will. Still, offering to take him to lunch is a nice gesture. If you'd like, I can come with you."

"Thank you," she responded, glancing back to where Kinkade had been standing, only to find he was no longer there.

The host's booming voice, amplified by a microphone, sliced through the chatter. As the charity auction commenced, the room hushed, guests' attention riveting to the stage, many clutching paddles. Sophie had always joked that charity began with purchasing a house on Long Island. It appeared that these attendees, possibly tired of investing in real estate, had discovered a renewed interest in philanthropy.

As the event neared its conclusion, Nick excused himself to mingle with unattended guests. Meanwhile, Sophie, glass in hand, gazed out the window, barely noticing Linda's approach until her voice, somewhat jarring, broke her reverie.

"Sophie, best make your exit by midnight, lest these dwarves curse you," Linda said, trying to catch Sophie's gaze.

"I hope I haven't inadvertently caused offense. Surely, I haven't spoiled anyone's engagement?" Sophie replied, half-joking.

Linda's smirk revealed she found Sophie's resilience amusing. "No, but you're clearly not as naive as you appear. You understand the situation perfectly."

"The evening has been delightful! I gather we have you to thank," they continued, their eyes fixed ahead.

"Thank you, dear. Greg likes to keep the tradition alive, but organizing isn't exactly his forte," Linda confessed.

Sophie chose not to probe further, yet she inferred the tradition was initiated by Greg's wife and Nick's mother. "It's a lovely tradition."

"Elaine was truly kind-hearted..." Suddenly, an engraving on the yacht deck flashed in Sophie's memory.

"I'm so sorry," Sophie said, turning to Linda with genuine empathy.

"One can never be fully prepared for such losses; they are simply unbearable," Linda responded, her gaze still fixed ahead. It was unclear to Sophie if her words stemmed from a true sense of loss for her brother's wife or if she was merely playing a part. "Excuse me, dear. I must check on the kitchen. I'm sure our paths will cross again soon."

With a sweet smile and a brief touch on Sophie's wrist, Linda departed. Left alone, Sophie contemplated the enigmatic nature of Linda's words. Discerning the true intentions of such individuals was challenging, perhaps because sincerity was foreign to them.

Meanwhile, Sophie noticed the curious glances of two girls standing slightly apart. Approaching them, she placed her empty glass on a table nearby.

"Good evening," she greeted them cordially, seeing no reason to ignore their attention.

"You must be Sophie? You're probably the second most discussed topic of the evening," one girl said with a hint of arrogance.

"Is that so? I was aiming for first... Who managed to surpass me?"

"Typically, charity events focus on the total donations raised," the other girl replied coolly. "And, of course, there's curiosity about who Nick's new girlfriend is."

"It's always better to meet in person, then," Sophie said, her gaze shifting between the two, inviting them to introduce themselves.

"Stacey Nicholson," the fair-haired girl announced, her tone uncertain, as if trying to mask her irritation with politeness.

"Bethany Harrison," the second girl stated, her voice carrying an overt rudeness, showing no intention of warming to Sophie.

"Bethany, I've heard your family name before. What do you do?"

"I... organize events, like this charity evening," she said, her discomfort evident.

"A noble endeavor indeed. And you, Stacey?"

"I assist my husband with his projects," Stacey said, a trace of pride in her voice.

"It's commendable. Women dedicated to their families are often heralded as modern-day heroines. It seems you're involved in a form of charity just as impactful as Bethany's."

The girls were momentarily taken aback by Sophie's sarcasm. They needed a moment to regroup, while Sophie looked on, a content smile on her face. She knew they had every reason to view her with skepticism. After all, no matter her identity, she was an outsider in their circle — a Brit with an ambiguous background.

Feeling Nick's hands on her shoulders, Sophie turned and kissed him on the cheek.

"Nick!" Bethany's voice was unusually loud. "We were just discussing work. I hear Sophie is part of your latest project. How interesting."

"Sophie graciously offered her expertise. That's how we met," Nick replied, returning the kiss and embracing her.

"How intriguing. A risky liaison," Stacey remarked, smiling.

"Indeed, but well worth the risk," Nick said, not doubting that survival games were unfolding here. "Ladies, I trust you've enjoyed the evening?"

"Absolutely. It was splendid, as always," Stacey replied.

"Wonderful. We're looking forward to seeing you again," Nick made a point of including Sophie in his farewell, "And now, if you'll excuse us, I'd like to introduce Sophie to someone else," he said, leading her away.

They made their way toward the more secluded side of the penthouse, away from the general throng of guests.

"Are you okay? They can be quite harsh…"

"Do you think I'm unfamiliar with such games? I excel at them," Sophie replied confidently.

"I do not doubt that. But I'd better not test the waters," Nick teased, adopting a mock British accent.

Sophie laughed, lightly tapping his forearm. Nick quickly captured her hands, drawing her in for a deep kiss. It was a reunion they had both been yearning for, having spent almost a week apart. This moment marked their first genuine kiss of the evening.

"Where are we headed?"

"I want you to meet my best friend."

"Why at the end of the evening?"

"It's part of our little tradition... we have an after-party. Consider yourself holding a VIP invitation," Nick explained, his arms still encircling her.

"With the official festivities concluded," Sophie said, slipping off her high heels.

They reached the staircase, and Nick nodded towards the top, signaling they should ascend.

"Of course..." Sophie chuckled.

Nick then swept her into his arms, carrying her up to the rooftop. The edge was unguarded, save for a lone figure seated near the west side, gazing out over the city. As Nick and Sophie neared, the man looked up and rose to greet them warmly.

"Sophie, meet Mike Harrison, a childhood friend of mine," Nick introduced, positioning himself between the two.

"Finally happy to meet you," Mike said, offering a friendly hug, his expression warm and amiable.

"It's a pleasure, Mike. I had the opportunity to meet your father earlier this evening," Sophie responded.

"We've got a small gathering going on here," Mike mentioned with a grin, indicating the pillows spread out on the ground.

Sophie settled onto a pillow with interest, carefully placing her shoes to the side. Her long dress restricted her from sitting in her preferred lotus position, so she gracefully tucked in her knees, keen to see Nick in the company of his best friend.

Mike then produced a tightly rolled paper from his jacket and lit it.

"So, this is the kind of after-party you have," Sophie remarked, smiling. "And how long have you been wrapping up social events like this?" She inquired, taking a puff and exhaling slowly after a moment.

"Ever since we were sixteen," Nick said with a laugh.

"I was the one who brought weed for the first time. Nick and I tried to smoke it in the guest bathroom, but then my younger sister Bethany barged in. She freaked out at the smoke and ran off to our parents. We certainly heard about it after that… That's why we joke about the tradition," Mike recalled with a grin.

"Honestly, I'm not much for it; is it strong?" Sophie asked.

"Don't worry, you'll find it relaxing," Mike advised.

"That sounds like exactly what I need…"

"Was it a tough night?" Mike asked Sophie, a slight smile on his lips.

"I'd say it's been a tough week. Plus, Edward Kinkade seems convinced I'm some sort of fraud, and the delightful Stacy and Bethany consider me nothing more than a nuisance. And I believe that's putting it politely."

"Stacy and Bethany?" Mike couldn't help but smirk. "Well, their kindness extends more to bank accounts than to people. And Bethany has her own reasons for not being your biggest fan."

"Did I cause some trouble?" Sophie's tone carried a hint of innocence.

"Only the minor issue of shattering my sister's lifelong fantasy of marrying Nick," Mike revealed.

"I've always treated her like a little sister," Nick interjected.

"Gossips and weed… I like it," Sophie said, her voice softening, more relaxed now. "Ever think hosting pre-parties might also be a good idea?"

"That's not a bad thought," Nick mused, exhaling a cloud of smoke.

Leaning back on her elbows, Sophie looked up at the sky, feeling this was the perfect way to end the evening – a rare moment of doing absolutely nothing.

"Then we'd end up spending all night here, making our bets," Mike suggested.

"It's not about bets; they're contributions," Nick corrected with mock seriousness, and they both erupted into laughter.

Sophie watched them, amused. It took only moments to see the bond they shared – a blend of warmth, independence, and mutual respect that made their friendship work. It reminded her of her relationship with Emily, and she pondered when things had begun to change between them.

"I envy you guys," she blurted out, "for having such a strong friendship."

The laughter stopped, and Nick gave her a look full of understanding.

"I know, baby," he said, gently placing his hand on her knee. "She's had a falling out with her best friend," he explained to Mike.

"And now she's heading back to London to be with her family, tired of pretending everything's the same between us," Sophie added, sitting up and wrapping her arms around her knees as she looked out at the view.

"That's rough," Mike sympathized. "But if she feels it's for the best…" he shrugged. "Personally, I'd choose my friends over relatives any day."

Nick chuckled, then cast a concerned glance at Sophie.

"I'm sorry..." he said softly.

"It's alright. Maybe we've just been living separate lives for too long now."

"Oh," Mike said enthusiastically, "That's a recipe for disaster. Eventually, someone's bound to give up. It's true for friendships, it's true for relationships. It's not just about compatibility; sharing a lifestyle is crucial too."

"Have you witnessed many instances of this?" Sophie queried, turning towards Mike.

"Quite a few. Twenty-five years of friendship with this guy who's head over heels for you," Mike gestured toward Nick.

Sophie nestled closer into Nick's embrace, seeking comfort.

"And his parents," Mike continued, his gaze drifting off to the city lights at night.

"He really loved her, didn't he?" Sophie's question lingered in the silence.

"Yes," Mike simply replied.

"Before Elaine's passing, you wouldn't recognize the man he was. It's like only half of him was left," Mike reflected.

Sophie squeezed Nick's hand tighter, feeling a slight easing of tension in her muscles.

"What was she like?" Sophie asked.

A moment of silence ensued before Mike replied.

"Extremely kind. She never reprimanded Nick and me for our mischief. Instead, she'd say, 'Mr. Davidson will have words with you.'"

"And my dad would lecture us, 'You're adults now, behave as such. Don't set a bad example for your little brother,'" Nick added.

"Yeah... Elaine was always supportive of Chris spending time with us," Mike took a brief pause, "Had she met you, she'd have found you charming and would've wanted..."

"To keep you forever," they said in unison.

Sophie felt a lump forming in her throat. She lifted her gaze to meet Nick's, her eyes brimming with tears. He pulled her closer, gently kissing her forehead.

19

IT WAS ALREADY NOON WHEN A PHONE CALL ROUSED SOPHIE FROM her sleep. The clothing rental store was on the line, asking when they could retrieve the dress. Glancing at the dress sprawled on the floor beside the bed, Sophie fell momentarily silent.

"I think I'll buy it," she decided after a pause.

"I understand. It's difficult to let go of such a piece," the voice on the other end responded.

"Yes, exactly. I want to keep it."

Ending the call, Sophie turned to Nick, who was still asleep beside her. The thought of leaving the warmth of the bed was unappealing. Snuggling closer, she relished his warmth.

"Morning," Nick murmured, his fingers gently threading through her hair.

"Good morning. Sorry if I woke you."

"It's okay."

"I need to head to the airport. Emily's flight is in a few hours."

"Do you want me to come?" Nick asked, his eyes still closed.

"Natalie's picking me up. Go back to sleep," she whispered, kissing his neck.

Outside, Sophie was greeted by a white Audi A6 parked at the entrance, with Natalie at the wheel. Lowering the passenger window, Natalie looked up at her sister with playful concern.

"You look worn out, sis!"

Ignoring the comment, Sophie got into the car and pecked Natalie on the cheek.

"Was up until 4," she explained.

Checking her reflection in the visor mirror, Sophie tried to tame her disheveled hair, but the strands refused to cooperate. Natalie reached into the glove compartment and handed her a black hairband.

"How did the evening go?"

"Not bad. Met his father, aunt, numerous guests, and family friends. Oh, and his best friend," Sophie recounted, while Natalie focused on the road. "He is really nice."

"That's good to hear. Sounds like you have no regrets."

"None at all. The time after was wonderful."

"I'm happy for you," Natalie replied, thoughtfully. "So, are you prepared for what's ahead? I've got a mini martini, just in case," she added, indicating the size of the souvenir bottle with her fingers.

"No, I'm good," Sophie said, looking at her sister quizzically. "What else is in that glove compartment?"

"Everything one might need."

"A martini solves about fifty percent of problems," Sophie quipped, folding her arms and turning her gaze to the road.

"You're catching on, darling."

"If you're asking if I'm ready to say goodbye to a friend I've lived next to for nineteen years, then no, I'm not. And I don't care if it sounds selfish. I can't wrap my head around her decision. It feels like she didn't even consider my feelings, informing me last minute as if my opinion didn't matter. It's so simple for some, isn't it? Deciding you no longer need your best friend. People ditch friendships for relationships, drift apart over differences in income, or because they're too busy. After all, friends are just another app you can replace. No problem, I'll go find another childhood friend…"

Sophie's words poured out uncontrollably. She was scared by how quickly she had lost control. Natalie drove in silence, casting a glance towards the glove compartment.

"You want to ask me something. I'll answer, but you need to ask it yourself."

"Do you think I'm a bad person? I ask because people dear to me keep leaving my life."

"No, you're not a bad person."

"Skip the therapy talk. What's your honest opinion?"

"Honestly? I think Emily's not fully matured. She's behaving childishly and wasn't prepared for motherhood. Right now, she needs someone to take care of her, meaning her parents. But my view doesn't solve your problem."

Sophie grew quiet, reflecting on her sister's perspective. She knew they had never been as close as she and Emily, viewing her more as her younger sister's friend.

"People are that way because that's just who they are, Soph. Don't overanalyze, like you did with Dean."

Natalie was worried about her little sister. Despite appearing strong, smart, and successful to others, she was only twenty-seven. Her maturity lent her a semblance of wisdom beyond her years, yet it was still insufficient for navigating such harsh life lessons. Natalie longed to alleviate her sister's pain but knew Sophie had to confront this initial stage on her own. Intentionally, Natalie brought up a name from the past, reminding Sophie of her first love's betrayal. That experience had deeply affected her. Natalie remembered visiting her family in London, only to find her younger sister hospitalized after a nervous breakdown.

They arrived at LaGuardia Airport with some time to spare, but they headed straight for the check-in counter. Not finding Emily and Mia there, Sophie instinctively knew where to look. Near the exit, a quaint bakery caught their eyes, known for its delicious cinnamon buns — a treasure Mia couldn't miss.

Approaching the bakery, they found Emily with Mia, who was already enjoying a cinnamon bun, her eyes sparkling with joy.

"Hey," Sophie greeted softly, embracing her friend.

"Hi. I didn't expect you to come. Thank you!" Emily's eyes moved from Sophie to Natalie.

Mia, buzzing with energy, began circling Sophie, though her excited chatter seemed to fade into the background for Sophie, her senses dulled by a creeping fog.

Emily checked her watch. "We're boarding in 30 minutes," she said, her glance lingering on Sophie before embracing her tightly. They remained that way for the whole minute. "Call me, okay?" Sophie nodded silently. "I will too."

The ensuing minutes blurred for Sophie; farewells were exchanged with hugs, and suddenly she found herself outside, unaware of how Emily and Mia had merged back into the crowd.

After days of preparation, it all ended in ten minutes, just like that. Feeling the urge to walk, Sophie said her goodbyes to Natalie and told her she would catch a taxi back. Upon reaching the city, she asked the driver to stop at Lenox Hill. From there, she slowly began walking toward downtown, wandering the streets until darkness fell.

She realized she hadn't eaten anything all day. She didn't want to eat alone, but she also had no desire to talk to anyone. Eventually, Sophie found herself at Battery Park, ascending to Nick's apartment. After a few minutes of ringing the doorbell, the door opened to reveal Nick, clad in casual pants and shirtless, clearly enjoying his day off. Without a word, Sophie stepped into his embrace. Words were unnecessary; he didn't need to see her face to know tears were streaming down her cheeks. It took her a moment to find her voice:

"You're the only person I want to be silent with right now."

20

THE NEXT MORNING, SOPHIE AWOKE AT NICK'S PLACE, REALIZING she had an early work meeting to attend. Hastily, she finished in the bathroom and quickly dressed. As she adjusted her hair while walking past Nick's office, his voice echoed from inside. Curious, she peeked in to find her boyfriend by the desk, draped in a towel, engaging in a multitasking ballet — flipping through documents with one hand and managing a phone with the other, his attempt at French breaking through the morning air.

"Eight in the morning in New York, and I'm without a lawyer by my side. Please, listen, I just need one document sent over... It's been a week of trying to get through to you, always hitting a weekend or lunch break..." His French faltered, interspersed with English for words he couldn't recall.

"Morning, baby, I've got to head out," Sophie announced, kissing him on the cheek.

"Hold on, don't hang up," he said, pulling the phone away momentarily. "Let's grab breakfast together."

"I can't today, I'm late for a meeting! What are you trying to sort out?" she asked, eyeing the documents.

"I need them to send over the Form 312 on intellectual property."

Taking the phone from him, Sophie switched to fluent French. "Bonne journée, madame!" she spoke rapidly, conveying her message efficiently before hanging up, as if the conversation was mutually unwanted. Handing back the phone, she left Nick staring after her, his expression one of utter surprise.

"How do you speak French so well?"

"Learned it in school. Got to run now," she said with a quick kiss goodbye.

Nick remained in place, phone in hand, as silence filled the line, his bemusement marking the start of the day.

In the afternoon, Sophie decided to pay a visit to her friends working at the Crence Gallery. As she stood in the hall designated for temporary exhibitions, she found herself captivated by a reproduction of Caravaggio's 'Supper at Emmaus.' The painting was more than mere art to her; it enveloped her, guiding her gaze and recounting its story with each viewing.

Behind her, a voice broke the silence, causing Sophie to startle. It belonged to the curator, who was also a friend.

"It catches you off guard every time, just when you think you've uncovered all its details," he observed.

Sophie sighed in response. Though she was reluctant to leave, the gallery was closing soon. "Leaving something beautiful behind is always difficult," she commented, her eyes still fixed on the painting.

"Tomorrow is the last day of this exhibition," her friend mentioned, folding his arms and positioning himself beside her.

They were similar in height and build, with him sporting a slender figure, accentuated by his loose-fitting attire. His chestnut hair and brown eyes complemented his handsome and elegant appearance, though Sophie found his overly feminine mannerisms slightly off-putting.

"Tomorrow's already Monday?" Sophie expressed her disbelief.

"Yes, is there anything you've left undone?"

"Derek..." She turned to face him, "Could I ask you for a favor?"

"I believe so."

"Would it be possible for me to use the gallery for a couple of hours tomorrow after closing? I'd like to give a personal tour to someone special."

"No problem," he answered nonchalantly, hands finding refuge in his beige cotton pants. "I'll give you the alarm code. However, I can't turn off the cameras," he added, his eyebrows raised suggestively, "Unless, of course, you're asking me to point out the blind spots…"

"That won't be necessary," Sophie responded with a laugh.

"It seems no man has yet had the privilege of that honor," he quipped.

Sophie faced him, "If that's the case, then perhaps the issue lies with me," she said with a smile. "I must be going now," she added, giving him a kiss on the cheek, "Please say hi to Melissa and let her know I wanted to catch up."

The woman she referred to was the gallery's director, who occasionally curated exhibitions herself. Her talent and vast knowledge of art history were remarkable, capable of answering any question and sharing stories unavailable through any search engine.

"Sure. Text me tomorrow."

Leaving the gallery onto 19th Street, Sophie messaged Nick: "I need you tomorrow evening. Can you make it?"

A few minutes later, he replied, "Of course."

The next day, Sophie sent him an address, intentionally directing him to a different street to locate the nondescript black entrance. She arrived early to meet with Derek and Melissa. Once the gallery was closed and everyone had departed, Sophie brought out a bottle of her favorite red wine along with two glasses. She then retreated to the staff room to change into a light cotton dress, beige in color with faint, almost imperceptible green lines tracing her form, giving the illusion of bare skin beneath. A delicate overlay of shimmering stones, small and sparingly placed, lent the outfit a minimalist elegance. With her hair let down, she evaluated her reflection in the mirror.

Nick called upon finding a parking spot.

"Do you see the black door at number 520? I'll meet you there," she instructed, hiding a smile at his evident confusion. Opening the heavy door, she found him waiting.

"Hey," she greeted, delighting in his bewildered expression.

"You always know how to surprise! What's this all about?"

"Crence Gallery," she replied, her arms tingling from the evening chill as she beckoned him inside.

As Nick stepped into the dimly lit space, his surroundings felt both familiar and surreal. The main lights were off, casting the paintings in a soft, mysterious glow accentuated by side lamps.

"This is the temporary exhibition hall," Sophie explained, gently pulling him towards a table set with wine and glasses. "Your personal tour starts right now, Mr. Davidson."

His attention shifted to her, finally taking in the details of her dress. "You're stunning," he remarked, looking deeply into her eyes. "This is incredible…"

"May I?" she gestured towards the bottle, ready to pour the wine. "Today is the last day of the Caravaggio exhibition. They're reproductions, obviously. And will be removed tomorrow morning."

"I've visited a few times, but never at night," he observed, taking in the hall once more.

"That's the beauty of it… I can't get enough of places like this. I may not be a skilled narrator, but I hope you'll feel the same sense of wonder," she said, handing him a glass.

"I doubt I'd find a better one," he responded, savoring a sip before gently kissing her cheek and wrapping his hand around her waist.

"Look at this painting," Sophie gestured toward the expansive canvas, "Supper at Emmaus. What do you notice?" She positioned them at the perfect vantage point from the artwork.

"Four men, and at the center, if I'm not wrong, is Jesus."

"Exactly. Caravaggio aimed to capture a pivotal Bible story with this piece. It's set just after Jesus was crucified and resurrected. His disciples, on their way to a nearby village in Jerusalem, meet him but fail to recognize him at first. Jesus joins them for dinner, and their expressions at the moment of recognition are immortalized here. Caravaggio's intent was for viewers to feel as if they could step right into the scene. Literally."

Sophie pulled Nick closer. "See the man on the left? Follow where he's looking," she directed, monitoring his gaze, "Now, you're looking at Jesus. Observe how his gaze leads to the lower right corner. Then, your eyes drift to the seated disciple, his arms wide open. From there, your gaze shifts to the table, where you scrutinize the fruits in the basket. It's only then you notice the basket is precariously perched on the edge of the table, seemingly on the brink of toppling."

With her hands encircling Nick's arm, Sophie sensed a slight twitch in his muscles and smiled at him.

"This is fascinating," he said, his eyes glued to the artwork.

"Caravaggio believed art should not only capture attention but also evoke a deep, emotional response. His mastery over light and shadow was unparalleled, bringing to life figures and objects that seem to extend beyond the canvas into our space. The characters' poses and gazes guide you to the elements designed to elicit a visceral reaction. It's as if you're drawn into the scene, sharing in the disciples' emotions."

"So, the fruit basket is there just to draw us in?"

"Not solely for that. Every item on the table — the bread, the wine jug, the chicken, the grapes, the apples, and particularly the pomegranate in the basket — has symbolic significance. Yet, the full meaning behind each remains elusive. What's evident is the story occurs in spring, but the assortment of fruits doesn't align with the season, suggesting they're laden with specific symbolism."

"Wow," Nick's gaze wandered to other artworks, "Did Caravaggio focus only on biblical themes?"

"Primarily, though he also depicted scenes from everyday life of the era," Sophie indicated a reproduction of 'The Cardsharps' nearby. "Now, you can see how he consistently infused his works with elements that bring them to vivid life."

They wandered through the next room.

"The permanent collection is housed here."

"I must have seen it, then," Nick said.

"Definitely," Sophie said, her attention captured by a striking canvas. She led Nick towards it, showcasing the distinct vertical stripes of varying colors and shades, a hallmark of artist Gene Davis. Sophie positioned Nick directly in front of the canvas, then moved to stand behind him, her hands gently resting on his biceps.

"Focus on the pink stripe in the center without looking away," they remained in this position for nearly a minute.

"The painting is coming alive," Nick marveled.

"On the sides, right?"

"Yes."

"Now, try shifting your gaze from side to side," she instructed.

"It's like playing a piano," Nick was mesmerized.

"Under natural light, the effect would be even more pronounced."

"This feels like basic physics, yet it's my first time really noticing it."

"You just needed to know where to look," Sophie wrapped her arms around him from behind, her chin on his shoulder. "But we're only scratching the surface of what's possible to see."

"Why's that?"

"Many galleries don't do justice to the artwork. They're essentially boxes with lights thrown on the paintings. But originally, artists painted in diverse natural light conditions. Back when artists crafted their paints only inside their studios and had to work swiftly due to the quick-drying pigments, they still sought natural light. The advent of synthetic tube paints allowed for outdoor painting, sparking the Impressionism movement to capture landscapes under specific angles of sunlight. Yet here we are, viewing this under minimal artificial lighting."

"You have a deep understanding of this," Nick said, holding her arms.

"Thanks! But I'm just passing on what I've learned. Some experts know more about art history than any search engine."

"It's clear you're passionate about it. That kind of dedication is unmistakable," Nick turned to face Sophie, who offered a warm smile in return.

"Our tour concludes here. How about we finish the wine by the pier?"

Leaving the gallery, they made their way to Hudson River Park. Sophie draped a trench coat over her dress, which added an air of elegance to her appearance, though it offered little in the way of warmth.

"Have you ever considered doing this professionally?" Nick gestured towards the wooden steps at the pier's end.

"Giving tours in galleries?"

Nick sighed, looking at her with patience as he tucked a stray strand of hair behind her ear. "I believe there are more avenues than just that."

"Well, I'm still committed to your project."

"Yes, but that's still within the realm of marketing."

"Perhaps that's where my issue lies. I have a myriad of interests, yet I don't feel a strong inherent draw towards any particular path. Entrepreneurship doesn't seem to fit me. I lack the compulsion to paint.

I revel in the study of art's theory and history, but teaching doesn't appeal to me — and that's mainly what those in the field do."

"I have to disagree. You're a great entrepreneur. I'm not just trying to flatter you. You possess a talent I've seldom seen in others. You tend to equate talent with tangible achievements, which is a misstep. Not amassing millions from a business or project doesn't negate your entrepreneurial skills," he paused, gazing into the distance. "You have an exceptional eye for detail, one that few can boast. As I can see, you've leveraged this skill across all areas. At the agency, clients are enamored with the system you've designed, streamlining processes without burdening them with unnecessary involvement. With the free port project, you've identified overlooked aspects and know precisely how to address them. And you're also very perceptive. Yet, you seem to conceal this profound ability to understand the world so intimately."

Sophie looked at him, speechless. No one had ever said such things to her before, possibly because no one had ever observed her so attentively. People are usually absorbed in themselves — their sensations, emotions, and feelings — rarely caring about others except in the context of interaction. Yet, we are all fortunate if we meet someone who sees in us what we haven't noticed before.

"This... I mean, these are the most beautiful and sincere words anyone has ever said to me," her voice softened.

"And what do people usually say? It seems like many have tried."

"I guess they say what they think I want to hear," Sophie lowered her gaze to her hands. "Attention is undoubtedly pleasant, but it doesn't necessarily lead to happiness. Perhaps it does for people like my sister. However, for those who prefer being in a relationship with one person, excessive attention can become overwhelming, even creating a sense of emptiness over time. It's like being constantly reminded of what you're missing," she paused, locking eyes with him. "Have you ever felt this way?"

"Yes, I have. More than once. But with you, that feeling is gradually disappearing," he offered a faint smile. "Back in a time, I decided to focus on myself, learning to better manage my attention and not lose sight of what's important."

"That sounds like a wise choice."

"It was, and it paid off," Nick agreed, nodding. "It's not every day you meet someone who organizes dates in art galleries."

"I'm glad you appreciated it. And I'm even more pleased that you understood what it was about. I felt like you did."

Nick leaned in closer to her, and after a brief moment, pulled back slightly to whisper, "What do you think teaches us to love?"

Sophie took a moment, lowering her gaze to his lips.

"The moment you realize you want to give someone everything. Your world. The best parts of it. The most stunning sunsets. Breathtaking views. The films and books that move you. The places you dream of visiting time and time again."

"Yes," he affirmed, kissing her tenderly.

21

WHEN SOMEONE CAPTIVATING ENTERS OUR LIVES, WE FIND ourselves more open to new experiences. Even if these experiences aren't entirely novel, we're enveloped in a wave of exhilarating joy, convinced that this time is different. Sure, it may have happened before, but never quite like this.

Thanksgiving had arrived. Nick and Sophie had hoped to gather with family, but his father was out of town, and her parents were far away in London. Consequently, they decided to invite only Natalie and Mike for dinner.

Sophie woke up early, with Nick lying beside her, facing her, clutching a pillow with both hands. She let her gaze wander over his arms, then gently touched his biceps with her fingertips, tracing them up to his shoulder. Sophie found herself enchanted by everything about him. His body, the shape of his muscles, his voice, his look, his laughter, and the dimples on his cheeks. Those fleeting nuances in his expressions, his charisma, masculinity, and kindness, all intertwined. His bravery in sharing his feelings, the generosity of his mind, and his self-awareness. She admired his confidence in the future and his certainty in his feelings for her. One might assume that individuals like him are free from internal struggles. Yet, there was something in his very essence that suggested otherwise. A certain indescribable sorrow that made him walk a fine line, adding to his allure. Sophie adored everything about him;

she just didn't know how to handle these emotions. She realized she was desperately holding back, trying not to dive headfirst into her feelings.

Nick stirred slightly, opening his eyes.

"I woke you up, sorry," she whispered softly.

"You were in my dream," he responded with a smile, looking at her.

"Really? What was the dream about?"

"It was about the night we met at the bar, remember? Only this time, you told me, 'I've been waiting for you for so long,' "he said with a faint smile. "It was strange because, in reality, you didn't even give me your number."

"You didn't ask…"

"You ran away," he raised an eyebrow.

"I ran away," Sophie agreed, smiling back. "I just realized something."

"What?" Nick lay on his back, placing Sophie's hands on his chest, she moved closer, resting her chin on her hands, and looked at him intently, "If you hadn't lied to me from the very beginning, we wouldn't have woken up together now. I wasn't ready for honesty with myself. And I wasn't ready to let a new person in my life," she unconsciously bit her lower lip.

Nick gently touched her face, running his thumb along her lower lip.

"It's okay. We all need those lies from time to time."

"I feel like you don't."

"You're wrong. I've lied to myself plenty."

"And now?"

"Now, I have something worth being honest for."

Sophie gazed into his eyes, feeling her emotions surge. Nick softly traced his palm along her cheek.

"Do you want to take a bath together?"

"Yes," Sophie shivered, her mind returning to the present. "Can you make coffee while I prepare the bath for us?"

Standing in front of the mirror, completely naked, Sophie felt an innate comfort in her body. This comfort was evident in her movements, her walk, and even her gestures. When Nick returned with two cups of coffee, placing them on the small table next to the bathtub, he kept his eyes fixed on her reflection and movements. Approaching without touching, his gaze shifted to her neck, then he began tracing the contours of her shoulders with his fingers.

"It's such a rarity for someone to feel so comfortable in their own body."

Sophie rested her head on Nick's shoulder, her eyes gently closing as he traced his hands from her collarbone down to her stomach.

"The coffee will get cold," he murmured, kissing her shoulder before heading towards the bathtub.

Sophie opened her eyes and smiled. "You still surprise me," she said, turning off the water.

"Because I don't leap at every thought of sex?"

The bathtub, set beside the window, offered views of the Hudson River. It was deep enough for the water to cover Sophie's shoulders, while for Nick, it barely reached his chest. He settled in front of her, hands resting on the tub's edges.

"That's part of it," she said with a smile. "I appreciate everything about you, even what others may not."

"Hmm," he observed as her feet glided up his body until they reached his chest. "Like what?"

"For one, you're consistently yourself, whether we're alone or among others."

"Some might find that boring," he said, his dimples showing.

"Not me. I also value the perfect balance of freedom we have. You don't disguise attempts to control with feigned concern and care."

"I've never appreciated that approach either."

"And you understand I don't like being fussed over in the conventional sense."

"But you do appreciate genuine care," he noted. "It's simpler to ask if you've eaten rather than to cook dinner, or to ask if you're cold instead of having a spare jacket ready. You prefer actions over words."

Sophie looked down, contemplative.

"You're right," she acknowledged, her hands finding his calves beneath the water.

"And here's something I like, though it might not appeal to everyone," Nick ventured.

"I'm listening."

"You're not jealous. You understand my long work hours, the late nights at the office or in meetings, without bombarding me with questions."

"I can understand this easily myself."

Their gaze locked; something tightened deep down their chests. Sophie searched for the right words to convey her feelings, but Nick spoke first.

"Come here," he whispered tenderly, reaching for her.

Sophie moved closer, enveloped by his embrace. She cradled his face, their kiss deep and longing as if making up for lost time. Nick gently pulled away.

"I love you," he said, shifting his gaze from her lips to her eyes. She whispered the same words in response.

It was well past noon when they remembered the impending arrival of their guests and the dinner that needed preparation.

Sophie, dressed in a white terry-cloth robe with a towel wrapped around her head, peered into the refrigerator. Nick, clearing cups into the sink by the kitchen counter, inquired, "What do we have for dinner?"

"Nothing," she replied, laughing.

"A few grand will rescue the evening," Nick quipped.

Sophie chuckled in response. "There were times I didn't even have that."

"Did your parents subject you to survival tests?" Nick teased.

"Not exactly, but before moving to New York, I gave them back the money they saved for me — they wanted to renovate our house in Scarborough. I left with a little that quickly ran out. But what made you think that?" Sophie hopped onto the counter near Nick.

"Given your family's background and your age, it's hard to picture you in such straits," he said, resting a hand on her knee. "My father, on the other hand, really did put me through such tests, both in high school and college."

"Making you work as a waiter?"

"No, he was keener on testing my entrepreneurial skills. At Harvard, it was easy to initiate or join projects, given the networks. Back then, we thought we were making good money, though it seems like pocket change now."

Sophie wondered about the difference in their financial standings. She knew little about his finances, realizing they hadn't discussed this topic before.

"And now?" She asked, "I think I'm playing at the level you consider a pocket change."

"We don't have to talk numbers. Just let me know when you need something," he said, kissing her lightly.

"People often say that until it's time to get serious."

"Oh, I forgot, you're a doer. Alright, let's suppose I earn more than you do; there's absolutely nothing wrong with that. And if you're thinking my words will just remain words, let's put that to the test right away," he said, his eyebrows lifted in challenge.

"What do you mean?"

They locked eyes in silence until Nick burst out laughing.

"Please, tell me you're working hard because you love what you do, not because you can't ask men for money."

Sophie's eyes widened; the unexpected turn in their conversation caught her off guard.

"What? Nick…"

"Alright, just tell me what you need," he said, taking her hands and intertwining their fingers.

"We're not doing this," Sophie attempted to steer the conversation away.

"Why not?"

"Because it's humiliating," she blurted out quickly.

"How does my offering support or help imply that you're weak or dependent? It seems I missed the memo where feminism took a step back. In case it's escaped your notice, society today paints women in two extreme lights: either as individuals who shoulder everything themselves, working tirelessly and refusing help despite the family's integrity largely depending on them or as those who contribute nothing, demanding money for manicures. What happened to finding a reasonable middle ground?"

Sophie listened, her initial discomfort challenged by his perspective. When did feminism take a wrong turn? It all seems so confusing now. Raised in a well-off family, she wasn't used to asking anyone for money. Generally, she wasn't accustomed to struggling. And, as it seemed to her, she was handling this life stage, including immigration, quite well. Why ask for money for something she could afford on her own? To her, this would be an admission of defeat, undermining her self-image as strong and independent.

She remained silent, unsure how to respond.

"I don't like this game," she said finally.

"Okay, imagine this... I know you love going upstate to spend time in nature, but you always borrow your sister's car. What if I buy you a car?"

In New York, just as in London, Sophie stuck to taxis without considering car ownership. When she needed to travel outside the city, finding options wasn't a problem. This purchase would simply be an unnecessary luxury.

"I'm not sure that's a good idea," she shrugged, taking off the towel and starting to comb through her damp hair.

"We found such an interesting intriguing topic. Now, I can say you still surprise me," he said, as he moved the collar of her robe aside.

"Nick," she began, wanting to change the subject, but he interrupted her.

"Just tell me... What kind of car do you want?" His fingers delicately pulled the robe from her shoulders, and as he kissed her collarbone, she took a sharp breath. He lightly touched her nipple with his fingers, then again, teasing her gently.

"Okay, let it be the same as yours."

"You have a good taste," Nick paused briefly, "A Porsche Panamera, in what color?"

"White."

"Why did it take you so long to answer something you already knew so well?" He looked at her questioningly.

"You're not going to buy me a car..."

"Why wouldn't I? We agreed to explore this hypothetical scenario you mentioned, remember? It's just a car, Sophie," he added after a pause.

"People view money differently."

"True. Yet, it seems we've stumbled upon something people called a soft spot," Nick said as he gently placed the robe back over her shoulders, helping her down from the counter.

"It's not a soft spot," Sophie countered, avoiding his gaze while pretending to untangle her hair.

"I'm not just referring to money. It's about how you'd rather purchase this car yourself than ask me for it."

She exhaled, finally looking back at Nick. "Asking for things isn't easy for me. Why ask for something I'm capable of obtaining on my own?"

"Because I want you to know you can rely on me. We're not business partners who split everything in half. We're not just friends, and there's more between us than just sex."

Sophie, still uncomfortable with the conversation, couldn't ignore the impact of Nick's words. She nodded in agreement.

"I'll grab my phone; we'll order some groceries, okay?" He suggested, giving her a reassuring kiss.

Returning to the living room, Nick seemed lost in thought as he opened the grocery app on his phone.

"Who were you with before me?" he asked suddenly. "My father used to say, 'Strong women are treasures for weak men.' Now I understand what he meant."

Sitting next to him on the couch, Sophie rested her head on his knee, looking up at him calmly. "Someone who gave love and care in the best way he knew. But it's not just about him. My parents always instilled in me the importance of resolving financial matters within the family," she explained, shrugging.

"I see. I'm sorry if I pressed too much," Nick responded, kissing her hand.

"If I'm to play along, can the car have a beige interior?"

"Whatever you wish. You'll have the freedom to customize it entirely, right down to the color of the seat stitching," Nick smiled, though a hint of sadness lingered in his eyes.

In the evening, Mike arrived first. The turkey was already roasting in the oven, and Sophie and Nick were busy finishing up the dinner preparations, wine glasses filled and ready.

"I was expecting everything to be ready by now," Mike quipped.

"And instead, you'll be tasked with slicing mushrooms," Nick retorted, playfully snapping a towel against Mike's forearm before he could dodge.

"How do you always manage to cause so much pain? Where are those mushrooms?"

Positioning himself at the kitchen counter beside Sophie, Mike found himself armed with a knife and cutting board.

"Do you receive the same treatment?" Mike asked Sophie, a playful tone in his voice.

"All the time," she laughed, wrapping an arm around Nick.

"Wait, are you telling me you two have moved in together?" Mike looked at them with his signature laid-back curiosity.

Exchanging smiles, Sophie was the first to respond. "Mike, you're starting off on the wrong note. How about some wine?"

"Oh, it completely slipped my mind! I brought a bottle of decent scotch. Check the bag," Mike remembered, then turned again to Sophie, still curious. "But seriously?"

"We didn't even think about it; we just enjoy spending time together whenever possible," Sophie explained casually.

Accepting this, Mike turned his attention back to the cutting board.

"This scotch is excellent! Mike, those mushrooms won't appreciate being sliced so slowly and solemnly," Nick joked, prompting laughter from Sophie.

"You guys are adorable; I never have this much fun around my sister."

"Well, she is a psychotherapist," Nick said, attempting a serious demeanor.

"Actually, when she talks about her psychology, her face is anything but serious. Yet, somehow, it always ends up making me a bit sad," Sophie added, eyebrow raised playfully as she held her wine glass.

"Is she coming tonight?" Mike inquired, continuing his methodical mushroom slicing.

"Yes, she's supposed to be here any minute," Sophie replied, taking a sip of her wine.

Just then, her phone chimed. Picking it up, Sophie read the incoming message aloud. "I'll be there soon, don't get bored. What do I need to buy?"

"Tell her we'll eat everything without her; that'll make her hurry," Mike suggested with a gesture.

Sophie looked at Mike, amused. "You certainly have a knack for this, but trust me, no manipulation works on my sister. She'd see right through it," she said, typing out a reply with her thumb.

Nick stepped out of the kitchen, leaving Mike and Sophie to themselves. Sophie leaned back against the kitchen counter.

"Do you mind if I ask you something?"

"It depends on the question," Mike looked up, puzzled.

"Was Nick's ex-wife working while they were married?"

"No, she was constantly studying, and I believe she did some volunteer work too. You know, you could've asked him directly."

"Yes, but then our conversation might have dragged on indefinitely," Sophie said, her tone reflective.

"I'm not sure what you're getting at, but it seems like you didn't find the answer you were looking for."

"On the contrary, it clarified a few things for me."

"I've been friends with Nick for many years. Believe me, whether working or unemployed, with or without a business, women from wealthy families have tried to date him... I've never seen his eyes light up like they do now. Especially after..." Mike's expressive look toward Sophie trailed off as he hesitated on his last words.

"Here, let me," Sophie offered, trying to end this conversation.

"What are you whispering about, ladies?" Nick called out.

He filled glasses with scotch, offering one to Mike, just as the doorbell rang. Sophie, wiping her hands on a towel, headed to the hallway. She opened the door to find her sister standing there with a bag.

"We were starting to lose hope!" Sophie greeted her with a smile and a hug.

"Don't start with me; I'm only half an hour late," Natalie retorted.

Upon entering, Natalie exchanged greetings with Nick, who helped her off with her wool coat.

"You have a cozy place here, or should I say, you guys do? I'm not quite sure," she chuckled, eyeing the fireplace in the hallway.

"You and Mike will get along just fine," Nick said with a smile as he hung her coat on the rack with other outerwear and umbrellas.

"Who's Mike?" Natalie inquired, her tone calm yet detached — a demeanor Sophie was accustomed to but often came across as novel and intriguing to others.

"Wine or whiskey?" Nick offered, gesturing towards the kitchen.

"Wine, please. Thank you!"

Entering the kitchen, they found Mike by the sink, washing his hands after preparing the veggies.

"Natalie, meet my childhood friend, Michael," Nick introduced him with a playful tone. "Mike, this is Natalie, Sophie's sister."

"Hi there!" Mike greeted, waving his still-damp hand towards Natalie, who responded with a polite nod.

"Hello," she said, her gaze quickly moving to his task. "I see why I didn't arrive earlier," she commented, indicating the busy kitchen scene.

"And she means it," Sophie added, coming up behind her sister and squeezing her shoulders. "Almost everything's ready, though!"

A large round table by the window was set meticulously with plates, utensils, various glasses, and napkins; the only thing missing was place cards.

"Nick, did you do this? Sophie has never been one for table settings," Natalie remarked, choosing a seat with her back to the window.

"Ladies and gentlemen, my sister," Sophie quipped, placing a salad bowl on the table.

"Actually, Sophie's responsible for all of this; I don't even know where she got all this from," Nick said.

Laughter filled the room as Nick pulled out a chair for Sophie and sat next to her. He positioned a bottle of wine in front of Mike and indicated a glass for Natalie.

"I can't imagine a cozier Thanksgiving than this," Nick toasted, raising his glass. "Here I am, surrounded by my best friend, my beloved, and her family. We have so many reasons to be grateful — more than one could ever dream of. And that's what we should remember to be thankful for, each and every day. Happy Thanksgiving!"

Echoing his sentiment, everyone raised their glasses, repeating his final words. Sophie leaned in for a kiss with Nick.

"So, how long have you two known each other?" Natalie's curiosity shifted from Nick to Mike.

"Seems like people don't live that long," Mike quipped.

"Since second grade, right?" Nick speculated.

"Our fathers are friends and even worked together for a while," Mike explained, readying himself with a fork, visibly starving.

"What do you do, if you don't mind me asking?" Natalie inquired, examining Mike closely.

"I'm in development. My father founded the company back in 1980," Mike responded, gripping his fork, a bit unsure.

"Has anyone ever mentioned that your personality seems atypical for your field?" Sophie teased, trying to suppress a smile, though her cheeks gave her away.

"It's quite the phenomenon, isn't it?" Nick joined in, amused. "He cracks jokes, the investors laugh; he invites them to dinner, and they laugh even more. Before they realize it, they've emptied their bank accounts by hundreds of thousands on yet another joke."

"They're just folks who don't know what to do with their money. They're happy to lose it. Then they meet me and think, 'This can't possibly end well.' Yet, in the end, they're always pleasantly surprised."

"Mmm," Natalie responded with a sweet smile.

"They're pleasantly disappointed," Sophie added.

"Nick, do you write?" Natalie's question came unexpectedly.

At that moment, Nick lifted his glass to his lips but paused, leaving the drink untouched. It was the first time Sophie saw him so visibly taken aback.

"What do you mean by that?"

"Writing, yes," Natalie continued calmly, meticulously picking at her salad.

"Why do you ask?"

"And you thought living with a psychotherapist is fun," Sophie interjected.

"Sure, you've suffered a lot," Natalie answered, without even looking at her sister. "You just seem very observant, paying close attention to the details and behaviors of those around you, and you possess a structured way of thinking — all essential traits for a gifted writer. Plus, you are involved in the publishing industry. My question is obvious." She fixed her gaze on Nick, waiting for his response.

"I do write a bit," he admitted, looking somewhat surprised. "But that's mostly because I've read so much. It gives you the illusion that you might actually be able to write something worthwhile."

"It's not an illusion. You should definitely write," Natalie encouraged, her words lingering in the silence that followed.

"I have no idea you write," Sophie broke the silence first.

"Wait, dude," Mike commented on Sophie's words, "I didn't know he writes," he expressed his surprise, drawing attention to himself.

"Because I haven't told anyone," Nick confessed, offering a faint smile.

Another pause filled the room, awkwardness hanging in the air.

"Well, your turn now. What's your secret? What do you do?" Mike directed his question at Natalie, his tone playful and teasing.

Nick and Sophie couldn't contain their laughter, and Natalie responded with a polite smile, echoing Mike's gesture by turning toward him.

"I make people's lives easier by prescribing them headache pills."

"And you excel at it!"

"Thank you!"

The evening unfolded more smoothly after Mike lightened the mood with his humor. Nick uncorked another bottle of wine as Mike entertained everyone with one of his comical tales. When Nick began to refill Sophie's glass, she declined with a shake of her head and a glance his way.

"I have a client meeting tomorrow. I'm going to end up with a headache," she said, standing to give Nick a peck on the cheek before excusing herself from the table.

"Are you sure?" he asked, his voice soft as he gently grasped her wrist. "It's still early."

Sophie responded with a kiss on his lips, her hands gently resting on his chest. As she walked toward the bathroom, Nick's playful retort followed her.

"Your sister's the one with the headache pills, remember?"

"They're so sweet together," Mike said to Natalie, deliberately ignoring Nick. "It's almost too much."

Natalie simply nodded, her thoughts elsewhere.

"She's earned it, though."

"And what about you?" Mike's gaze lingered on Natalie, full of curiosity.

Nick observed her closely, noting the fatigue in her eyes and her reluctance to engage in the game that Mike had started at the very beginning.

"Why do they make me feel like a stranger in my own house?" Nick rolled his eyes playfully.

As midnight approached, Natalie and Mike prepared to leave. Nick was tempted to suggest Mike stay longer, but he could tell Mike was keen on spending time alone with Natalie.

Exiting the building, they were greeted by the night as the doorman secured the door behind them. Mike continued the conversation with enthusiasm.

"It's still early, how about another drink?"

"It's already late, maybe some other time."

"Which direction are you heading?"

"I'm over in Dumbo."

"I've got my car. Let me drive you."

"It was great meeting you, Mike. But, I'll pass."

"Let me guess, 'some other time'?"

"Exactly."

They lingered on the sidewalk, awaiting a taxi.

"No taxi yet? Are you cold? There's a cozy spot nearby. It's small, but the jazz is fantastic, and the whiskey is top-notch."

Natalie pondered for a moment before responding with a smile.

"Why don't you ask if I'd go there with you on Saturday?"

"Would you like to join me there on Saturday?"

"No," she said, her smile broadening.

"So, when?"

"Sunday. It's my only day off."

"Sunday it is," Mike agreed, just as a taxi arrived. He courteously opened the door for Natalie.

Meanwhile, in the Battery Park City apartment, Sophie stood by the bedroom window, watching the rain start to drizzle. Emerging from the bathroom, Nick wrapped his arms around her from behind. She felt the warmth of his bare chest against her back and covered his hands with hers.

"Did you enjoy the evening?" he whispered.

"Absolutely. I feel so grateful for it," she leaned back into him, her nose against his cheek. "Sorry about Natalie. She can be a bit..."

"Straightforward?" Nick offered, chuckling.

"Yeah. But honestly, I was surprised."

"Nobody knew, except for one person. My mom had always known I write, ever since I was a kid. She was my only editor."

Sophie turned to face him, her gaze full of bitterness, but Nick was looking away.

"Do you see now? All those other things seem trivial, don't they?" he said, finally meeting her gaze.

She nodded, now understanding. Recalling the sadness in his eyes, she was horrified by her previous distance from the pain her loved one had endured.

"I've been waiting for you for so long. I should have said that the night we met at the bar."

"I should've stopped that interview and never let you go from the moment we met."

"I would have been terrified," Sophie said, a laugh escaping her.

"You seemed so out of reach. Nothing's changed, though."

"Well," she paused, finding the courage to express feelings she'd held back, "Loss teaches you to appreciate. Betrayal makes you guarded. But you, with all your kindness, shouldn't have had to go through what you did," her voice trembled.

Nick gave her a warm look.

"Can you share your story with me?"

"Will you let me read your book?"

He smiled.

"It's hardly a book. Just a bunch of scattered thoughts."

"I'd still love to read them."

"Okay," he said, gently tucking a strand of her hair behind her ear. "There's no rush."

"I wish that were true," Sophie said with a flicker of fear in her eyes.

"I'm certain of it."

"How can you be so sure?"

Nick sensed the emotions she was holding back. "Meeting you made everything meaningful again."

22

Sunday came, and Mike offered to pick up Natalie, wanting to ensure their date had all the proper touches. Yet, she claimed errands would delay her, promising to meet him at the bar at their agreed-upon time. Her deliberate distance only piqued his interest further.

A steady rain set the scene, epitomizing a typical November day in New York City with its gentle drizzle. The cold and damp seeped through, making even the heaviest coats feel insubstantial. It was the kind of day that made venturing outdoors comfortable only when wrapped in the warmest blanket.

Mike lingered at the bar's entrance, finishing a cigarette. He hunched his shoulders, the collar of his wool coat turned up against the chill. The bar, chosen for their date, was far from fashionable or modern. Nestled in an old basement, it featured a small stage and bar counter, its ambiance suggesting the furniture hadn't moved since the 1920s. Stepping through its door was like entering another time, a space indifferent to one's social standing or wealth. This was a haven for intimate conversations, classic jazz, and the rare freedom to smoke indoors, reminiscent of bygone days. Mike had noticed that the guests, whether by choice or chance, often donned business casual attire that hinted at the Prohibition era. From his first visit, he was utterly smitten.

He stubbed out his cigarette just as Natalie emerged from a cab.

"Hey!" she greeted, her smile warm, eyes reflecting calm.

"Hi!" Mike responded, his smile matching hers as he waved. "You look great!"

"Thanks. Should we head inside? It's freezing tonight."

"Yeah," he agreed, leading the way to the entrance, letting her enter first.

Inside, Natalie scanned the cozy space, noting the modest stage and bar counter. The bar was snug, with patrons settled into their preferred nooks — around small tables or at the bar, including two men by the door engrossed in deep conversation.

"What a charming place!" she remarked.

"It is," Mike agreed, taking her coat. "What'll you have?"

"Wine," she started, then, looking at the bartender, added, "Actually, a dirty martini sounds better."

"Got it, I'll be right back," he said, heading to the bar.

A woman at the bar glanced at Mike, her interest piqued, but she looked away quickly, noting he wasn't alone. Natalie found a seat at a small round table. As Mike ordered their drinks, she observed the guests, swiftly discerning details about them — details they'd likely be astonished to learn from a stranger. It wasn't mind-reading; rather, she intuitively understood their fears, desires, and intentions. It was almost automatic for her, a routine observation that had become somewhat mundane. Her genuine interests had narrowed to her profession, scientific research, and interactions with colleagues. Social excitement and personal dreams had faded into the background of her professional life. Yet, some realities still stung: the concern for her younger sister, watching her parents age, and the disappointment she often brought to men harboring hopes of a future with her. That Thanksgiving evening, waiting for a taxi, she recognized a familiar hope in Mike's eyes.

He returned with their drinks, pulling her back from her thoughts.

"This place is so cozy! How did you stumble upon it?" she inquired.

"After I came back from Boston post-graduation, a friend brought me here. He claimed he needed to get wasted before heading home," Mike recalled with a laugh, acknowledging the absurdity of the memory.

"Seems it was the best option at the time," Natalie observed, looking around.

"And it remains the top choice," Mike said, his gaze lingering on Natalie with a smile.

"You're a lot of fun," she remarked playfully.

"Huh, you know how strange it is to hear that during business meetings," he quipped.

Her laughter filled the space, showcasing her bright smile.

"And what happens when the jokes stop?" she asked, watching his reaction closely.

Mike paused, her question catching him off guard; he was usually never at a loss for words.

"Did you expect a date with a psychotherapist to be fun?" she teased.

"Is this a date?"

"I'd rather not label it, though you seemed keen on it being one."

"Why doesn't that idea appeal to you?" Mike asked, focusing intently on her, his hands resting on the table. Natalie glanced at his hands, then met his eyes.

"Why chase someone whose values and desires don't align with yours?"

"You're certain they don't align?" he probed.

With a sad smile and a bitten lip, she responded, "An evening with you and Nick was enough to see our differences."

"But if it's just my values and desires at stake, shouldn't I be the one to decide?" he countered.

As they spoke, the piano began to play, and the bar gradually quieted, giving way to the first set. The musicians savored the attention of the guests, knowing that as the evening progressed and drinks flowed, attention would wane, with guests becoming absorbed in their own worlds.

23

A WEEK LATER, ON THE SAME DAY, SOPHIE WAS CONCLUDING HER workday at the office. She decided against staying late, as Nick had promised to pick her up. Closing her laptop, she looked out the window. From her fifth-floor vantage point, she observed a young woman walking her dog, who was too engrossed in her phone to notice a raccoon stealthily approaching her tiny terrier from behind a trash can. "New York," Sophie mused with a faint smile on her lips.

"Wrapping up for the day?" the account manager inquired.

"Yes," Sophie responded, smiling.

"Me as well," said the blonde woman with round glasses, her hair neatly tied in a bun, as she addressed the young man sitting at the long table in the office's center. "Looks like you're in for a long night, Derek."

"I'm aiming to finish it today," he answered without looking up.

"Don't forget to set the alarm," Sophie reminded, rising from her desk, laptop in hand.

Meanwhile, Nick and Mike were en route to the office, with Nick having just picked up Sophie's new car from the dealership. The service was exceptionally prompt, clearly aimed at pleasing a valued customer.

"Are you serious? A Panamera? Why does she need such a big car?" Mike queried.

"She wanted it," Nick replied with a chuckle, aware of Mike's superior knowledge about cars.

"A coupe would have sufficed."

"It doesn't bother me, as long as she's happy with it. I was intrigued by her reaction, though. She seemed so out of her element; I've never seen her like that."

"Women who've earned everything on their own aren't accustomed to gestures like this. Makes sense, right?"

"Not in my book. But I appreciate her taste. This car is timeless. So, where can I drop you?" Nick slowed at a traffic light, signaling for a turn.

"Just around the corner," Mike said. Nick sensed his friend might have more on his mind but chose not to delve. He had an inkling of what it could be.

"Good luck, Romeo," Nick teased as Mike prepared to exit.

"See you, brother," he clapped Nick on the shoulder. "And thanks for the ride. Never thought I'd get to cruise in a Porsche!"

With that, Mike stepped out of the car. Nick smiled at the jest and drove to Sophie's office, arriving just as she was exiting the lobby.

Upon seeing the car, Sophie's face lit up with a smile. Even though she knew every detail about it, she hadn't anticipated receiving it so soon. As Nick approached, she looked at the car with fondness.

"Is everything in place?" Nick asked, standing beside Sophie and attempting to mimic her focused expression.

"If I just say thank you, it wouldn't be enough! What do people say in situations like this?"

"Just be genuine," Nick shrugged. "I could've just bought it for myself, but thanks, Nick. You definitely found the way to surprise me."

Sophie chuckled, wrapping her arms around Nick's neck, her eyes twinkling mischievously.

"Do you really think you need to surprise me? I still can't believe we met!"

"We would've crossed paths eventually," he replied, looking at her.

Sophie gently placed her hands on his cheeks and kissed him.

"I love you!"

"I love you more! Let's head home."

She nodded in agreement.

"Would you mind giving me a lift?" Nick asked playfully, tossing her the keys.

On their way home, Nick shared Mike's reaction to Sophie's new car.

"What does he drive?" she asked, eyebrows raised in disbelief.

"A Lamborghini Urus. He's quite the car enthusiast, with a collection that includes both automatic and manual transmissions. You might even spot him on the track occasionally. Arguing about cars with him is futile," Nick said with a smile.

"So, he drives a Lamborghini Urus while I have a coupe? And when did you guys meet up today?"

"He stopped by my office towards the end. It turned out we were heading the same way, so I gave him a ride. It seems he has a date with Natalie tonight."

Sophie was silent for a moment. Her sister hadn't mentioned anything about seeing Mike again. Considering it hadn't been long since their first encounter, Natalie probably hadn't had the opportunity. Besides, she wasn't one to openly share personal details even with Sophie.

"I hope he knows what he's getting into."

"I get what you're implying, but I don't know Natalie that well," Nick responded.

"She's very clear about what she wants, and there's a high chance they want different things."

"It seems so."

"Mike's a good person. I wouldn't want him to get hurt."

151

"He's an adult; he knows what he's doing. They'll figure it out," Nick said, refusing to explore the topic further.

Sophie didn't need to see how this story unfolded to feel empathy for Mike already.

Upon arriving home, Sophie enveloped herself in a blanket to fend off the evening's damp chill, noticing the apartment felt cooler as well. Entering Nick's office, she found him engrossed in a letter among several scattered on his desk. Wrapping her arms around his shoulders and draping the blanket over him, she said, "Is everything okay?"

"Yeah, I was searching for a particular letter and mistakenly opened the wrong drawer. Instead, I found this," he said, turning the letter over in his hands.

"What is it?"

"It's a letter from the British embassy, granting approval for a business visa. Five years ago, we were negotiating an acquisition with a British publishing house. They invited me over for negotiation," he reminisced, "but I declined the offer."

"How did everything turn out?"

"My business partner went in my stead. It's strange; I had completely forgotten about this."

"You don't suppose..." Sophie hesitated, sensing the direction of his thoughts.

"That we could have met five years earlier?" Nick finished her thought, still looking at the letter.

"It's remarkable how we're often presented with more opportunities to make decisions than we realize," she mused.

"And we don't always choose wisely."

"You had your reasons, though. Weren't you married by then?"

"I had just gotten married. She was reluctant to travel, and it seemed unreasonable to marry and then leave the country for an extended period."

Sophie let the blanket slide from her shoulders and perched on Nick's lap.

"As for me, I never imagined leaving London."

"What changed?"

"I yearned for a fresh start, to transform my reality until it was unrecognizable," Sophie trailed off, shaking her head, "Perhaps it's for the best we didn't meet sooner."

"Why's that?"

"Five years ago, I was entangled in trivial matters — complicated relationships, lacking self-confidence, you name it. I was lost in that mess. And you, you were likely enduring one of the toughest chapters of your life. We wouldn't have had much to offer each other then."

"Maybe, but I still wish we had met earlier," he said, leaning back into the chair. "I remember a time when interacting with people felt like a burden, lasting several years. My life seemed to pause while everyone else's moved on. I couldn't bear hearing people complain about missed opportunities, cheating partners, dull parties, drug-induced lows, and more. It made me nauseous. My therapist prescribed medication, but I never took it."

"Why? They say it helps."

"It felt like, without that pain, I'd be left with nothing. My father had become unrecognizable, cold and distant. I didn't love my wife; being with her felt incredibly lonely. Even sex felt like an obligation."

"Were you scared of that feeling?"

"No, quite the contrary; it seemed appropriate. But there was a day when I looked in the mirror and saw my eyes reflecting only light, nothing more."

"When did things start to change?"

"Deciding to divorce was a turning point. Mike took me to the mountains for a few weeks. For the first time in a long while, I felt like I was truly breathing. That's when the healing started."

"Thank you," she said, pressing her forehead to his.

"For what?"

"For sharing this with me."

"The healing process is ongoing," he mused. "I'm rediscovering things I had lost interest in, adapting and finding new replacements. Do you understand what I mean?"

Sophie nodded silently. Nick seldom spoke of his mother and brother's deaths, but whenever he did, she hung on every word. She admired his resilience and willingness to open up, something she once thought impossible.

"I find myself eager to come home in the evenings again," he continued. "Though it's infrequent, we have breakfast together. This apartment once felt so empty, but now, it's beginning to feel alive. I'm experiencing emotions during sex again," he said, kissing her wrist and feeling her pulse.

Sophie smiled, waiting for him to continue. "Is this like rediscovering how you used to feel the world?"

"Not exactly. I hardly remember my old perceptions of familiar things. I likely took them for granted, which means I didn't truly appreciate them," he said, placing his hand on her cheek, thumb brushing her lip. "Let's leave reflection for another time. Come here."

She gazed at him intently, wrapping her arms around his neck. "I never realized how spacious this chair was before," she joked, her smile betraying her playful mood.

24

THE NEXT MORNING, DESPITE IT BEING A SATURDAY — A DAY SHE often worked at least until noon — Sophie awoke early with altered plans. Opting to use the extra time to visit Natalie, she dialed her sister's number, awaiting her answer amidst the long rings.

"Morning! Can I swing by? I've brought your sweater and my designer just printed the first version of your article's cover," Sophie said when Natalie picked up.

"Hey! Thanks, dear. I'd have made us coffee, but I've unexpectedly got a patient at 11 am, so I'm already out," Natalie replied.

"I see. I'll drop everything at your place anyway. Take a look tonight and let me know what you think."

"Will do... and something else," Natalie hesitated, "You'll probably meet Mike at my place."

"Mike?" Sophie's surprise was genuine, despite having half-expected such news.

"Yeah, he wasn't in a hurry this morning, unlike me."

"I understand," Sophie replied, her tone hardening — a sign Natalie knew meant her sister was pressing her lips together in frustration. After a sigh, Sophie continued, "Why are you doing this? You know Nick sees him as a brother."

"How does their friendship preclude Michael from making his own decisions?"

"You know what I mean. It's not about their friendship; it's about the possibility of you hurting him. And Nick is caught in the middle."

"Which concerns you more? Michael's feelings, Nick's position, or your own sense of awkwardness?"

"Do you always have to be such a bitch?"

"Sophie, you know who I am. Are you accusing me now of being myself?"

Their conversation fell into silence. Sophie often found herself at a loss for words in arguments with Natalie.

"I was clear with him from the start, back at that bar. I said we weren't going to be serious. He chose to stay."

"Fine, you'll sort it out," Sophie conceded.

"Thanks!"

"By the way, did you enjoy Thanksgiving evening?"

"Yes," Natalie sighed, sensing the direction of the conversation.

"It just seems like we won't have more evenings like that."

"I know. And I'm truly sorry to dash your expectations, guys. It's not amusing to me at all. In fact, I see little tragedy in it."

"Maybe things will change with Mike?"

"Let's not go through this again. You know my stance. I'm at peace with my choices, and I hope everyone finds what they want in life sooner rather than later."

"Yeah, I get it. It's just hard for me to fully grasp your decision."

"That's understandable," Natalie replied, her voice competing with background construction noise, "I'm nearing the office, so I'll have to hang up now."

"Okay, call me tonight."

After hanging up, Sophie was left pondering. This topic seemed endless between them. Their differences were stark. Sophie always wondered how two people, raised in the same environment, the same family, with the same values, could grow up to be so different. Natalie had always been the contemplative and curious one, fully engrossed in exploring new things for the sake of the process itself, without needing anyone else's involvement.

Sophie, on the other hand, had always been deeply emotional, craving the presence of others and constantly engaging in communication. An offensive remark from a classmate could occupy her mind for days, a sign of interest from a boy could fuel her daydreams, a reprimand from her mother about chores would weigh heavily on her, and her stepfather's broken promises of returning home early would deeply distress her.

Despite growing older, their differing personalities continued to fuel conflicts between them. Sophie struggled to comprehend how her sister could remain so detached in situations, especially when her actions could potentially hurt others.

Arriving at Natalie's apartment, Sophie hesitated at the entrance. She glanced between the keys and the doorbell. With a sigh, still irritated by the situation, she opened the door with her key. Inside the kitchen, she placed her bag down and noticed there was still coffee in the machine. Listening for any signs of company, she heard noise from behind the bedroom door just before Mike appeared.

"Good morning!" she greeted, managing a smile.

"Hey! You probably weren't expecting to see me, huh?" Mike looked a bit uncomfortable.

"Nat mentioned you might be here. I just need to drop some things and then I'll head out," Sophie replied warmly, adding, "It's a bit surprising to see you, though."

"Yeah, I can imagine," Mike said, glancing at the coffee machine. "Are you hungry? Or maybe you'd like some coffee? There are a few nice spots nearby if you're not in a rush."

Sophie teetered on the brink of refusal, but a fleeting glimpse at the clock coupled with a sudden swell of curiosity swayed her decision. "Actually, coffee sounds great!"

Her curiosity often led her into complex situations, distinguishing itself by a lack of detachment. This time, it was mingled with empathy and a wish to be of help.

They found themselves at a café a few blocks from Natalie's apartment, discovering a shared preference for espresso as they ordered. In the Dumbo area, authentic and cozy places were plentiful. Yet, this café on Henry Street stood out, radiating European charm with its quietness and simplicity, setting it apart from the many spots nearby. People engrossed in relaxed conversations at petite tables, seemed to have nowhere urgent to be. Near the exit, bar-height tables stood for those who preferred to swiftly finish their coffee before dashing off. Sophie and Mike chose one of these standing spots.

"This place feels uncharacteristically calm for New York. What made you choose it?" Sophie inquired.

"I've heard they brew excellent coffee, and it's worth standing around for that."

"I recall similar cafés in France where our parents sent us for summer school."

"Yes, it does feel surreal, especially in New York. It's as if stepping through the door transports you to a parallel universe where time slows down," Mike observed.

"You're quite similar to Nick," Sophie remarked. "Your lifestyles, habits, preferences…"

"He's been my best friend my whole life. It's natural we've picked up habits from each other. Yet, I haven't managed to get him into racing, and he hasn't convinced me to love running," Mike said, his smile making Sophie empathize more deeply with him.

"Mike, you seem like a genuinely good person. You share similarities with Nick, but you're very different from my sister."

"It's amusing how you say the same thing in different words. She's mentioned our differences before, something about values and desires," He said with a wry expression.

"And it's true. I'm glad she told you."

"Why?"

"She might appear smitten, but I sense you both view your feelings through different lenses."

"Maybe it is so," Mike replied, his interest waning.

"Knowing you don't share her outlook, aware it might hurt you, why pursue it?"

"I'm not sixteen anymore, Sophie. Assuming I'm halfway through life without 'the one,' I'm simply exhausted. Tired of searching, of fighting the current, trying to steer life in a direction it refuses to go. Perhaps there's wisdom in accepting the present. Right now, I have Natalie. She's incredible — intelligent, ambitious, independent, and uniquely charming. Why should I walk away from that?"

Sophie fell silent, a frown creasing her brow as a chill swept through her. She stared down at her hands, words burning on her lips. "And I've spent my whole life fighting. Never giving up, right?" Crossed her mind.

"I'm sorry," she said, meeting his gaze. "You don't need my advice. I guess... maybe I wish someone had warned me once."

"Don't worry about it. I usually don't take kindly to unsolicited advice. But coming from you, it feels different."

"Really?" Sophie's smile was tinged with guilt.

"Yeah. Now I see why Nick fell so hard for you. You have this endearing quality," he sighed. "After meeting you, all he could talk about for weeks was your name and a new project of his. Watching a grown-up man, laden with responsibilities, fall head over heels like a teenager was incredibly amusing. His eyes lit up like those of a cartoon deer," Mike said, his smile warm and genuine.

"I try not to dwell on it too much when we're apart."

"Why's that?"

"Discipline isn't exactly my forte, yet I possess an abundance of emotion," she grimaced, "Just keep it between us. It's a big secret."

Mike chuckled, realizing the woman in front of him was far more complex and endearing than she first appeared, marked by kindness and sincerity that contradicted her initial facade of detachment. "And how old are you?"

"Twenty-seven."

"Interesting. So, Nick, Natalie, and I are about the same age, but you're the youngest," he mused, his gaze drifting. "Being under 30, it's natural for emotions to be more intense. Everything, even falling in love, feels different. Nick could tell you about that." Checking his watch, Mike sighed. "I should head out. I've got a work dinner tonight and I need to freshen up a bit," he said, rolling his eyes playfully.

Sophie hugged him. "Thanks for the coffee and the chat," she said as they parted.

25

THAT EVENING, MIKE'S PLANS TOOK AN UNEXPECTED TURN. HIS partner canceled their dinner with what seemed like a flimsy excuse, leaving Mike skeptical of the truth behind it. Compelled by a strong desire to see Natalie, he pushed aside his reservations and sent her a message.

She responded promptly, informing him she was wrapping up at the clinic.

"Hey," Mike's voice sounded through the phone, opting for quicker communication. "How about dinner tonight?"

"Hello," Natalie's voice, ever calm and unhurried, came through. "You're quite persistent, aren't you?"

"Yeah, well, what do you say? Should I come pick you up?"

"Alright. Give me half an hour."

Mike couldn't help but smile, a wave of joy washing over him. He wondered if this was how girls felt waiting for a call or a date with someone they were smitten with. Natalie seemed indifferent about whether they met again, a stark contrast to the excitement he felt. On his drive to her work, he pondered what exactly drew him to her so powerfully. Was it her free spirit? The idea of changing her? Or perhaps something deeper he had yet to discover. Maybe Sophie was right, and it would indeed hurt him when Natalie stopped responding to his calls.

Arriving at the clinic, he had just parked when Natalie appeared. She greeted him with a wave and a smile, moving towards the car with a lightness and grace that seemed to emanate not from her physical movements but from her very being. Her eyes sparkled with an insatiable curiosity and a complete indifference to how she was perceived by others. Mike was captivated, eager to be part of her world.

As she settled into the car, her gaze met his. "You look great, so happy!" she observed, her attention fully on him.

For a brief moment, Mike felt a twinge of discomfort at not being the first to offer a compliment.

"You look charming. How was your day?"

"Not very good, to be honest."

"Do you usually work on weekends?"

"Hardly ever. Today was an exception due to an unplanned morning session. Then, I learned one of my patients, whom I've been treating for six months, was transferred to day hospitalization at another clinic without any improvement."

"That sounds tough. I'm sorry to hear that."

"It's particularly disheartening since it feels like a victory for some of my colleagues. To them, drug treatment is the be-all and end-all," she said with a hint of sarcasm.

"I must admit, I'm not well-versed in your field, but I can sense your frustration."

"To put it in terms you might relate to, imagine if you caught a cold, and instead of a mild treatment, you were immediately bombarded with antibiotics."

"Was her case straightforward?"

"Not exactly," she said, clearly frustrated, "My approach often diverges from the standard practices here in the U.S."

"It's challenging to be taken seriously when you're slightly over thirty but look like twenty-four, huh?" he commented, hands firmly on the wheel.

"Exactly. Plus, your entire country is on Adderall. Guys, this is not okay," she adopted an exaggerated American accent, "It destroys mental health. You don't always need to be on your A-game. Overworking to the point of not being able to focus is a sign you need rest," she explained, before adding, "I guess you're prepared to listen to my venting without interrupting, so I'll stop here."

"I'm captivated by your passion. It's clear you care deeply about your work."

"It occupies a significant part of my life, by choice. Don't you feel the same about your job?"

"Not really," Mike admitted, eyes on the road. "I feel like I never got to choose. There wasn't a moment to consider my options. You and Sophie, you were fortunate to have that chance from your parents. I didn't, and neither did Nick, though he found his passion in the family business."

"Hmm," Natalie pondered, preparing her next question, "What would you change about your job, if you could?"

"I'm not sure. The company's fine. It's just that sometimes, I feel out of place. My dad expected a more serious demeanor from me. But maintaining a grave facade all the time, pretending I'm tired of life, that's not me," he glanced at her, "That's what draws me to you. You seem to navigate life with a lighter touch."

Natalie nodded, understanding dawning on her.

"Now it all makes sense. I see why you're drawn to me."

"Because you're free, vibrant, and your eyes... they're captivating," he smiled, meeting her gaze.

"Oh, Mike," she sighed, a hint of regret shadowing her expression, "I've been practicing psychoanalysis for a decade. Which eyes, you ask? Flattering, sure, but attraction goes beyond the eyes."

"What then?"

"It's about unresolved internal conflicts. Our psyche is driven to evolve, influenced by survival instincts and the need to release energy from mental blocks. Reproduction is a basic instinct, that's clear. But the intricacies of attraction — whom and why we're drawn to — is where it gets complex," Natalie paused.

"And?"

"What we often find is this: let's say you're struggling with an internal conflict about your social identity. You're unhappy in your career and unsure of your path. Then you meet someone whose life is the polar opposite. She doesn't just enjoy her job; she's devoted to it. And I, more than anyone, highlight this discrepancy. We haven't known each other long, but imagine a future where I'd be staying late, working weekends, preferring work meetings to our dates."

"Well, there are many girls who love what they do, but I'm drawn to you specifically."

"The concept of 'love' can be misleading. You won't get far with concepts like these. Consider Sophie. Does she love her work?"

"It seems so."

"And I can confirm this. Yet now, with a significant relationship in her life, she finds herself spending less time at work. The same goes for Nick. The fact that they both love their work didn't negate that their late nights at the office were prompted by the absence of something significant in their lives."

Mike absorbed her words, contemplative.

"You've just demystified romance," he said with a smirk.

"I warned you, darling. Reality is often more complex than simple explanations. Our internal conflicts and the influence of our surroundings are just the tip of the iceberg. But I'm not giving you a therapy session, forgive me," she smiled.

"That's the last thing on my mind. I'm starving. Let's eat."

Mike was silent during the drive, keeping their destination a secret. He was taking Natalie to his favorite steakhouse near City Hall, a spot she'd never tried before, which made the surprise even more delightful.

After dinner, at Natalie's suggestion, they headed to her apartment for coffee.

"Why choose this?" Mike inquired, his fingers lightly tracing a path from her neck to her shoulder.

"Not the usual approach, you mean?" Natalie responded, a playful smile on her lips.

"Sorry, but the odds are in my favor," Mike said.

"You're right. It's hard to articulate. How do you know you need only one partner?"

"It's a feeling. I find solace in the presence of one woman in my life, learning about her, building trust, and growing together."

"I'm just different. It's not boredom; I'm more intrigued by people and the various connections I can have with them," Natalie explained, her voice hinting at unspoken thoughts. "Once, I realized I don't want children."

"When did you come to that decision?"

"About eight years ago. Our cousin brought her newborn son over for the weekend. The entire house revolved around him. I felt like a stranger in my own home. After years of self-observation, my feelings towards motherhood haven't changed."

"Do you believe you might change your mind someday?"

"Those things don't just change out of the blue. A dramatic shift can only happen if a person lied to themselves before. True feelings, even the slightest, are recognizable early on unless someone else's influence comes into play."

Mike gave a resigned roll of his eyes, as Natalie's hand gently brushed against his cheek, feeling the texture of his stubble.

"What my work boils down to is helping people be honest with themselves. Many, like me, prefer not to pursue traditional family or relationship commitments, but they find it scary to admit it."

"That must be a common question for you."

"Yes, and out of my whole family, only my stepfather really gets it. My mom has come to terms with it, somewhat forcibly. Sophie, to this day, still doesn't quite grasp it."

"It seems she's worried about what's happening between us."

"Oh, she's more concerned about herself, and Nick, than us, believe me."

"Have you noticed how she tries to mimic your way of interacting with strangers? But she ends up just seeming cold and distant."

"I know. She's trying to use that demeanor as a shield, though it's not a conscious decision. She was deeply hurt by someone close, once. Ever since she acts as if she's indifferent to many things, but that's far from the truth," Natalie said with a soft smile. "So, if you ever think she doesn't love your friend enough, that's not the case."

"I came to that realization today when I bumped into her at your apartment this morning. She felt obliged to caution me against getting involved with you," he said, chuckling.

"Of course…"

"I have no regrets about it, though," Mike said, leaning in for a kiss, his hand trailing along her thigh.

26

MIKE AND NATALIE SPENT MANY EVENINGS LIKE THESE, ENJOYING themselves. Natalie felt seen and understood in her beliefs and their unique relationship dynamic. Mike seemed to have released his concerns, fully present and authentic. And for the first time in quite a while, he liked the guy he was.

One evening, they returned to the underground bar of their first date, now hosting a stand-up comedy night instead of jazz. After the final monologue, the comedian announced an open mic opportunity and anyone who wished could take the stage. Natalie looked at Mike, smiling gently and giving him time to realize.

"Come on, what are you waiting for?" she nodded toward the stage.

Mike hesitated, his skepticism visible, yet a smile betrayed his contemplation. Finding no real reason to hold back, he made his way through the crowd and ascended the stage in just two steps.

"Go for it, man," the previous performer encouraged, passing him the microphone.

"Wow, I'm actually doing this," he said, taking the microphone and scanning the room. The audience chuckled in response. "After those pros, you'll probably laugh at anything."

Mike raised his hand, counting off fingers, drawing light laughter from the crowd. "See, it works!" He paused, his gaze dropping. "Do you know what stops us from doing things like this? From stepping onto the stage, grabbing the microphone, and making a complete fool of ourselves? It's the fear of awkwardness. All those terrifying scenarios and doubts running through your head... 'Who let him up there?' 'He's not funny at all.' 'Put your pants on!' Can you imagine how many unforgettable experiences we deny ourselves just because we fear judgment and non-acceptance? As I was climbing up here, I bet you felt more awkward for me than I did. We all fear living out our worst nightmares. So, what haunts us in those nightmares? Stepping outside only to realize you forgot to put on pants. Ever happen to anyone here?" He focused on the guests near the stage. "And then, you leave your house in the morning, your heart skips a beat, you look down... phew, pants are on. But then, you quickly check around, 'No, just checking for my keys.' "He patted his pockets, eliciting growing laughter. "Got any other awkward nightmares?"

He directed his question to a woman sitting at the nearest table.

"That someone will undo my bra in the subway," she responded with a hint of jest.

Repeating her words for all to hear, he added, "Seriously? How do you cope with that? Maybe it's time to leave New York City, or at least reduce your subway rides; it's taking a toll on you! Sadly, I can't relate; I don't wear one... yet," he shrugged. "What else?"

He then looked across the hall, where a middle-aged chubby man was seated.

"That 'little guy' falls during sex," Mike echoed the man's words, eliciting laughter from the audience. "Oh, my friend, we'd need all night to cover that topic! It's beyond nightmares..." he shook his head, "If you're even dreaming about it... It's like opening a door only to find yourself back in the same room," Mike chuckled. "But let's leave the inevitable fate of 'the guys.' There is another one... Remember those fears from school? You go in for a kiss, and she turns you away. Been there?"

The man in the center of the room nodded. "Been there and after school years," he shouted.

"You mean recently?" Mike asked, with a hint of amusement, "And then you think, 'Well, at least tonight I don't have to worry if it'll rise or fall,'" he paused, observing reactions, "But here's a twist: I met a girl who told me straight up not to kiss her," he glanced at Natalie, "and it turns out, it was more than worth it! Thanks, folks!" He bowed slightly in response to the applause.

Once Mike came down from the stage, they left the bar behind for a leisurely walk through the city.

"I can't be the first to notice you've got a knack for this," Natalie remarked, one eyebrow arched as she gazed at him.

"I'm not sure. Some people mentioned my sense of humor," Mike responded, being skeptical.

"But it's more than that… It's your confidence, your charisma, your eloquence. You could host a TV show or a late-night gig… There's a world of possibilities where you could apply those skills."

"Becoming a stand-up comedian might mean I'd have to pay for the privilege," Mike joked.

"Oh, come on. You can always juggle this with your main job. But let me tell you something. People who do what they love blossom to their full potential. They earn more than they ever could elsewhere. Imagine waking up daily to something that fills you with peace and authenticity."

"That sounds dreamy," Mike sighed, the thought distant. "I've long forgotten what that feels like with my current job. But mixing it with something else? I can already see my dad's reaction — now, that'd be worth the price of admission."

"Confronting our parents, especially as we age, can feel like battling the voices they've implanted in our heads," she observed.

"True. My dad's era believed in passing the baton from father to son. That's why Nick never told anyone he writes. I figured that out later. Creative paths aren't easily embraced by those destined for a specific role."

"Are you an only child?"

"No, I have a younger sister, Bethany."

"I see," Natalie paused, considering her next words carefully. "You do realize that sooner or later, you have to address this issue? Stop waiting for your opportunity to be free in the form of... your father's passing."

"Yeah, that was an option."

"He doesn't deserve that. Besides, he has the opportunity now to pass on his business to whomever he deems fit."

"Oh, Nat," he shook his head, looking ahead, "You know, you're really turning me into a wall-climber with all these antics!"

"No, I'm guiding you towards finding yourself. But let's change the subject; we have more interesting things to do."

Stopping, she squinted playfully, a spark of mischief in her eyes. Mike caressed her face, cold from the damp air of the night.

"How could I ever let go of someone like you?"

"I don't know... but from what I see, you'll decide that on your own," she whispered.

"Not today," he leaned in, feeling her lips eagerly meet his.

27

AS CHRISTMAS DREW NEAR, THE HEART OF NEW YORK CITY BEGAN its magical metamorphosis into a dazzling tapestry of twinkling garlands and glistening plastic toys. Every few minutes, someone was lugging a tree twice their size down the street or strapping it onto the roof of their car, blocking the rearview. In every establishment, the relentless repetition of Christmas songs filled the air, creating an inescapable festive symphony. The flashy store windows screamed about how this holiday had become yet another marketing tradition. Despite the glaring absurdity of this tradition, one that seemingly encourages lavish spending, Christmas is adored with unwavering affection. Even the staunchest skeptics held a quiet excitement, buried deep within their hearts. They fondly recalled the fragrant Christmas tree from their childhood, the one their father used to bring home on Christmas Eve. And, without hesitation, they could list all the dishes their mother would lovingly prepare during those festive days. Anyone with cherished childhood Christmas memories had an unconditional love for this holiday. When everything around was aglow with warm lights, even if just for a moment, that joy felt as if it were experienced for the first time.

Sophie treasured her Christmas traditions, each one steeped in warm, fond memories of celebrations with her family. However, for the second consecutive year, she found herself unable to travel to London to be with her parents. Recalling her first Christmas in New York sent shivers down her spine; it had been a difficult time. Indeed, our most cherished holidays often bring our shortcomings into sharp focus, highlighting how our lives can diverge from our desires. One may long to celebrate with a beloved companion, only to find themselves embarking on a solo journey. Similarly, a recent move to a new city can disrupt plans to reconnect with old friends. Amidst our daily routines, we often distract ourselves with pressing matters, but the holidays have a way of stripping away these distractions. It feels as though everyone has gone home, engrossed in family affairs, leaving little room for connection in the coming week.

During that challenging Christmas, Sophie questioned whether her profound affection for the holiday was worth the emotional toll it took on her. And yet, exactly twelve months later, she felt genuine delight and hope once again. Throughout, Natalie had been a constant presence, though she never shared the enthusiasm for family ties or festive customs. However, this Christmas was different; Nick was next to her. His appreciation for her warmth and festive spirit seemed sincere, or perhaps he simply adored the spark in her eyes whenever he proposed something to enhance the holiday mood, no matter how small. Bringing a live tree into the apartment, selecting garlands in her preferred shade of warm yellow, getting tickets to a classic Christmas movie, or navigating his way through her mulled wine tutorial without knowing the first thing about it. For Nick, these moments unveiled her true essence, free from the constraints of vulnerability.

One quiet evening, just after work, Nick stopped by Sophie's office. Everyone else had already left for the day.

"I'm having dinner with the chief editor of Puzzle Publishing. You should come," he suggested, perching on the edge of the long table at the office's center.

"It's a business dinner, though. What would I be doing there?" Sophie inquired.

"It's not strictly business. He's a close friend, and we've been working together for years. Sometimes, we have dinners just to catch up, though we might talk about new authors we're publishing," Nick explained.

"In that case, I'd love to join," Sophie responded, moving closer to Nick. "You know, I could listen to you talk about literature for hours."

"Then, that's exactly what I'll do," he said, meeting her eyes with a steady look and taking her hand to draw her nearer.

"Thanks for..." She hesitated, glancing down.

"For what?" Nick prompted, pulling her closer and gently lifting her chin.

"For the sense of home, you've given us. For making me look forward to coming home during Christmas."

"I should be the one thanking you. Do you know what really sets the holiday mood?" Sophie gave a small shrug.

"Your emotions. They're adorable. I never imagined I'd be so captivated by someone," he said, his voice soft, a smile playing on his lips as he watched her cheeks dimple with a blush.

"The best thing is falling in love at Christmas," Sophie whispered, pressing a light kiss to his lips, then lingering on his lower lip, moving in sync with his.

"There's something even better," Nick murmured, holding her just a breath away. "Finding true love at Christmas."

They arrived at an intimate Italian restaurant in SoHo for dinner, set to meet the chief editor of Puzzle Publishing. He had held the position for the past five years. Around sixty, the man had russet hair and a beard flecked with gray. Slightly plump and wearing round-framed glasses, he had the air of a university professor. At first, Sophie couldn't place his familiar look, but then it clicked: he reminded her of her fine arts history professor.

"Fred, good to see you!" Nick greeted him with a warm handshake, then stepped aside slightly. "Let me introduce my girlfriend, Sophie Lind. Sophie, this is Fred Ottenberg."

"It's a pleasure to meet you, Mr. Ottenberg!" Sophie reached out her hand.

"Just Fred, please. I hope my age doesn't preclude a bit of informality!" he replied with a broad smile.

Their introduction was briefly interrupted by the waiter, who guided them to their table.

"What a lovely evening," Fred commented, perusing the menu.

Nick smiled, familiar with Fred's tendency to fill the silence with such observations.

"I've dined here before. Their salmon ceviche is not to be missed," Fred added.

After they had placed their orders, Mr. Ottenberg leaned back and looked from Sophie to Nick.

"Sorry to spring this on you, Nick, but I'm a bit surprised! You've never brought a girlfriend to any of our literary evenings before," he said.

"That's reassuring to hear! I was worried I might not be able to keep up with your conversation," Sophie responded.

"I'll pretend I believe you," Fred said with a chuckle, then paused as a thought struck him. Turning to Nick, he retrieved a bound stack of papers from his briefcase. "This is the first part, and it's quite impressive! It reminds me of early Hemingway."

Nick took the papers and glanced over the cover page.

"There might be issues with the title," Nick observed, scrutinizing the text.

"We can probably persuade the author to change it. That's the least of our concerns. The book's merit is undeniable. Such writing is increasingly rare."

"What do you mean?" Sophie interjected, taking a sip of water and grimacing as she encountered ice.

"As you read this manuscript, you sense the author's confidence. He articulates his views on the world and society with conviction, occasionally in categorical terms. Crucially, he explores enduring values — courage, honesty, bravery — portraying masculinity through a classical, conservative lens. This approach offers a refreshing change. In contrast, contemporary literature often veers toward introspection, with authors sharing nuanced views on subtle and mystical phenomena. Literature has increasingly become more reflective."

"Oh," Sophie remarked, "that's similar to trends in the visual arts. Once, galleries predominantly featured landscapes with multi-layered perspectives; now, they mostly showcase abstract expressionism."

"Do you work in visual arts?"

"No, I'm in advertising."

"Though she tends to downplay it, she has a deep understanding of visual art theory and history," Nick interjected, still focused on the papers.

"There are plenty of experts in that field," Sophie said with a smile towards Fred.

"Well, we all find our way to our true calling, sooner or later," Fred concluded, clasping his hands together.

Upon hearing Fred's words, Nick's gaze drifted into the distance. He was transported back to the moment he first told his mother about his dream of becoming a writer. He was only fourteen. She had smiled gently, kissed his forehead, and reassured him that he could achieve anything he set his mind to. Yet, for a fleeting moment, he had noticed a shadow of sadness in her eyes, a silent acknowledgment that his father would never support his ambition. This memory had resurfaced often since Thanksgiving, after Natalie's revelation. Nick had long since found solace in pursuing his passion privately. Now, as he pondered the possibility of sharing his work with the world, he questioned whether there was deeper fulfillment in contributing something meaningful, something that truly aligned with his soul. Everyone has their unique medium of expression, whether it's through writing, saving lives, or creating new technologies. Yet, Nick's lingering doubts suggested he might not be fully prepared to take that leap.

"Would you like to see a magic trick?" Fred's deep voice cut through, snapping Nick back to the present. He was addressing Sophie.

"Absolutely!"

"What's your favorite book?"

"Dandelion Wine, by Bradbury."

"Ah, that tells me you had a delightful, carefree childhood, likely spent summers away in the countryside with your parents or grandparents. Those memories are precious to you. You have little rituals that bring you comfort and a sense of safety, echoing those days. You're a romantic at heart, given to nostalgia. Rather than reveling in fleeting pleasures or whims, you treasure enduring connections, longstanding friendships, and the idea of building a family."

"That's astonishing. It feels like being exposed in front of everyone," Sophie laughed.

"It's a remarkable book, and you, too, are remarkable. Holding such values is rare and invaluable in today's world. However," he motioned with his hand, "there's one aspect of people like you that I can't quite envy. You find it hard to deal with loss and the end of relationships. I can deduce that from your favorite book, but I can only imagine what you truly experience in those moments."

Fred cleared his throat, shaking his head in mild disbelief. His tone was as casual as if they were discussing something mundane, like the salmon ceviche or the weather outside. Yet, a knot formed in Sophie's throat. A brief shadow of confusion flickered across her face, but she regained composure when she felt Nick's leg brush against hers under the table. He gave her a look, silently asking if she was okay.

"It's often more challenging than words can express," she paused, gathering her thoughts. "But I'm more interested in hearing about your new find," she added, gesturing towards the stack of papers.

"Ah, an incredible author, Neil Newman. This is his second book. Unfortunately, we missed out on his first," Fred responded.

"His debut didn't fare well," Nick said. "He chose the wrong publishers. By the time he approached us, the book's ratings had plummeted and it had barely caught anyone's attention. However, Fred's personal assistant took a chance on it, promising Neil she would give it a read."

"A few days later, she burst into my office, insisting I read his work," said Fred.

"When you scheduled a second meeting with him, you invited me along, hinting you'd discovered something special. I was struck by his youth, barely forty, yet his writing possessed a depth of wisdom and insight. He has this rare ability to observe and articulate details that many overlook, consumed by their own realities. I remember his words that night," Nick gestured toward Fred, "He said, everything I've ever prayed for was just to become a good writer."

Nick's voice trailed off, his gaze drifting. Surrounded by understanding companions, he sensed they would grasp his thoughts even if he faltered mid-sentence. Sophie sought to uplift him, and maintaining the flow of conversation seemed the best support she could offer at the moment.

"Finding someone truly passionate about their craft is indeed fortunate," she remarked, turning to Nick.

"And you're absolutely correct," Fred agreed.

After dinner, Sophie and Nick stepped outside, walking a couple of blocks to the car. Sophie buttoned her coat, shivering in the brisk wind. Nick wrapped an arm around her, planting a kiss on her forehead.

"Let's head out; it's not too far," he suggested, his gaze drifting to a store window they passed. "Christmas is around the corner. Do you have any special wishes?"

"No... You don't have to get me anything," she replied, her voice tinged with hesitation as she eyed the items in the display. "But, if you insist, something personal would be nice."

She paused, taking his hands in hers.

"Maybe... your book," she suggested, looking into his eyes, searching for his response.

"Sophie..." Nick smiled, diverting his gaze. "It needs a lot of editing; I never imagined sharing it."

"I just want you to know I'd love to read it," she said, standing on her toes to plant a quick kiss on his lips.

Nick shook his head, a wave of emotion washing over him. It felt as though something inside him breaking apart as if there wasn't enough space for it. His feelings for Sophie surpassed everything he'd ever hoped for. The realization that she felt the same was overwhelmingly powerful.

28

THE FOLLOWING DAY, NICK FOUND HIMSELF THINKING ABOUT Mike, realizing it had been weeks since he'd last seen his friend. He had a hunch about what Mike might be up to and sent him a text, suggesting they catch up over lunch. The reply he got was unexpected, an invitation to meet at a bar that evening instead. Although Nick wasn't a regular at this bar, he knew it well.

Upon his arrival, Nick scanned the room for Mike but was unprepared for what he found. The bar was hosting a stand-up comedy night, and to Nick's astonishment, Mike was the next performer. Nick quickly grabbed the nearest available seat, eager yet surprised to see his friend take the stage.

Concealing his amazement was challenging as Nick watched, once more struck by Mike's natural charisma and eloquence. Onstage, Mike seemed to escape the discomfort he often exhibited in his family life, at work, during partner negotiations, and in other roles that never quite fit him.

Before beginning his performance, Mike caught the look of astonishment on Nick's face, which momentarily heightened his own apprehension about revealing this different side of himself in familiar company. However, as he turned to face the audience, their eager anticipation fueled his confidence. Jokes began to flow, and with a smile,

Mike brought the microphone to his lips. After his set, he rejoined Nick at the table.

"You are something else, man! That was fantastic! How long have you been performing here?" Nick inquired, genuinely impressed.

With a playful punch to Nick's forearm, Mike began to share the story of his unexpected debut on this very stage, sparked by an evening spent with Natalie.

"Wow, you caught me off guard, but it was incredible! Natalie seems to be having a great impact on you. I've always thought you needed a hobby like this, something that truly brings you joy."

Mike gave a hesitant nod, feeling the pull of the stage more intensely than he had anticipated. Once he experienced the thrill of being in his element, the thought of returning to his previous state of confusion, uncertainty, and perpetual discomfort seemed unbearable. It was becoming clear to Mike that he didn't want to regard this newfound passion merely as a hobby.

They relocated to a quieter place down the street for a private conversation. Once the waiter had set down two glasses of whiskey before them, Nick's gaze wandered, drawing him into memories. His last visit to this place was with his ex-wife and her parents over dinner. He had never taken to her parents — typical, arrogant Republicans. Her father had amassed his wealth through the stock market, occasionally crossing ethical lines, always shielded by an army of lawyers. Coming from affluence, her mother boasted an impressive education and a flawless smile. Yet, her husband's unfaithfulness was hardly a secret, betrayed by his leering glances at waitresses, hostesses, and other admirers. Nick seldom interacted with them, but he couldn't ignore how his father-in-law would slyly pocket phone numbers from waitresses after leaving the restaurant bathrooms. In stark contrast, his mother-in-law was the picture of kindness. Her impeccable manners, gentle voice, and thoughtfully curated topics of conversation spoke volumes. Unemployed, she devoted herself to charity work, though this seemed a secondary priority next to ensuring her daughter's advantageous marriage. She considered her own marriage successful, despite likely being aware of her husband's affairs. Nick suspected she chose to overlook his indiscretions, perhaps clinging to the hope he might change, or maybe because the thought of surviving alone was unfathomable to her.

Ironically, the feeling was mutual. They also held a certain disdain for Nick, viewing him as someone born into prestige with a silver spoon in his mouth. Despite this, they were determined to marry their daughter off to someone of his stature. Perhaps this was the motive behind sending her to Harvard, investing not only in her education but in her prospective marriage as well. Nick frequently wondered whether his feelings for his ex-wife were genuine, especially given his aversion to her parents.

"Why are you so lost in thought today?" Mike's voice snapped Nick back to the present.

"Just reminiscing… The last time I was here, I was with Diana and her parents."

"Ah," Mike drawled, "Speaking of which, I bumped into Matt recently."

"Did he pass along any warm wishes?" Nick asked with a smile.

"He did, actually. But honestly, I think it's time you let go of that guilt."

"I made a mistake and paid for it. Still, being labeled as the guy who broke someone's heart and supposedly caused all their problems isn't a great look."

"I think you made the right call. You're happy now, and I'd bet Diana is too. Things turned out for the best, didn't they? Do you have any regrets?"

"Not a single one," Nick stated firmly. "You kidding? Towards the end, I dreaded going back home, not to mention everything else…"

"How are things with Sophie?"

"Better than just well. They're great, actually… especially when it comes to everything else," Nick said with a chuckle.

"Then that's fantastic," Mike replied. "So, are you done dwelling on your ex-wife and her parents and all that?"

"You're right," Nick sighed, redirecting the conversation. "So, what are your plans with this comedy venture?"

"I'm not entirely sure. For now, I'm just enjoying the open mic nights. It's all so new to me; my whole world feels flipped on its head."

"Seems like it shouldn't really impact your day job, though."

"That's just it, Nick," Mike replied, shaking his head. "I'm not sure I want it to stay that way."

"You're not seriously considering leaving your father's firm — your firm," he quickly corrected, "to pursue comedy full-time, are you?"

"It's what I dream about. I haven't vocalized it much, but," he paused, collecting his thoughts, "I've reached a point where I no longer want to wake up in the morning and go to that job."

Nick looked thoughtful, pondering the situation. He couldn't imagine making such a leap himself; it seemed too impulsive. He was ready to lay out a list of reasons why Mike should reconsider such a sudden move. His primary worry was Mike's father's reaction. He was certain the man wouldn't understand, or worse, he'd be utterly unable to accept it. With some people, you don't need to test the waters to predict their reaction — they ensure you already know. Nonetheless, Nick chose to approach the subject from a different angle.

"Don't get me wrong, but have you considered what you're up against? Your current lifestyle isn't sustainable on a comedian's salary — in fact, it's hardly sustainable on any salary. And bank accounts run dry quicker than you'd expect."

"Nick, do I really need a second Lamborghini? If it doesn't bring me genuine happiness, it's not worth a lifetime," Mike responded.

Nick nodded slowly, taking a sip of his whiskey. "You have a point... Mike, you know I support you fully. I'm just asking you to consider whether the cost might be too high."

Mike's gaze fell as he swirled the glass in his hand. He yearned to close his eyes and awaken in a new reality, free from obstacles, where he could truly be himself. But life is anything but a movie. He had spent enough time dreaming; it was now time to take steps forward and turn those dreams into reality.

"Dad invited you and Greg to the Long Island house for Christmas. And Sophie too, of course," Mike mentioned.

"Thanks! Are you thinking of inviting Natalie?"

"I'm not sure."

"It's just for one day. Just make sure not to tell Arthur that she's the reason you're considering leaving the company. Otherwise, we'll have a Christmas to remember," Nick chuckled.

"Yeah, and only Nat would stay calm and collected, as always," Mike replied, his smile radiating warmth.

Nick noticed but remained silent. What was there to say? Advising someone in love to slow down is akin to asking them to stop breathing. Love envelops us, influencing not just our feelings but even the expressions on our faces. It seemed impossible for him to mention her name without a smile.

29

MIKE STEPPED OUT OF THE RESTAURANT INTO THE COLD, DAMP AIR. Despite the late hour, the idea of going home to sleep was unappealing. Deciding to leave his car in the parking lot for retrieval in the morning, he opted instead for a walk to gather his thoughts on the day's conversations.

He halted by the roadside, undecided on a direction. Natalie's place was about an hour's walk away. Without calling or texting her — hoping for a surprise visit — he wasn't sure if she'd be home or if she'd be alone. Yet, the urge to see her was overpowering. It might have been passion, maybe infatuation, or perhaps it was the way she seemed to belong to a different, simpler universe that appealed to him amidst his complexities.

He didn't notice how he covered this distance. The ambient city noises — the hum of traffic, distant sirens — were all muted, replaced by the music in his ears. If asked later, he couldn't have described the route he took. Standing in front of Natalie's house, he looked up, feeling the chill wind but remaining still, hands buried in his coat pockets.

A girl approached and positioned herself beside him, hands tucked into her pockets and gaze directed upward, just like his.

"I guess she's not home," came Natalie's voice.

Mike turned with a smile. The cold had tinted her cheeks and nose a slight red, yet she radiated profound comfort and contentment.

"Why are you here? It's well past midnight," he asked.

"Did you think you were the only one in New York not sleeping tonight? Come on, let's get something warm to drink," she suggested, extending her hand.

They settled into the kitchen with steaming mugs of tea, Natalie evidently eager to soak up every detail of Mike's evening at the bar: his performance, Nick's reaction, if he was surprised.

Observing her, Mike felt a pang of envy for her unburdened freedom. Natalie navigated life with a self-first principle, which seemed to shield her from the weight of external judgments. She made choices based on her own well-being, largely indifferent to others' opinions. Ultimately, Mike realized, that when people talk about someone, they are just revealing parts of themselves.

"Nat, does it get any easier?" he asked, his smile tinged with melancholy.

"It'll hit you even harder," she responded with a nod. "But, you know, life is simpler than we make it out to be. It's just that realizing this is the complex part. And, by the way, you'll never have more time than you do right now."

"Do you have someone to lean on too?"

"Sure, but I rarely feel the need to complain. The 'cage' you feel is all in here," she said, circling her finger around her head.

"Why do I get the feeling you hide your emotions, playing the therapist for everyone instead?"

"Only for those who come to me with problems. You need to sort yourself out before trying to handle anyone else's issues," she replied, her tone firm yet detached, breaking the moment's intimacy. She contemplated her next words. "I'm not interested in accompanying you through the challenges you're currently facing. I can be a temporary friend, perhaps the only one you'll confide in about your struggles."

His initial shock at her blunt honesty gave way to reflection. His life was indeed in disarray, his past relationships were merely distractions from deeper issues. Natalie's words were a sobering realization; he was using their connection as an escape rather than facing his reality. Regaining his composure, he turned to the window.

"You're right. I've been avoiding what I need to face head-on."

"It's going to be okay," she assured him, placing a comforting hand on his. "Though it might not seem like it now, things will work out."

"I want you to join me for Christmas at my parents' house on Long Island. Your sister and Nick will be there too."

Natalie hesitated, then finally nodded. "I think we'll manage to brighten up the holiday. I have some news myself," she added, sharing a meaningful look with Mike.

30

On Christmas morning, an unexpected snowfall blanketed the roads, creating picturesque traffic jams. This festive morning was truly cherished by those without the urgency to rush anywhere. Sophie, still groggy from sleep, wandered to the window, her fingers brushing against the cold glass, her eyes widening in wonder. The sound of activity from the kitchen was followed by Nick entering the bedroom with two mugs in hand. He leaned in for a gentle kiss before handing her one of the mugs. She inhaled deeply, the rich aroma of cocoa warming her senses.

"The snow must have fallen just for you today," he said with a smile, giving her nose a playful peck.

"You're the sweetest," they stood by the window, enveloped in each other's embrace.

"To be so sweet, my heart has to go ten beats faster," he chuckled. "Let me tell you a secret... I'm not so nice to everyone. Some people find it hard to imagine me being like that."

"I won't believe it," she replied, planting a kiss on his stubbly cheek. "What time are we leaving for Mike's parents' place?"

"We should head out now. It's a bit of a drive, and we'll grab breakfast on the way."

"This early?"

"Yes, they kick off the celebrations with a late lunch. Do you mind if we stay overnight?"

"Why not?" she agreed, the prospect of an extended celebration adding to the day's excitement.

The journey to Bridgehampton was lengthy, the traffic relentless. It seemed everyone was in a rush, their nerves frayed, momentarily forgetting the holiday spirit. Sophie took the driver's seat.

"Now's a good time to fill me in," she said, focusing on the road ahead.

"Fill you in on what?" He asked, not quite in the mood for seriousness.

"Like, are there any topics we should steer clear of at dinner? Any sensitive issues?"

"Just don't bring up your threesome on ecstasy. Other than that, you're safe."

"What? Nick..." She feigned shock, her expression exaggeratedly outraged, but feeling it lacked conviction, she added, "I never had a threesome on ecstasy."

"You missed out then."

"Nick, I'm being serious..."

"Have you ever noticed that when you get angry, you start talking with a British accent? It's rather charming."

She exhaled, giving him a calm look, though the corners of her mouth betrayed her amusement.

"If I end up saying something I shouldn't at the table, I'm blaming you."

"How quickly you pass the buck," he sighed softly, taking her hand. "Love, I just want you to enjoy the day. Say whatever comes to mind, in any accent. Just feel at home with family."

They arrived past noon, welcomed at the doorstep by Mike's mom, Melissa, who was dressed in a charming dusty pink midi dress adorned with a white apron, straight out of a Christmas card scene. Nick introduced Sophie, and following warm greetings and hugs, they entered the house. To Sophie, the house appeared spacious from the outside, but its interior seemed to boast the grandeur of ballrooms. They were soon greeted by Mike's dad in the hall, someone Sophie had met previously at a charity event.

"Nick! Sophie! Delighted to see you, kids," he greeted, shaking Nick's hand and hugging Sophie.

"Thank you for having us," Sophie responded with a genuine smile.

"The traffic was horrendous," Nick mentioned. "Are we the last ones to arrive?"

"No worries," Arthur reassured. "Mike's bringing your sister, right?" He glanced at Sophie.

"Yes, Natalie's her name."

"Ah, Natalie," Arthur nodded, leading them towards the living room.

It felt as if lifted from a Disney Christmas film, centered around an enormous Christmas tree decorated with red, white, gold, and silver ornaments, shimmering under the lights of numerous garlands. Sophie had to remind herself to keep moving, despite wanting to gaze at the tree in wonder. Feeling Nick's hand in hers brought her back.

Seated near the window, Nick's dad and Mike's younger sister were engaged in conversation. Greg rose to embrace his son and Sophie.

"Merry Christmas, you both," Greg returned the greeting, smiling at them. "You're late."

"Traffic was a nightmare," Nick admitted, then greeted the girl on the couch. "Hey, Bethany."

"Hi," she responded, quickly getting up to hug him, "Merry Christmas!"

Her gaze flickered to Sophie, offering a cool, distant hello.

"I'll grab the presents, and you all can catch up," Nick suggested.

At that moment, Nick's aunt Linda entered, her joy apparent upon seeing them.

"My darlings, you've arrived," she exclaimed, embracing them.

"Merry Christmas, Linda," Nick reciprocated the hug.

Linda's attention briefly lingered on Nick before turning to Sophie. "Would you like a glass of wine?"

"I'd love one," Sophie accepted.

"Then let's join Melissa and me in the kitchen," Linda proposed, offering Sophie a welcome escape.

They made their way through the hall into the kitchen, where Melissa was busy checking the oven. The aroma of roasted turkey and fresh basil filled the air.

"It smells delicious in here!" Sophie couldn't help but exclaim. Turning to Melissa, she added, "Your home is so warm and inviting."

"Thank you, Sophie! We're delighted to have you and Nick with us today," Melissa responded with a smile.

Linda, meanwhile, poured wine into a glass and handed it to Sophie.

"Thank you! We're happy to be here, though I noticed Bethany seems less than thrilled about my presence."

Melissa dismissed the concern with a wave of her hand, though her irritation was evident. "No one's forcing her to act that way and dampen the holiday spirit for everyone."

With those words, Melissa shifted her attention to a kitchen cabinet, clearly displeased with the direction of the conversation. She was frustrated with her daughter's lack of tact. In this household, manners were paramount, a value Melissa and Arthur had ingrained in their children from an early age. Disagreements were inevitable, but they were always expected to conduct themselves with grace.

"Everything's nearly ready for us to sit down at the table. Has anyone seen Michael?" Before Melissa could reach for her phone, Michael's voice filled the hallway.

Sophie went to welcome them and found her sister and Michael at the front door. Nick followed, his arms laden with colorful boxes and gift bags. Joyful anticipation lit up his face, seemingly unconcerned with the possibility of anything going wrong.

"Merry Christmas, little one," Natalie greeted her sister with a kiss.

"Mike," Sophie embraced him warmly, "I'm so happy to see you!"

"Me too, especially since Nick and I managed to bring you two here together," Michael observed the room, noting his mother standing slightly apart.

He approached her with open arms, his movements radiating warmth. "Merry Christmas, Mom."

"Merry Christmas, Michael," Melissa replied, her eyes tender. "What took you so long?" Her tone was gentle yet reproachful, like a parent chiding a late child.

"Mom, I'd like you to meet Natalie," he said, positioning himself between them.

"Hello, Natalie," Melissa greeted her with measured warmth.

"It's a pleasure to meet you," Natalie responded cheerfully.

"Well then, let's all gather around the table now," Melissa concluded.

They made their way into the dining room, where the table was elegantly set with red napkins and gilded silverware atop a white tablecloth. Sophie glanced around the room, admiring the intricate French arch windows and the light-toned decorations that exuded freshness and elegance. This reminded her of her parents' recently renovated country house, echoing a similar color scheme. Memories from the photos her mother had sent washed over her, leaving her with a profound sense of emptiness. She longed to be with her family, to be home, even though everything seemed perfect today.

As they settled at the table, Arthur proposed a toast. "There is nothing more beautiful than gathering your family around the table, nothing more beautiful than watching your family grow. For thirty-three years now, this holiday has filled us with love and kindness. I pray that this tradition continues. Merry Christmas," they all said, clinking their glasses.

Nick glanced at Sophie, who was seated next to him. He gave her a subtle smile and placed his hand on her leg under the table. She returned the smile, keenly aware of Bethany's intense gaze on her.

"How's the new project going, Nick?" Arthur inquired, taking another sip of his whiskey.

"Everything's on track. The grand opening is set for March," Nick replied.

Arthur beamed with pride. "Impressive! It's a joy to see our children succeed, right, Greg?"

"Absolutely," Greg agreed, nodding.

It was then Natalie spoke up, her voice cutting through the amiable chatter. "Do you ever worry your children are paying too high a price for their success?"

Sophie coughed on her drink, attempting to subtly signal her sister. Despite her efforts, Natalie continued to hold Arthur's gaze, unflinching.

"I'm sorry?" Arthur asked, taken aback.

"Have you considered whether your children are truly happy?" Natalie pressed, her tone calm yet firm, making it clear she was not to be dismissed lightly.

The air was charged with tension following Natalie's declaration.

"I believe I've done everything within my power to ensure their happiness," Arthur said, his brow furrowing. "Your question catches me off guard. What do you do, if you don't mind me asking?"

"I'm a practicing psychotherapist," Natalie replied.

"Ah, I've always found your folk a bit tricky to understand," Arthur said with a light chuckle, glancing at his wife's amused smile. "And where might you work?"

"I'm currently at the Henry Willson Clinic, though I'll soon be heading to Germany."

"Germany?" Sophie echoed, her surprise evident. "When were you planning on telling me this?"

"Today," Natalie responded with casual ease. "I've accepted a one-year position at a prestigious clinic in Berlin. It's a tremendous opportunity for my doctoral research," she added, her smile unwavering.

"That's quite an achievement," Arthur acknowledged, offering a nod of respect.

Sophie turned her gaze towards the window, lost in thought. This was typical of Natalie, seemingly oblivious to how her decisions and words impacted others. Nick sighed and raised his eyebrows, sensing the growing tension in the room.

"I have some news as well," Mike started, casting a glance at his parents.

"Perhaps we should start eating first?" Nick interjected, throwing a meaningful look towards his friend.

"I've made the decision to resign and leave the company," Mike announced, his eyes dropping to his hands.

"What do you mean, son?" Arthur asked, his brow furrowing as he stared intently at Mike.

"I'd like to explore different avenues," Mike answered, bravely meeting his father's gaze.

"Michael, could we perhaps talk about this later?" Melissa suggested, her eyes darting between them, filled with concern.

. "And what avenues might those be?" Arthur no longer heard anything else around him.

"I'm considering comedy, possibly on television."

"Is money no longer a concern for you?" Arthur asked; his hands flat on the table.

"Arthur, perhaps this is a conversation for later?" his wife stressed, emphasizing her point.

The room fell into another bout of awkward silence, punctuated only by the occasional clink of utensils against plates.

"Melissa, Linda, the basil in this salad is a brilliant touch! It's absolutely delicious," Sophie smiled, attempting to break the silence.

"Yes, I first tried this recipe at Raclette. It took quite a bit of persuasion to get the chef to divulge the sauce's ingredients. But eventually, I was successful," Melissa replied with a subdued smile. "It's a place you should definitely visit."

"I believe I've been there once, for a wine-tasting event, possibly."

Their late lunch was filled with tense conversations, as everyone seemed keen to tackle the recent revelations. When they finally rose from the table, it was noticeable that much of the meal remained untouched. Sophie turned to look at Natalie.

"Let me show you to your rooms," Melissa said, approaching the sisters and gently placing her hands on their shoulders.

She led them through the house to two neighboring bedrooms, which were nearly identical save for the bedding. After offering a warm smile, Melissa exited, leaving Sophie and Natalie alone. Tension crackled between them, fueled by Sophie's brewing anger.

"I wish you had told me earlier. It would have been nice to hear about your plans directly from you, like sisters should," Sophie said, her voice thick with frustration.

Natalie exhaled heavily, feeling weighed down by the expectation to always consider her younger sister's feelings, a burden that felt heavier at the moment.

"And how exactly would it have made a difference if I told you sooner? Why does the timing matter?" she asked.

"It matters because I wouldn't have felt like an outsider at the dinner table…"

"You and Nick really are well-suited," Natalie cut in sharply, her gaze turning frosty. "You're both so wrapped up in yourselves that you fail to see when someone else might be struggling."

Sophie's eyes fell. She recognized that Natalie was referring to how Nick had seemingly not provided Mike with the support he might have needed.

Sophie left the room without another word. Her throat felt parched, and she yearned to navigate the sprawling layout of rooms just to reach the kitchen for a glass of water. Upon entering, she found Bethany there. Sophie reached for a glass, filling it quietly with water.

"We don't have to be enemies," Sophie ventured.

"No, but I don't like you," Bethany responded, her gaze cold and emotionless. "And I'm convinced this odd fascination Nick has with you will soon fade."

Choosing to remain silent, Sophie refrained from further conversation. It was clear they wouldn't find common ground, and she didn't want to respond rudely.

From the eastern wing of the house, where Arthur's office lay, loud voices intermittently broke the silence. Mike's voice could be heard at times, but it was Arthur's that dominated the conversation. As time passed, Mike realized that he wouldn't be able to get through to his father that day.

"I've made up my mind," Mike said with a heavy sigh.

"I thought you had moved past these teenage impulses. What is this nonsense?" Arthur retorted.

"Dad, this is my life! Can't you at least try to understand where I'm coming from?"

Arthur paused, crossing his arms and leaning against the edge of the table. "I'm beginning to see... What drugs are you on?"

Mike just shook his head in frustration. "We'll discuss this tomorrow."

As evening fell, Nick waited for a lull in the commotion before approaching Arthur's office.

"Hey! Is it okay if I come in?"

"Nick, of course, come in," Arthur responded with a smile, gesturing toward a chair.

"We had quite the eventful Christmas, didn't we?"

Arthur let out a snort, his grin fading. "Let me ask you this," he said, his expression turning serious, "If Mike is dealing with an addiction he's keeping hidden, now's the time to tell me."

"There's no addiction," Nick replied, leaning forward earnestly. "I recently saw him perform stand-up at a bar. He was really in his element."

"Shouldn't he pursue whatever he's passionate about? Am I standing in his way? But why would he jeopardize his future?"

Nick stayed quiet, sensing the frustration in Arthur's voice; it was a mix of misunderstanding and disappointment, not with his son, but with the realization that the legacy he had envisioned was inevitably crumbling.

"Nick, you're both adults," Arthur pressed on. "Doesn't this seem absurd to you?"

"The only thing I wish for is that my father would stand behind me, just once. After all, there's no one closer to me than my family."

Arthur remained silent, looking off into the distance.

"The only point I disagree with Mike on is that his decision overshadowed Christmas for you and Melissa," Nick said. "Aside from that, he has my full support."

A few hours later, everyone gathered in the living room around the Christmas tree to open presents, providing a momentary respite from the day's tensions. It seemed as though, for a brief time, all personal worries and disappointments were forgotten.

Sophie chuckled as she unwrapped Mike's gift, revealing a pair of Porsche driving gloves.

"Do you really think I'm that skilled at driving?"

"Give it a couple of months, then come to the track. We'll find you the right car," he replied with a wink.

"I've got a surprise for you too. I heard you're a fan of the late-night show with Marcus Ray," she noted his reaction, "I have a few friends there, and they'd be happy to give you a tour."

"Wow, that's awesome!" Mike embraced her warmly in response.

Sophie then noticed a small package with a card that read, 'I love you - Nick.' She picked it up, feeling the contours of a hardcover book beneath the festive wrapping. Her heart skipped a beat, then pounded with anticipation. Eagerly, she began to unwrap it, wondering if it could be the book she was thinking of. The wrapping paper, a vibrant mix of red and green, concealed an old book with pages yellowed by time and edges adorned in gold. Sophie glanced at the cover: Ray Bradbury's 'Dandelion Wine,' a first edition. She paused, briefly overwhelmed. Just then, Nick entered the room and their gazes locked.

PART 2
LONDON

7 MONTHS LATER...

"ARE YOU OKAY? YOU SEEM UPSET," NICK SAID AS HE SAT DOWN ON the bed next to Sophie.

They were in the same bedroom where they had spent Christmas night. After everyone had retired to their rooms, Sophie found herself alone, holding a copy of 'Dandelion Wine' her gift. Before she had met Nick, such a thoughtful present, a first edition of her favorite novel, would have filled her with joy. But now, doubts gnawed at her, consuming her from within. Bethany's words echoed in her mind, "This strange fascination will end soon." Suddenly, it hit her: these words encapsulated all her fears, everything that made her feel insecure.

"I'm just lost in thought... Thank you for the book," she said, managing a weak smile.

"Were you expecting something different?" Nick asked, his gaze shifting away.

Sophie looked down at her hands, shook her head no, and then, gathering her courage, she agreed with him.

"Yes, I was. I was hoping you'd reveal something that's truly important to you."

"It might be best to leave things as they are. Why would you want to know me better? You're so afraid of being disappointed," he said, his back to her as he stood and walked towards the window. "Moreover, I'm unsure about my feelings for you. I doubt I'm capable of truly loving you. Do you think anyone can, Sophie?"

Feeling a wave of dizziness, she was suddenly nauseous. She attempted to stand but stumbled.

Sophie woke up with a start, the nausea still clinging to her. The physical sensations were unsettlingly reminiscent of her dream, especially his haunting question, "Do you think anyone can?"

She made her way to the bathroom and leaned over the sink, feeling the cool marble beneath her hands. Splashing cold water on her face helped snap her back to reality.

Back in bed, she lay in the middle staring at the ceiling, accompanied only by the faint hum of the air conditioner. It was July, and New York was engulfed in summer heat. Sleep seemed uninviting now. To distract herself from the unsettling dream, she recalled how the evening had actually ended: she had shared her doubts with Nick, and he had just smiled in response, suggesting they move in together. Everything had unfolded as planned since the new year, and for a time, the troubling dreams had ceased. Yet, tonight, they had resurfaced.

Feeling for her phone under the pillow, she checked the time: two in the morning. A message from her mom awaited, sent at 7 a.m. London time. Taking her phone, she wandered to the kitchen for water.

"Hi, dear," came her mom's ever-lively voice. Sophie couldn't remember a time it sounded any different.

"Hi, Mom. Aren't you headed to work yet?"

"Just on my way. How are you? Wait a moment," she imagined her mom checking her watch, "Why are you up? It's well past midnight there."

"I can't sleep, but I'm fine. Mom, what would you think about coming to visit us during your vacation?"

"To New York? But we've already planned everything. Plus, your sister's coming from Germany; she's even booked her flight to London. What's prompted this?"

"It's just a thought, really."

"That would be lovely. We'll be at our place in Scarborough. You love it there, plus we could celebrate your birthday. You'd get to see all your friends…"

"Yes, you're right. I forgot I wanted all that."

Their conversation wrapped up quickly, as usual.

"Sweetheart, I must go. Patients are waiting."

After ending the call, Sophie sighed and finished her glass of water. She looked out the window into the night. Despite the absence of lights in her room, the city's nocturnal glow filled the space, illuminating it as if a spotlight shone directly at her window. In this city, it was never truly dark. Leaning forward, she rested her elbows on the table and gazed at the World Trade Center tower, which stood tall at the center, dwarfing the surrounding buildings. Sophie smiled, finding comfort in the view. New York had become her sanctuary, a breath of fresh air amidst struggles with depression and intrusive thoughts. The decision to move here marked a pivotal escape, bringing not only new people into her life for whom she was grateful but also introducing her to a city brimming with potential. She was thankful to New York for reigniting her self-belief and helping her rebuild from the shadows of doubt cast by those who had never believed in her. It was an ironic truth that those closest to us can sometimes reflect our deepest doubts and insecurities.

All these years in the city had unfolded like a chapter of carefree beauty. The challenges she faced were typical of an average New Yorker: business dilemmas, project deadlines, and event planning. Then Nick came into her life, and the city unveiled a new dimension to her. It showed her how life could shift dramatically and how relationships between men and women could evolve. Sophie found herself smiling again in the dim light of the kitchen. Their year together had breezed by as though it were merely a day. Her mother's recent call snapped her back to reality, reminding her of the inevitable return home. Until now, she had skillfully avoided it, convincing her family to vacation elsewhere than England. But this year, she had failed to make alternative plans in time. Now, there was no escaping it. Life, once again, appeared as an intricate labyrinth of challenges and uncertainties. The brief spell of joy she had known seemed already in the past.

31

THE JARRING MELODY OF THE ALARM CLOCK PIERCED THE MORNING quiet yet again. When he'd finally replace that irksome tune, Nick wondered. It was time for his morning run, yet fatigue clung to him, a remnant of a grueling week. The Los Angeles heat, coupled with endless meetings and negotiations, had drained him. He yearned for the comfort of his bed back home.

He silenced the music, catching his breath, just as a FaceTime call from Mike lit up his phone screen.

"Hey! How are things in the so-called happiest state?" Mike quipped.

"I wouldn't know, I've been all work. What's up with you?"

"Same old… But actually, I have some news. That's why I called," Mike's voice wavered slightly, a rarity that Nick couldn't recall hearing before.

"What's going on?"

"NBS is launching a new late-night show, and they've invited me to be the host."

"No way, that's... That's incredible, man!"

"Yeah, I've gone through the entire casting process. Now, all that's left is signing the contract."

"I always believed you'd make it to the stage… but this is beyond."

"I'm really looking forward to it."

"I'm thrilled for you, truly," Nick paused for a moment, "And hey, just remember, you made this happen. It's all on you, regardless of what anyone else might say. Hold on to this moment."

Mike fell silent, struggling to respond.

"We've got to celebrate. How about you and Sophie join us at the Ritz tomorrow?"

"Sounds great!"

After ending the call, Nick's breathing nearly settled back to normal. He had another appointment on his schedule for today. An old friend and business associate of his father's had extended an invitation to their new residence in Santa Barbara. Nick felt reluctant to attend, but his father had mentioned discussing some work matters, making it impossible to decline.

The house was nothing short of spectacular, seemingly too grand for just four occupants. Its sheer size and excellent location made it clear that cost was not a primary concern in its selection.

Upon entering, Nick was welcomed by the wife of Charles Trenton. She radiated warmth and appeared remarkably joyful, leaving Nick to wonder if her happiness was a result of the luxurious home or her prosperous marriage. He estimated her age to be around his or possibly Sophie's, making her look more like an older daughter to Charles than his spouse. Given that Charles had a twenty-one-year-old daughter, most would mistake this youthful woman for her friend rather than her stepmother.

"Nick, can I offer you something to drink? Charlie is just finishing up a call."

"A soda would be great, thank you."

She guided him to the expansive living room, where large windows framed in white overlooked the beach. The gentle breeze caused the translucent chiffon curtains to dance lightly. The decor seemed lifted straight from a Fitzgerald novel, a stark contrast to Charles' previously modest New York apartment.

"Nick! It's been too long!" Charles emerged from what appeared to be his office.

"Charlie!" They exchanged firm handshakes.

A young woman approached from the kitchen, bearing two glasses filled with drinks.

"Thanks, dear," Charles said, planting a kiss on his wife's cheek. Nick, accepting his drink, discreetly looked away, feeling the display of affection was somewhat exaggerated.

"Thank you, Hannah," he said, offering the girl a polite smile.

She returned the smile and exited the room.

"So, what do you think?" Charlie swept his arm around, showcasing his new acquisitions.

"It's impressive!" Nick responded, his lips forming a thoughtful expression. "Truly beyond what I had envisioned."

"Yeah, I may have gone a bit overboard. But at least we have room to breathe now."

"Congratulations, then!" Nick lifted his glass in a toast.

"To dreams realized!" Their glasses chimed together.

After a momentary silence, Charlie fixed Nick with a contemplative look. "So, what about you? Have you started looking for your place outside the city yet?"

"No, I'm still in New York."

"Nick, my boy, give it fifteen years and New York will start to wear on you. Right now, you're all about the fast pace, having the office close by, and the instant gratification of your needs. But that allure fades fast. What then?"

Nick gazed out the window at the point where the dark blue ocean kissed the sun-drenched sky. The question lingered in the air. How often had he pondered it? Had he ever truly considered it? In business, thinking long-term was second nature to him, but this was about his personal life. Where did he see himself in fifteen years? Did he want to leave New York one day? One thing was clear — he wanted to be with Sophie. But what did she want? To return to London and be closer to her family? Questions began to swirl in his mind with unsettling urgency.

He couldn't recall his response to Charlie, brushing off the topic to navigate back to the familiar terrain of business discussions, where he felt more secure.

The day flew by, and before he knew it, Nick was on his way to the airport, eager to leave a city that felt distant to him. He sighed deeply, rolling his eyes at the announcement of a two-hour flight delay.

32

NICK WALKED INTO THE HOTEL, MAKING HIS WAY THROUGH THE lobby with a few bored guests around and employees at the front desk. Mike's penchant for renting the first-floor pool for private parties was well-known, and tonight was no exception. Guided by signs to the spa, Nick could already hear the distant echo of water splashing.

He stepped into a grand hall, where a pool was flanked by four marble columns. Familiar faces dotted the crowd; Mike had a knack for inviting an eclectic mix of acquaintances, including those he barely knew or hadn't seen in ages, especially if a recent encounter had rekindled their connection. Though Mike never fully understood his own rationale for such expansive invites, he found no compelling reason to curtail them. Consequently, his parties were invariably larger than anticipated.

As Nick surveyed the room, his gaze found Sophie. She stood by the window, engaged in conversation with Mike and his girlfriend, a glass of champagne in hand. Dressed in her typical business casual attire, it seemed she had come straight from work without even a thought of bringing a swimsuit. He watched her laugh, smile, and listen intently to her companions. Feeling his gaze, Sophie looked around the room until her eyes met his, and a distinctive smile graced her lips. She briefly lowered her gaze, only to look up at him once more. At that moment, someone approached Nick to greet him. He responded with a handshake, his attention unfalteringly fixed on Sophie.

Nick had always considered himself fortunate, never truly experiencing loneliness. So why was it that, in a room bustling with people and with Sophie's gaze meeting his, he felt a profound sense of relief wash over him? It was as if he had just been rescued from the grips of overwhelming isolation.

"Nick," Mike called out as he joined them, "What took you so long?"

"California wouldn't let me go. They even rescheduled my flight," Nick replied with a chuckle, exchanging handshakes with Mike and greeting his girlfriend, Stacy.

He gave Sophie a kiss on the cheek, allowing himself a moment longer than usual before pulling back. Wrapping his arm around her waist, he felt her whole being lean into him. Now, he found himself looking for her in crowded rooms, even in her absence.

"Hi."

"Hi..."

"You two are adorable," Stacy observed. "If I didn't know better, I'd think you had just met."

"We might as well have," Nick quipped, shifting his focus from Sophie to Stacy. "I've been away for a week. But tonight's not about us," he raised his voice slightly, "Tonight, we celebrate my best friend's dream becoming reality. And that's just the beginning of his journey."

"Let me grab some champagne for you," Mike interjected, scanning the area for a bottle.

"It's fine," Nick said, taking Sophie's hand which held the glass, "This moment is all yours, Mike. Here's to countless more celebrations."

"To Mike," Sophie echoed, sipping her champagne. She nestled closer to Nick, his kiss landing softly on her forehead.

Later, when Sophie and Stacy found themselves alone, Stacy initiated the conversation.

"You and Nick are wonderful together! I must admit, I'm kind of envious…"

"Thanks! You and Mike seem great too," Sophie responded, offering encouragement despite not having considered it before.

"No, we're just friends…" Stacy hesitated, "Well, friends with benefits, perhaps. But I'd give anything to look at someone the way Nick looks at you. Sometimes, you meet someone who seems perfect for you in every way, but the spark just isn't there. Then, unexpectedly, you find your entire world in someone you never planned on meeting."

"I get it; it's all so complex… I once felt that way about someone, but our stars didn't align. When Nick came along, I fought it as hard as I could, yet here I am…" She gave a small shrug.

"Don't fight it. Once you let go of the fear of losing, there's no point in resisting."

"Maybe you're right," Sophie mused, observing Stacy closely. The girl was insightful, pursuing desires that weren't easily satisfied. She wasn't drawn to Mike for his status or wealth; she was after something more profound, something beyond the reach of money. Perhaps they both understood that, each carrying a sense of longing within them.

At the other end of the room, Nick noticed his friend stealing glances at Stacy.

"Is there something serious going on between you two?" he inquired.

Mike's expression turned contemplative as if trying to dismiss the idea. "Nah," he responded. "It's nothing like what you and Sophie have, you know?"

"I understand," Nick said, wanting to provide support without making empty promises like 'You'll definitely find someone.' After all, who could foresee the future?

"Meanwhile, I encourage you and Sophie to take business trips together," Mike said with a friendly smile.

"Sophie's been talking about visiting her parents in London this September. It coincides with her birthday and our anniversary. And I've been thinking..." Nick's expression softened into a shy smile as he shared his thoughts with his best friend.

"Oh, come on, man!" Mike exclaimed, his voice rising with emotion. He often didn't realize when his feelings overtook him.

"Shh," Nick laughed, his dimples showing. "I thought about it while in LA and saw no reason to delay any longer."

Nick woke in the dimness of their bedroom, the bathroom door ajar, spilling a narrow beam of light across the room. After the party, he had managed a few hours of sleep, his body heavy with the week's workload and the added weight of jet lag.

Rising, he followed the sliver of light that now seemed to pierce his eyes painfully. There, Sophie stood in front of the mirror, brushing her hair, clad only in black lace panties. Nick wrapped his arms around her from behind, the discomfort in his eyes fading away. His hands rested on her stomach, and he breathed in the familiar scent of her hair. Sophie leaned back into him, her head finding refuge in the crook of his neck. She closed her eyes, overwhelmed by a deep sense of longing. She had missed him more than she ever admitted to herself. His scent, his touch, his gaze — it was a yearning she found could not be replicated elsewhere.

"I didn't sleep well without you. I kept waking up," she admitted.

"I'm sorry, baby," he murmured, his hands exploring her body, pausing at the spots where her skin seemed to come alive under his touch.

"Just the other day in LA, I stumbled upon this incredible bar with a live pianist. The music was mesmerizing. I wish you were there with me... But since you missed it, you owe me a dance," he said, his smile gentle as she turned to face him.

"Tomorrow, I promise," she assured him, planting a kiss just below his ear.

Once back in their bedroom, Nick gently laid Sophie on the bed, lifting her arms above her head and lightly holding her wrists. He noticed the goosebumps forming on her skin and smiled subtly. Leaning down, he kissed along her collarbone, chest, and ribs, paying extra attention to the areas where the goosebumps were most pronounced.

"Finally, I'm home," he breathed, maintaining his slow exploration. Sophie reclaimed her hands, weaving her fingers through his hair.

"Welcome back, love," she whispered back.

"What do you want?" he asked softly.

"You," her voice trembled. "Just you."

For a brief moment, Charlie's words flashed through Nick's mind, causing his gaze to momentarily stiffen. Sophie's gentle touch on his arm pulled him back to the present. He dismissed the intrusive thoughts. Looking into Sophie's eyes, he moved away slightly and placed her leg over his shoulder, slowly tracing the inside of her thigh with his lips.

Sophie rested on Nick's chest, relishing the calming sensations in her body and the gradual release of tension from her muscles. She looked up at him.

"You seem pensive today."

"I was just thinking... we've never really discussed the future," he said, pulling her closer.

"The future?" She elongated the words, prompting him to elaborate.

"Our future together," he specified.

Sophie exhaled, trying to ease the tension that had crept in. "But we're here now, in the present. Isn't that what matters most?"

"Of course. However, there are questions worth considering. Like, do you envision spending your life in New York? Or maybe returning to London?"

"Whole life... it sounds like a big commitment," she shifted, sitting up and hugging a pillow, seemingly unfazed by her nudity. "Was tonight that bad that you're lying here questioning our entire existence?" She teased, trying to turn it into a joke.

"Soph," Nick replied with a gentle smile, though his eyes conveyed deeper contemplation, "It's not a difficult question."

"It's a very difficult question. The truth is, I don't know," she admitted, looking down at her hands. "Have you thought about spending your entire life in New York?" Her tone turned slightly ironic.

"I've never really considered it."

"After a few of my plans didn't pan out, I stopped making such long-term commitments," Sophie shared.

Nick's gaze returned to the ceiling, aware that sleep was far off.

"I'm happy here, in this city, with you. In my experience, making plans often leads to disappointment. They seem to dissolve as soon as we voice them, and I don't want that for us. I just want to be with you," she concluded, and Nick's smile grew at her words.

"It seems one of us does need to think about the future," he mused.

"Nick, it's only been a year."

"But it's been a wonderful year."

"So, you're suggesting we end it on that note?" she laughed, dodging his playful attempt to tap her arm with his pillow, only to cover him with hers and lie atop him, their faces inches apart.

"I love you. Let's focus on the here and now. Tomorrow is uncertain. All I want is to have a few weeks off with you and my family. Isn't that enough?" she asked, biting her lip anxiously as she awaited his response.

"It's more than enough. I'm sorry if I pressured you. It's just that, lately, I've been thinking about more."

Sophie absorbed his words, which she would reflect on frequently in the days ahead.

"I'm so glad you walked into that bar a year ago."

"And you haven't regretted it yet," she responded with a playful tease.

33

THE FOLLOWING DAY, AS SOPHIE WAS PURCHASING TICKETS TO London, she received a call from Natalie.

"I hope you've secured the tickets by now," Natalie's brisk voice came through, often bypassing customary pleasantries.

"I'm on it," Sophie responded.

"Great! Our parents keep asking what they should gift you for your birthday."

"And you've told them I need nothing, right?" Sophie asked.

"Actually, I told them to give you money. Judging by how much you work, you need it," Natalie said, amused by her quip.

"I'm not working just for the money," Sophie countered.

"You're assimilating into American culture too quickly. Remember, you were born in Europe. We value traditions, drink a lot of alcohol, and plan holidays well in advance."

"That's precisely what I'm doing now. Nick and I will be arriving on the 20th."

"Speaking of which, it's peculiar that your boyfriend hasn't inquired about what gift to get. It's unusual."

A silence followed. Sophie gazed off into the distance before finally speaking.

"I think I know what his gift will be. Nat, I believe he's planning to propose."

"That's quite a gift. I can almost hear you asking to be more serious. Sophie... don't you think it's a bit soon to bring him along?"

"It doesn't seem so. It's the perfect time to introduce him to the family," she said, her voice tinged with doubt.

"And to confront any unresolved issues you left behind."

"There are no unresolved issues," Sophie stated more firmly.

"Sure, little sister. As always, I pose the questions, you provide the answers. Quick and painless."

Feeling irritated and eager to end the call, Sophie hurried through their goodbyes, hanging up less than a minute later.

The unresolved issues — that's all that was missing. But why do such things never come with an expiration date? Beloved products in the fridge always have theirs, and you're compelled to throw them away. Yet, stories from the past carry no time limit. They're akin to bulky, old suitcases that occasionally tumble out of the attic with a crash.

Sophie grasped the implication behind her sister's words but was puzzled as to why Natalie chose this moment to bring it up. After all, so much time had elapsed. Sometimes, her sister's intuition was eerily accurate, sending shivers down her spine. Was it too keen for a therapist, or did the amassed life experiences of her clients imply that everything in life followed set patterns? Sophie shook off these thoughts, telling herself, "No, I've already spent too much time dwelling on this..."

That evening, Sophie chose to stay in and prepare dinner before Nick's arrival. Surprisingly, he came home early, catching her as she sorted through sprigs of rosemary.

"What a pleasant surprise! I'm almost afraid to ask what brought you home early..."

"I just wanted a night in, to enjoy dinner in a cozy setting."

"Do you think maybe it's age?"

Sophie playfully aimed to swat his forearm, but he caught her hand and drew her close with a gentle yet firm pull at her waist. Sophie adored this gesture; Nick's soft smile captivated her, causing her gaze to drift to his lips.

"Your smile... I find myself waiting for it all day, thinking just a bit longer until I see it again. It feels like the one thing in this world I truly understand," Sophie whispered, her expression emotionless.

It appeared her feelings were deeply buried under layers of courage and resilience, necessary to persevere through even the most painful moments. Nick frowned. A strange, subconscious feeling of concern for her washed over him. He inhaled deeply, seeking composure, then embraced her tightly. Gently lifting her chin with his thumb, he kissed her.

"It smells amazing," he murmured, pulling back slightly.

"I'm making steaks."

Sophie barely touched her dinner, aimlessly pushing her fork across the plate, her mind elsewhere. It became increasingly clear to her that she couldn't taste her food and was plagued by nightmares. Her thoughts were preoccupied with the dread of what awaited her back home.

After cleaning up, Sophie stood by the kitchen counter, lost in thought as she watched the flickering candles. Nick joined her, trying to follow her gaze.

"Talk to me," he urged, meeting her eyes.

"Um," Sophie hesitated, shaking her head with a sigh, "I'm not very good with all this psychological stuff."

"Just forget about that. Tell me what's on your mind," he encouraged.

Sophie slid down to the floor, leaning her back against the kitchen counter, and Nick did the same.

After a brief silence, Sophie finally opened up, "You can't ever run away. If you do, it'll haunt you forever. I don't want to go back home," her voice quivered with emotion, "There were good times, but I also don't want to relive the bad."

"You won't have to," Nick reassured her, "I'll be there with you. Sophie, I observe more than I let on. I noticed you continued paying rent for your apartment for three months after we moved in together. I see the effort you put into your work, and how you rely solely on yourself. Initially, I thought I should wait; allow trust to grow between us. But now, I understand it's more than that. It seems you feel unworthy of happiness or a peaceful life."

"It's just... People I care deeply about have walked out of my life as if we had no connection. Each time, the world turns gray again, and I have to learn how to rediscover joy. And yes, you're right, perhaps I've grown too accustomed to relying only on myself."

"How long have you been struggling to sleep?" Nick inquired.

"Ever since Natalie reminded me about our promise to visit our parents. They're planning to stay in England for their vacation, so..."

"You woke up tonight, suddenly jumping and trembling. What were you dreaming about?"

"I dreamt about the year before I left London when I was hospitalized due to a nervous breakdown. I remember those dreadful needles, piercing my skin. They kept hooking me up to IVs meant to calm me down. Have you noticed how hospitals always have such cold, bright lights? They're blinding," she recalled with a shiver, "My mom works in a hospital. She was convinced I needed that treatment."

Sophie curled up, hugging her knees to her chest.

"It feels like there are things I'll never be able to cope with," she said, tears streaming down her face.

Nick wrapped his arms around her, wishing he could comfort her, to tell her it was all just a nightmare and that none of it was real. But that would be a lie. Everyone carries their past, and you can never fully understand the depth of someone else's scars.

"If only I knew how to help you," he murmured. "Pills and therapy don't always provide the answer. True healing requires the bravery to confront your deepest fears. But only you can decide when you're ready."

Sophie stayed quiet, nestled in his embrace, soaking in the comfort of his warmth.

"And one more thing, love," Nick added softly, "I'm not going anywhere."

Hearing his words, Sophie looked up into his eyes. Even in the dim light, she could see their familiar depth that always seemed to draw her in. She nodded and laid her head back on his chest.

"Regardless of what the future holds, thank you for this past year," she whispered. "My love for you has made me a better person. But I find it hard to think about the future when I'm still afraid of it."

34

THE WAITER OPENED THE DOOR, ALLOWING THEM TO STEP OUTSIDE. Nick and Sophie had just left a new restaurant in Tribeca after brunch, a place recommended by Mike.

"Since when does Mike frequent these quaint cafes where couples share a single glass?" Sophie asked, her eyebrows raised in playful skepticism.

Nick chuckled at her jest. "They even gave you a second glass to avoid any complaints," he said, his attention then shifting to a couple approaching them.

Sophie followed his gaze and spotted a tall man with dark-brown hair dressed in a suit, looking as if he had stepped off the cover of Forbes. His direct gaze and confident walk seemed to underscore that image. Next to him was a woman of medium height with golden, slightly reddish hair, delicate features, and light-green eyes that frequently glanced at her companion. When her eyes finally met Nick's, she appeared to momentarily freeze, her gaze flitting nervously. They were close now, with no obvious way to avoid each other.

"So, that answers your question about the clientele here," Nick murmured, watching the couple intently.

"What? What's going on?" Sophie asked, a frown forming as she sensed the tension in the air.

When they finally crossed paths, Nick was the first to speak. "Diana! It's great to see you. This is Sophie, my girlfriend. And Diana, my... ex-wife."

Sophie hesitated briefly, her mouth slightly agape. She greeted Diana but refrained from extending her hand, gauging her reaction to the introduction. Diana, appearing nervous, began tucking her hair behind her ear, subtly showcasing the ring on her fourth finger. Sophie's eyes instinctively darted to the man's left hand, noting a matching gold band. He caught her glance, but Sophie responded with a sweet smile.

"John, meet my ex-husband, Nick," Diana's gaze shifted to her husband, filled with adoration.

"John Gage," the man said confidently, extending his hand to Nick, who shook it with genuine warmth.

"It's a pleasure to meet you, John. Diana, you look lovely! Are you still living on Madison Ave?" Nick inquired, directing his attention solely to Diana as if eager to catch up. Sophie observed, intrigued by their interaction.

"No... no, I sold that apartment," Diana replied, placing a hand on her stomach.

"Of course! I'm happy to hear you're doing well," Nick replied.

"Likewise. But we really should be going, darling, right?" Diana turned to her husband, seeking confirmation in his gaze.

"Yes, we were just about to get something to eat. It seems the place we're looking for is around here," he indicated, gesturing toward the direction from which Nick and Sophie had come.

"Italien place?"

"Yes, that's the one," John responded, his tone indicating satisfaction as if he had just solved a puzzle.

"It's just around the corner," Nick said, gesturing. "I'm sure you'll enjoy it!"

Sophie bit her lip to stifle a laugh.

"Well, take care!" John nodded, while Diana averted her gaze.

Nick and Sophie continued on their way, leaving the couple behind. Nick let out a sigh, intertwining his fingers with Sophie's.

"That was quite the encounter!" Sophie observed, studying Nick's expression closely.

"Definitely! Seems like today's Sunday brunch special included a rendezvous with exes," he joked, meeting her curious gaze.

"Why did you ask about the apartment?"

"It used to be our place; I left it to her after we split."

"Well, she went through a difficult divorce process…"

Sophie reflected on the stark differences between herself and Diana. Nick's ex-wife had remarried swiftly and appeared to be expecting. It was as though she were a satellite, perpetually in need of a planet to revolve around. Meanwhile, here was Sophie, a girl who dreaded even the mundane discussions about the future, standing beside Nick. Yet, Nick never ceased to steer the conversation towards those very topics. It was his voice that snapped her back to the present.

"Some people find the world a lot more complex than you do," he said, gazing into the distance. Then, turning back to Sophie with a gentle squeeze of her hand, he added, "Sorry, that came out wrong."

"No, you're right. She's delicate, vulnerable… and distinctly feminine. I'm nothing like her," Sophie admitted, looking away.

Nick halted, positioning himself in front of Sophie, and gently took her hands in his. "Are you kidding me? I've yet to encounter a woman as strong and independent as you. Being with you feels like an ongoing adventure, and sometimes, I worry I might not make it to the end," he said with a light chuckle. "Diana is great, and what I'm about to say may sound terrible, but if I want a golden retriever, I'd get a golden retriever. Sophie, you're the one who I need!" He stressed, his voice earnest. "You inspire me daily. Even on days when I feel like I've achieved so much, I look at you and see your endless drive and ideas, your passion to make them a reality! And to think, you left all those flowers and gifts from your admirers at the office, thinking I was unaware of them. And you talk about someone's femininity?"

Sophie's smile widened as she gently squeezed Nick's hands.

"I caused Diana a lot of pain by making her feel as if something was inherently wrong with her. But in reality, there was nothing wrong. I was expecting from her something she couldn't give and didn't need to. Leaving her that apartment and removing myself from her life was the least I could do after everything," Nick confessed.

Sophie listened attentively, her eyes welling up with tears as if someone from her past was tugging at her heartstrings. When Nick hugged her, she pressed against him for the first time, as if he were her only chance at survival.

"I need you. I might not have your way with words, and expressing how much you mean to me can be hard. It's as though I dialed a random combination of numbers and hit the jackpot when I met you. In some alternate reality, I'm still waking up every day to someone trying to make me believe there's something wrong with me."

Sophie gazed into the void over Nick's shoulder, sending shivers down his spine. For several weeks, Nick had noticed a change in Sophie's behavior, becoming more pronounced as their trip to London approached.

35

"HOW DO YOU TURN THIS OFF?" SOPHIE ASKED, REACHING FOR THE fan's control knob above her seat.

Traffic in Brooklyn had delayed them, and their rush-hour departure meant they were the last to board, earning disapproving looks from early passengers eager to take off.

"Are you cold?" Nick attempted to press the switch, but it malfunctioned. "Maybe this will be easier. Excuse me," he flagged down a passing flight attendant, "Could you bring a blanket, please?"

"Certainly, sir. Just a moment," the attendant replied, her British accent noticeable.

"I'll need to get used to that accent," he said, smiling.

"You can start practicing now," Sophie suggested. "Everyone here is British. Look." She leaned towards the man in the neighboring seat. "Excuse me, sir, might you have an extra bottle of water?"

The middle-aged man, glancing up from his e-reader, looked puzzled. "Water?" His rich British accent confirmed Sophie's observation. "You might want to ask the flight attendant."

"Yes, of course. My apologies for disturbing you," Sophie said politely, withdrawing.

Hearing Nick chuckle, she placed her hand on his knee, turning back to him.

"Pretty soon, you'll be briefed on all the things you can't do on this flight," she emphasized the word 'can't,' elongating the 'a.' "After that, expect an offer of an alcoholic drink that seems to accept nothing but a 'yes'."

"What do you mean?"

"Just watch. Someone will request wine even before the snacks come around. In this country, braving the dreadful weather calls for a drink," Sophie quipped, determined not to let the long flight dull her spirits.

"And for those who don't drink?"

"Technically, they should've never let you on board," Sophie said, her puzzled look tinged with amusement at Nick's reaction. "Non-drinkers aren't exactly celebrated here... Give it a week, and they'll convert you. British airlines might as well add this to their safety briefing: 'No smoking in the toilets, and at the bar, never admit to abstaining from alcohol.' Otherwise, you'll find everyone eager to introduce you to platform nine and three-quarters," she joked.

"In that case, I'll have to adopt a British accent and take up gin."

Sophie eyed him skeptically, her arms crossed.

"Let's hear this British accent, Mr. Davidson."

"Oh, please, it can't be that hard," he said with a smirk.

"So, you believe after my year of mastering an American accent, you can instantly channel Downton Abbey?" She raised an eyebrow skeptically, then turned once more to their neighbor. "Excuse me, sir, my friend here has a pressing question that's been on his mind since we boarded."

The man looked up from his reading, scrutinizing them both.

"Yes, indeed, I wanted to ask you..." Nick hesitated, then continued in a somewhat awkward British accent, "Don't you think the United Kingdom has gone too far in granting privileges to social minorities?"

Sophie's eyes widened in surprise.

"What exactly are you referring to? If you're talking about the bill to ban all forms of conversion therapy, it hasn't passed yet. Moreover, I believe its success would mark a significant advancement in making society more humane," he became more animated. "I'm sorry, but you Americans really should take better care of each other. The so-called unity in America varies greatly from one state to another. In one state, they'll put a gun to your head; in another, they'll get you high; and in yet another, they won't even give a homeless person a piece of bread."

"It's hard to disagree with that," Sophie said, nodding in agreement.

"Miss, since you're British, aren't you proud that our country is a pioneer in gender equality?" The man leaned across the aisle toward Sophie.

"I am indeed proud, more than you can imagine," she replied earnestly.

"Our progress has been centuries in the making! So, the next time such thoughts cross your mind, sir, remember the world can never have too much tolerance and love," he stated solemnly, settling back into his seat and turning on his tablet.

Sophie shot Nick a meaningful glance.

"God, save the Queen!" Nick murmured softly.

Sophie laughed, resting her head on his shoulder.

"And this is the first time I've heard you speak with a British accent," Nick smiled.

"How does it sound? Does it echo a spirit of gender equality?" Sophie raised her gaze to Nick, comfortably nestled on his shoulder.

"I like it," Nick leaned in, tenderly kissing her while slightly biting her lower lip. "There's something special about it," he smiled.

"Exciting?"

"Intriguing," he corrected, brushing his fingers against her chin.

"I once went on a date with a guy who, upon finding out I'm British, immediately asked me to speak with a British accent, his eyes alight with excitement. I never saw him again after that," Sophie laughed.

Nick grinned, glancing away.

"But you'll have to endure my accent for seven whole days," she teased, placing her hand on his neck.

"Truthfully, I've never had a vacation quite like this."

Sophie chuckled at his words.

"What will you be drinking, sir?" the flight attendant inquired, leaning slightly and looking at Nick.

"You were right... the question doesn't seem to allow for refusal," he admitted to Sophie. "A gin neat, please."

Sophie laughed at the solemn tone with which he made the request.

"And for you, ma'am?"

"Red wine, please," she replied with a nod. But before the flight attendant could turn away, Nick stopped her.

"Excuse me, but I'd prefer some whiskey."

"Of course, sir," the attendant nodded again and moved to the next row of seats.

Nick took Sophie's hand, intertwining their fingers, and lightly brushed the back of his hand against her leg.

"So, what about a gin neat?"

"It's on the menu," Sophie looked at Nick with a meaningful glance.

They arrived in the evening, with Natalie awaiting them at Heathrow Airport. The usual slog through passport control and baggage claim stretched for over an hour — a process yet to be expedited in any country. Emerging into the main entrance, they found no sign of Natalie. A call to her revealed her impatience:

"You could've taken even longer with your duffle bags. I'm at the bar near the east entrance."

Sophie, rolling her eyes, led the way, Nick following with undiminished spirits, excited for the night ahead. It had been six months since they last saw Natalie. Spotting the bar, there was no mistaking Natalie would be there, wine in hand, eagerly anticipating their holiday rituals. Sophie embraced her tightly.

"I missed you, nag," she said, enveloped in the familiar scent of Natalie's perfume.

"Hey, little one," Natalie returned the embrace warmly.

Sophie closed her eyes for a moment, hearing the thought she had longed to hear and, at the same time, feared: "I'm back home." It's always held a special place in our hearts. Home is a sanctuary where cherished moments come alive again, where we wrap ourselves in the comforting memories of childhood, laugh once more at past mishaps, and bravely face the fears that once had us hiding under the covers. It embodies the warmth and love that flood back to us at the mere thought of it.

Nick joined, greeting Natalie with a kiss.

"So, what's the plan?" he inquired, looking at them both.

"You didn't tell him?" Natalie raised an eyebrow at Sophie.

"Nope," came Sophie's smiling reply.

"Well, darling, you're in for the best tour of London yet."

"Aren't your parents expecting us?"

"They're in Scarborough already. We're heading there tomorrow," said Sophie, looping her arm through his.

"A tour, huh? Alright," Nick grinned.

"Let's drop off our luggage, and you'll see for yourself," Natalie said, grabbing her suitcase's handle.

The taxi ride to their destination was enveloped in silence, punctuated only by the hues of the setting sun. Sophie seemed distant, her gaze fixed on the passing scenery, lost in thought. From the front seat, Natalie turned to engage Nick.

"First time in London for you?"

"I've passed through, but never really explored," Nick admitted.

"I see. Maybe it's just not meant to be," Natalie nodded knowingly, glancing at the road. "There's Big Ben, Piccadilly Circus, and Buckingham Palace. Our parents' place is in Chiswick, in the west."

"Did you grow up there?"

"Yes, mom and Charlie settled there right after their wedding. I have vivid memories of moving in, but Sophie was probably too young to remember."

Sophie, suddenly alert at the mention of her name, looked puzzled. "Remember what?"

"Our move to Chiswick. Do you recall anything?"

"No, I was barely two," she replied, her attempt at nonchalance betrayed by a brief, strained smile. Nick reached out, covering her hand with his.

The taxi veered off Grove Park Road onto a narrower street, coming to a halt near the Thames. Natalie paid the fare in cash, explaining to Nick, "Our house is by the waterfront, in a pedestrian zone. We'll need to walk from there."

"In the US, pedestrian zones like this are rare, and taxis usually drop you right at your doorstep," Nick observed.

"I've always wondered why Americans don't walk more," Natalie commented with a slight frown.

"And why do Europeans walk so much?"

"Because there's so much beauty to take in on foot," she replied with a simple shrug.

Natalie led the way, pausing at the stone steps in front of a door numbered 5522. It was painted a light beige, harmonizing with the green ivy climbing the walls. This building, with its multiple entrances, stood proudly along the Thames, separated from the river by just a wide sidewalk.

"It's beautiful here!" Nick marveled.

"Yes, but come winter, you'd face a bone-chilling wind. Living by the water adds an extra layer of dreariness to the already challenging weather," Natalie responded.

With her key, Natalie unlocked the door, holding it open wide to ease the entrance of their suitcases. She noticed Sophie lingering at the threshold, absorbing every detail of the familiar doorway, each notch and groove a part of her memories. Approaching her sister, Natalie placed a reassuring hand on Sophie's shoulders.

"I'll show Nick around."

"Thanks, Nat," Sophie replied, touching Natalie's arm, yet her gaze remained fixed ahead.

"Take your time, okay?"

Once Natalie and Nick disappeared inside, Sophie began her ascent up the stairs, her fingertips gliding over the newly painted wooden banister. "They must've painted it recently," she mused, aware that such household tasks were rare for her stepfather, likely the work of hired hands this time. She knew that upon entering the hall, she'd find a vase on the round table, filled with a lavish and beautiful bouquet. Their mother always said that flowers create a welcoming atmosphere in a home. However, this bouquet was meant for guests. Meanwhile, in the kitchen, there were eustomas, chamomiles, or lilacs — her favorite flowers, which she bought for herself.

The first home occupies a special place in our hearts, persisting through life in memories and dreams. Sophie adored her home, with its perpetual warmth and floral fragrance. Departing it, she felt a tinge of melancholy. Yet, she recognized that staying longer would only replace warm memories with the inevitable challenges life presents: the initial stumbles, disappointments, and losses. She preferred to preserve this place as a cherished chapter from the fairy tale of her childhood.

Upon entering her room, Sophie gently closed the door behind her, leaving the lights off. The windows overlooked the waterfront, with the streetlights outside casting a beautiful illumination inside. This was something Sophie always treasured, especially since she had battled a fear of the dark in her childhood. Her room used to have semi-transparent chiffon curtains, which softly diffused light into the space.

She stood still, embracing the silence. It was always serene here, a tranquil haven. Her gaze drifted to the bed nestled in the far corner, the sudden urge to curl up and sleep until Christmas overwhelmed her. The thought of attending more gatherings with old friends or celebrating birthdays held no appeal. Everything essential was right here: a room echoing with her parents' voices, treasured toys, and a comforting, familiar scent. Just through the wall, her sister was nearby, always knowing just the right words and ways to offer support. For a brief moment, Sophie's current life felt incredibly distant, almost dreamlike, and the constant hustle she had been living in seemed utterly trivial.

Sophie lingered in her childhood room before eventually joining the others downstairs, where she found Natalie and Nick chatting in the kitchen.

"Hey," she greeted with a wave, a shy smile on her face. "Sorry, I disappeared for a bit."

Approaching Nick, she wrapped him in a hug. He was clad in a black long-sleeved shirt, the sleeves rolled up to his elbows. Sophie ran her hand along his arm, her gaze lingering on him.

"Today, all the women in London will be envious of me," she remarked, her eyes still fixed on Nick.

"Has she been this out of it the entire day?" Natalie asked with an eye roll. "Shall we?"

As Natalie exited the room, Nick gently lifted Sophie's chin and kissed her.

"You're always charming," he whispered.

36

AS DARKNESS ENVELOPED THE CITY, THE TRIO MADE THEIR WAY TO the city center. The uncertainty of whether the night would turn out to be memorable or forgettable lingered in the air. Nick was the first to pierce the silence.

"So, this isn't actually a tour, is it? You're just looking to catch up with your friends."

"Yeah, but you're going to enjoy it too!" Natalie assured him with a wink before instructing the taxi driver, "Please, stop right here on the corner."

The taxi pulled to a halt in South Kensington in front of an old pub, its entrance adorned with a steel sign featuring golden, swirling letters. Two girls and a guy, cigarettes in hand, stood by the entrance. Their faces lit up upon spotting Natalie and Sophie, and they approached with enthusiastic greetings.

"What took you so long?" one queried.

"Sophie, Nat," the second girl greeted, warmly embracing both friends.

"Nick, these are our friends Dave, Kate, and Rosie," Sophie introduced with a beaming smile.

Nick extended his hand to Dave and offered a friendly nod to the girls, smiling.

"We were starting to get worried! She's never mentioned anyone over the years," Dave commented, eyeing Nick. "For all we knew, she could be married with two kids by now."

"Don't you worry about Nat as well?" Nick said.

"Oh, dear, you've got a lot to catch up on," Natalie put her hand on his shoulder, "Let's head inside."

It was a typical old English pub, nestled on a quaint cobblestone street. Upon entering, they were enveloped by the warm embrace of polished oak beams and worn wooden floors that had borne the weight of countless revelers over the years. The low ceilings, adorned with dark wooden beams, and the soft glow of brass lanterns cast a warm and inviting ambiance. The walls were adorned with an eclectic assortment of memorabilia, from vintage photographs of local events to dusty hunting trophies and antique clocks that seemed to have frozen in time.

They made their way to a couple at the bar counter. The girl with the short haircut turned around at the sound of familiar voices. "These are my girls!" she exclaimed, embracing Sophie and Natalie warmly. After introductions, they settled at the bar and ordered drinks.

"Is Emily going to make it tonight?" Kate inquired.

"No," Sophie replied with a sigh, a gesture that seemed to release some of her tension. "She couldn't find anyone to watch Mia, so she won't be joining us."

"Yeah, that's tough," Matt chimed in from next to the girl with the short haircut.

"So, when are you two thinking of...?" Natalie teased with a sly smile.

"Ah, here come the awkward questions," Matt responded, looking slightly embarrassed.

"Are you guys married?" Nick inquired, looking at the couple.

"Yes, since college," the girl answered.

"Is she always like this?" Nick asked, nodding toward Natalie with a smirk.

"Yeah, but get her drunk, and she'll start focusing more on herself," Kate laughed.

"Sorry, not happening tonight," Natalie interjected, raising her wine glass in a toast.

Sophie was leaning on the bar counter when a guy who seemed barely out of college made his way through the crowd towards her.

"Hey! You look great!" he exclaimed, attempting to shake her hand.

Sophie turned, her expression a mix of surprise and bemusement as if he had appeared out of thin air.

"Hey! Thanks. Sorry, I'm here with friends and my boyfriend,"

The guy, looking embarrassed, apologized and retreated back through the crowd.

"How do you deal with that?" Dave, standing beside Nick, asked with a skeptical tone. "Seems like she's always getting hit on. And not just by guys," he added, casting a meaningful glance around.

"Is that supposed to bother me?" Nick responded, his curiosity piqued.

"It'd bother me. That's why I steer clear of dating women who are too attractive."

"Because you're worried you wouldn't be the center of attention?" Nick retorted, a playful smirk on his face.

"Looks like they're a perfect match," Dave remarked, raising an eyebrow.

"Absolutely!" Natalie chimed in.

"Yeah, but it's not like *he* avoids dating 'too attractive' women," Rosie said, looking at Dave.

"Oh, and what would you know? Do you think a beautiful woman doesn't realize she might stand out in a place like this? And of course, she takes advantage of it. Those arrogant looks, the eye-rolling…"

"Notice, I'm staying silent," Natalie murmured to Nick.

"Maybe now's a good time to weigh in," he whispered back.

"Approaching someone with that mindset is bound to be off-putting," Rosie countered.

"Do you often make the first move with guys?" Dave challenged, his eyebrow arched inquisitively.

"I haven't kept count... How about a bet? Tonight, I'll approach the most attractive guys and get their numbers, and you do the same with the most beautiful girls. Whoever ends up with more numbers wins."

"Here we go," Dave said, crossing his arms.

"What's the wager?" Kate asked, eagerly joining in.

"If I win," Dave began, pointing at Rosie thoughtfully, "you'll call over the bartender, ask him to lean in, and then whisper, asking if you can pay for the drinks and give him a kiss."

Rosie snorted, a grin spreading across her face.

"But if I win," she paused, considering, "you'll do the same."

Laughter erupted from the group. Rosie and Dave shook hands on the bet.

"You don't stand a chance," Dave scoffed. "Let's go!"

Kate separated their hands as Rosie and Dave diverged, each scanning the crowd for their first victims. Dave quickly locked eyes with a girl standing solo at the far end of the bar and shot Rosie a confident wink before approaching the stranger.

"The lengths we go to see a best friend kissing a guy," Rosie sighed, turning her attention to a group of guys across the room.

"Is it just me, or is Rosie's win a foregone conclusion?" Sophie interjected. "She's irresistibly charming."

"True, but if she wins, it'll be because she picks guys she's actually drawn to, not just to inflate her ego, unlike Dave, who'll target the most attractive girls," Natalie countered.

"Do you think that's why Dave and Rosie aren't together?" Nick asked, scanning their frozen expressions. Natalie offered a small smile and averted her gaze.

"What are you implying?" Kate asked, pretending not to understand.

"It's quite evident Dave has feelings for Rosie," Nick explained, maintaining his calm demeanor.

The conversation paused for a moment.

"Alright, you're new here," Anne, with a short haircut, teased lightheartedly.

Laughter filled the air, and Nick, in a gesture of surrender, raised his hands. Sophie nestled closer to him, laying her head on his chest.

"You two are adorable," Anne commented. "Ever considered moving to London?"

"No, why?" Sophie felt a strong desire to change the subject.

"What does New York have that London doesn't? We're much more fun," Anne challenged.

"Oh, I'm starting to see that," Nick laughed, casting an observant glance around the room before noticing Sophie's gaze fixed on the floor.

"You'll forget proper English if you stay away too long!" Anne jested with a playful smirk directed at Sophie.

"That's up for debate," Nick responded smoothly.

"Don't bother arguing," Anne's companion interjected. "She holds a Ph.D. in English language and literature."

"That's what's so refreshing about them — the absence of preconceptions," Sophie reflected. "There's a sense of ease there, a lightness that's hard to find elsewhere."

"On a scale of one to ten, how challenging do you find immigration?" Anne inquired, her gaze fixed on Sophie.

"A solid twenty," Sophie confessed.

"Yet, you appear to be managing quite well!"

"Maybe. It's just that people often only see the achievements, not the struggle that led to them. It's sad how much disappointment this brings. If people knew the whole truth from the start, few would agree to go through it. Frankly, for many, there's no compelling reason to endure such hardship as immigration."

"And what about you, Natalie?" Matt turned his attention to her.

"It's not fair to compare. I relocated for a job, so I had a measure of stability from the outset. Sophie, on the other hand, dove into complete uncertainty, and rebuilt her career from the ground up. Even Emily had more of a basis for her move."

"Emily hasn't reconciled with her child's father, has she?" Anne asked, her tone tinged with sorrow, as though she anticipated the response.

Natalie shook her head. At that moment, Rosie returned, her smile beaming, as she reached for her drink.

"How's it going?" Kate asked with a smirk.

"I've got five numbers, and one guy's particularly cute," Rosie replied, giving her friend a meaningful look.

"Five numbers?" Nick interjected, surprised. "Considering there's barely sixty people in this bar."

"So, how much time do I have left?" Rosie asked, placing her drink down with renewed energy before diving back into the crowd.

"Five more numbers till we witness Dave's legendary kiss with the bartender," Kate said, chuckling.

Half an hour later, Rosie and Dave rejoined their friends, ready to see who had won.

"I hate to break it to you, Rosie," Dave started, "but tonight might not be your lucky night."

"Let's hear it, how many?" Rosie prompted.

"Eight," Dave announced with a proud wink at Rosie.

"Sorry to disappoint," Rosie responded, her smile unwavering. "I got ten."

As Matt clapped Dave on the shoulder, everyone else offered their congratulations to Rosie. Natalie caught Dave's eye, silently warning him against arguing.

"Well, it looks like there's no escaping it now," Matt said, laughter filling the air.

Dave made his way to the crowded bar counter, surrounded by people.

"Looks like I'm buying for everyone tonight," Dave conceded with a sigh.

He approached and signaled the bartender, who leaned in closer due to the noisy, crowded bar. The bartender's reaction to what happened next was unexpectedly hilarious — Dave, with a look of mock disgust, quickly pecked the bartender on the lips. The bartender, clearly shocked, froze, leaving their lips in an awkward moment of contact. Suddenly, a tall, stocky man nearby, easily twice Dave's size, yanked him away from the bar by his shirt collar and tossed him into the crowd, nearly sending two other patrons tumbling. They looked at Dave, bewildered, asking what his problem was.

"It's time we left!" Matt announced, moving to retrieve Dave.

"What about the rights of social minorities?" Nick joked, glancing at Sophie.

"Not in this place," Sophie said, taking his hand. "Any suggestions on where to next?"

"Liam and his brother have a party tonight," Anne suggested.

They quickly exited the bar, and within minutes, Dave and Matt caught up.

"Smile," Rosie commanded, her laughter peaking as she pointed her Polaroid camera at Dave.

"You all really know how to make a night memorable!" Nick observed, eyeing the group.

"That was just the warm-up! Off to Liam's we go," Matt declared, giving Nick an encouraging slap on the shoulder.

Nick hadn't expected a massive mansion right in the heart of the city, but there it was, ablaze with the bright lights of multicolored projectors shining from its windows. People milled about in small, animated groups near the entrance. The whole house seemed to pulse with the beat of the music.

"You didn't leave this place because it was dull, that's for sure," Nick remarked to Sophie.

"Oh, please. Remember Mike's antics when he got bored? And I only caught a glimpse of that in a year."

Inside, they entered a crowded hall that opened up into a vast room with a wide balcony. There, a group of guys gathered around a table featuring an ice sculpture. One was drizzling a drink over the sculpture while another drank directly from its icy contours. The host of the party, spotting the newcomers, greeted them enthusiastically from the balcony.

"Hey, glad to see you!"

Approaching them was a tall guy in a light shirt, his dark hair in stark contrast. He greeted Matt and Anne warmly, then acknowledged the rest of the group.

"American girls! What brings you here?" Liam wrapped his arms around their shoulders.

It was clear he was the architect of the evening's wildness, living up to his notorious reputation.

"We couldn't miss your parties," Natalie responded with a hug.

"Liam, this is Nick," Sophie introduced, stepping back from Liam's embrace.

"Nice to meet you," Nick offered his hand.

"Love the accent!" Liam grinned. "Glad you could make it. Enjoy yourselves!"

A guy with a glass in hand joined them, nodding silently to the group.

"Help yourselves to anything behind the bar. If you're after something stronger, ask for Rob," Liam gestured towards his taciturn friend.

The group began to scatter, with Sophie and Nat moving towards some familiar faces they spotted.

"Hey, mate," Liam addressed Nick, "How about a round of poker?"

"Not tonight. I'd rather hang out with the girls," Nick said.

"Suit yourself," Liam responded, hands raised in a gesture of acceptance. "We'll be downstairs if you change your mind!"

The house was a labyrinth of endlessly occupied rooms. In this complex array, Nick and Matt stumbled upon a pool table, while Sophie and Anne cozied up in armchairs for a conversation. As midnight neared, Natalie joined them with a friend in tow.

"Some kids managed to punch a hole in the hallway wall," Natalie commented with an eye roll.

"Seems like one tried a somersault," her friend chimed in.

"What's good?" Natalie inquired, looking at the group.

"Just chillin'," Anne responded, stretching out.

"Fancy a lift?" The man next to Natalie offered, shaking a small box of minty candies. "Nat, I know you want some too," he teased.

"No thanks, I'm good tonight," she declined with a smile. "Lately, I've been enjoying doing this sober... Better give it to them," she suggested, nodding towards Nick and Sophie. "So you kids have some fun!"

"What's this?" Nick asked, his skepticism barely concealed.

"MDMA, no impurities. Trust me, you'll enjoy it," the man assured.

"The doctor gave his approval for tonight," Natalie said with a wink.

Sophie gave Nick a look, subtly nodding towards the door.

37

IN THE DIMLY LIT KITCHEN, WITH ONLY A SOFT GLOW FROM BENEATH the cabinets illuminating the space, Nick watched Sophie fill a glass with water.

"Don't forget the knife," he said.

"You seem quite experienced with this," Sophie noted, observing him skillfully divide the pill into two uneven halves.

"Not really. My days of partying with ecstasy ended back in college," he replied, downing his half before passing the glass to Sophie. She took hers with a tilt of her head. "So, are we heading to your place?"

They exchanged glances and burst into laughter.

"No, I've got a better idea," Sophie said.

He responded by drawing her closer, one hand at her waist and the other gently caressing her hair. "I wish we'd met sooner, to have spent our twenties together. It would have been incredible," he mused.

"I have no doubt about that," Sophie replied, her heart calming in his presence. "Everything just quiets down around you. All the noise just disappears."

"I remember the first time I tried this; the next morning, I was almost overwhelmed by the realization that everything is always fine in the moment. However, as soon as your brain kicks in with fears, expectations, and anxieties, you stop truly living," Nick reflected.

Sophie felt an electric jolt through her body. She couldn't quite tell if it was Nick's words or the substance in her system.

"I've spent my whole life being afraid of something, running from something, waiting for something," she confessed.

"That sounds like a perfect reason to stop right now. And we don't need any pills to do that," he said with a casual shrug.

"Everything is always fine in the moment," she whispered, her gaze drifting into the distance.

They ascended to the top floor, finding a single bedroom tucked beneath the slanted roof. As they stepped inside, Nick took in the simplicity of the space: whitewashed walls, a slender window, and a mattress laid directly on the floor, illuminated by a lampstand Sophie switched on.

"Wow, of all the places in London, you chose to show me this," he remarked.

"Yes," Sophie moved closer. "This is home. This is where we've been ourselves. The last time we were here, with Emily, about six years ago... we were drunk and barely made it up to this room. Those memories are among the last warm ones we shared."

Feeling dizzy, Nick sat down on the floor, and Sophie joined him.

"My heart is racing," she confessed, her gaze meeting his.

Nick took her hand, feeling for her pulse. He glanced at his watch, timing it.

"190," he noted, observing a newfound brightness in her eyes. "What do you usually experience?"

"Everything," she said with a smile. "I want to capture the moment and hold it still. I've never understood the urge to dance on this."

"It sounds like you've always had a pill with a similar effect," he mused, resting his head against the wall. "Now, I can feel my pulse racing."

Sophie lifted his hand to her lips, kissing his wrist gently before tracing her fingers delicately along the veins.

"Have you ever had sex on this?" Nick asked, captivated by her touch.

"No, I never wanted to," she admitted.

"Me neither. But I think in this state, you reveal your true feelings towards someone."

"Still, you might find yourself wanting to cuddle and kiss, without it leading to sex."

"Yeah," Nick sighed, a hint of seriousness underlining his tone. "Could you tell me what happened before you moved to New York? While we're still coherent," he added with a chuckle.

"You chose now, when we are high, to ask about my past?"

"It's the one topic you've consistently avoided. Your past."

"Do you think I'm hiding something?"

"I believe it's difficult for you to discuss, and I'm curious about the reasons. Honestly, I'm interested in everything about you. I didn't delve into such questions on our first date, nor during the months we dated, or even after we started living together. But here I am, across the ocean, in a house filled with your college memories, eager to understand what drove you away."

Sophie gazed into the distance, her expression thoughtful. She swallowed, her voice wavering slightly as she spoke.

"There were many reasons," she started. "My time here with Emily encapsulates the last of my warm memories. Shortly after, she married and had a child within a year, and Natalie relocated to New York for work. They both drifted out of my life. During that period, I was in a deep, complex relationship with someone very important to me. We met when I was eighteen. My God...," she sighed, "I had never fallen in love like that before. It's that moment when you're ready to die for someone. He was older and, for as long as I can remember, played with my feelings all the time we were together. We argued a lot, but we were the kind of couple everyone thought would end up together. Even my parents believed we were meant to be. Everyone except for Natalie. Before she left, we had a major argument. The breakup led me to a nervous breakdown and hospitalization. When Natalie visited, she confessed she couldn't watch me destroy my life anymore and refused to be a part of it. In response, I pushed her away."

"What led to the breakup?" Nick said quietly.

"It was a series of breakups, really. Once he called to say we should cease all communication. Just like that. It was the second breakup. There was a third one ahead. Despite his odd beliefs and influence over me, I was drawn back to him, forgiving his infidelities, his absences, and his sudden reappearances. Looking back, I can't fathom how I tolerated it all."

"Forgive my confusion, but the person I met... You always seemed to embody self-assurance, self-respect, and a profound appreciation for your own time."

"I guess those qualities didn't just manifest overnight. Leaving him marked a turning point for me, and my decision to move was almost immediate. It was a complete upheaval of my life."

"And you've never spoken to him since?"

"No, not at all. I clearly remember when he attempted to reconnect, still oozing charm and charisma. I realized that things might seem okay for a while, but inevitably, we'd fall back into the same destructive cycle. I made the decision to completely sever ties. Moving to New York was challenging, but I'm eternally thankful to this city for helping me find my self-belief. It taught me that I could be beautiful, intelligent, and skilled in many areas," she said, her voice tinged with emotion.

"Are you kidding me? Sophie, you're incredible. And I'm not just saying this. I've seen how people react to you; you possess a truly unique allure. It's been amazing to witness how often you leave people speechless, mesmerized by your presence. It's even boosted my ego, though it shouldn't. If I had realized you needed to hear daily affirmations of your beauty, intelligence, and charm... I mistakenly thought you were well aware. I didn't want to be just another voice echoing what I assumed you already knew. Surely, many have told you the same. And yet, you let the words of one person overshadow all that?"

"I've spent a long time pondering why I gave his words so much power. I still don't have the answer."

Nick embraced her, pulling her close. He could feel the anxiety and indignation within him starting to battle the substance, gradually relaxing his consciousness.

"There will never be anyone like you again. I know this... please hear me."

Sophie closed her eyes, breathing in the familiar scent of his sweatshirt — the scent of her new home, of cozy evenings by the fireplace, lazy weekends in bed, heartfelt conversations, and trust.

Nick's fingers combed through her soft, silky hair as he closed his eyes, letting go of the mundane world and its expectations. Concerns about time, sleep, meeting Sophie's parents, and what awaited him back in New York faded away. In this moment, nothing else existed but them and their profound connection, as if it had always been meant to be.

Leaning back against Nick, Sophie took his hand, tracing the lines on his palm. "If only we could stay in this room forever," she murmured.

"Then nothing else would really matter," he sighed.

"Have you ever wished you could stop being defined by people from your past?" Sophie asked softly, deep in thought.

"Yes. It feels like a heavy burden to carry sometimes."

"For the first time, I feel I could let go of it. Free myself from being tied to all these people. Just to exist. Not even as myself, but just this feeling right now. And when it changes, to simply continue existing."

Nick listened to her voice fill the room, eyes closed.

"Sophie?" he whispered tenderly.

"Yes, love?"

"Do you ever feel our lifestyle consumes us?"

"No," she said, a frown creasing her forehead as she continued to explore their intertwined fingers, reveling in the warmth and softness.

"What would you do if you weren't bound by work, projects, and the city's relentless pace?"

"I haven't thought about it."

"We could live life in countless ways, yet we choose just one."

"I'm sorry, it's hard to focus right now, even harder to grasp why this matters so much."

"It mattered, but now it doesn't anymore."

"Let's remember this conversation and talk about it tomorrow," she smiled, leaning in toward his lips, pausing just inches away, her fingers lightly touching his stubble.

This place, this moment, was all that mattered. Gradually, it became infinite. The past and future dissolved, leaving only the present. Questions became unnecessary. Clarity and simplicity reigned. Time ceased, and space contracted to this single room, capable of containing an entire universe. Perhaps this state is what people truly seek, striving to free themselves from the constraints of their own minds.

We often yearn for endless tranquility and a carefree existence, sometimes forgetting our inherent purpose, the unique gift we are meant to share with the world. This purpose, our true calling, might compel us to face challenges and obstacles. In those moments, it can feel like suffering, a deep desire to shed all concerns. Yet, it is within this struggle that our greatest potential lies — the act of creating what we were born to achieve. Unfortunately, we frequently overlook this opportunity. We take it for granted, doubt our abilities, or stray from our path. We shy away from commitments, fearing to immerse ourselves in profound love and devotion. We wish to remain serene and detached, venturing into enigmatic realms of knowledge where emptiness seems to prevail.

Sophie opened her eyes while lying on the mattress, with Nick right beside her. She looked up at the ceiling, which seemed to dissolve into soft, shimmering light. A compelling urge to touch the light washed over her. Extending her hand, she was instantly bathed in warm, yellow-orange radiance pouring in through the window. The beauty was breathtaking. If only the whole world could witness the beauty of this moment. Turning her head towards Nick, she found him looking back at her. They chose silence; words now felt too heavy and futile. They could sense each other's emotions as if the barriers between their physical forms and consciousness had vanished. Nick recalled the first moment he saw Sophie, her large eyes gleaming with a gentle sparkle. Only now did he understand that he had never doubted they would share a moment like this. He closed his eyes again, running his fingers through her hair.

It's difficult to say how much time has passed. Nick rose and walked toward the window, peering out at the cobblestone street lined with lanterns. Squinting against the bright light, he let his gaze wander down the street, realizing that beyond this room lay an enormous, boundless world that simply took his breath away. This world was extraordinarily beautiful, just as it was. It demanded no alterations, changes, or expectations from him. He felt an integral part of this world, sensing a piece of himself in everything he saw. Gradually, his vision sharpened.

Sophie wrapped her arms around him from behind, pressing her forehead against the back of his neck. Her breath was steady and calm. Nick placed her hands on his chest. Sophie's lips brushed softly against his neck, her touch gentle against his delicate skin. Turning to face her, Nick was drawn to her lips, reaching out to meet them. Their lips, almost parched from a long period, heightened the intensity of the feeling even more.

"Right now," he whispered.

"Yes," Sophie murmured, feeling the warmth of his breath.

Sometimes, we want to fall asleep lying on the chest of the one we love, listening to their heartbeat. Sometimes, we wish to slip beneath their shirt and stay like that for a while. And sometimes, we want to crawl under their skin and dissolve within them.

Nick slid his hand under Sophie's blouse, then withdrew it, slightly tousling her hair. He began to brush it away from her face, kissing her simultaneously.

"I've never felt like this before," she said, her eyes wide and shimmering with purity.

"Me neither," he said, running his hands over her body.

Gently, Nick kissed her forehead, her eyes, her nose, and finally her lips. At that moment, he felt as if he had completely merged with her. Sophie removed his sweatshirt, tracing her fingers over his chest and collarbone. She rested her head against his chest, tuning into the rhythm of his heart. It was the most beautiful sound, and for a moment, time stood still. She couldn't recall the moment they lay down or when he removed her jeans. She felt his lips kissing the inner side of her thigh. Instead of feeling ticklish, every cell in her body responded to his kisses. When he was on top of her, their eyes met. He unbuttoned his jeans and paused. The next moment was an explosion in the universe where they had spent the night.

"I will always come back to this room," she whispered in his ear.

38

SOPHIE AWOKE TO THE NOISE OUTSIDE; THE SUN HAD ALREADY climbed high above the horizon. Searching for her phone, she noticed Nick still asleep beside her, undisturbed by the noise.

"Love, it's time for us to go," she whispered, gently kissing his forearm.

"Already?" Without opening his eyes, he reached out, attempting to pull her closer.

"Yes, we need to head out before noon to beat the traffic."

"Is there coffee in this house?" He sighed, rolling onto his back.

"No, but I know a place where we can get some, and we'll find my sister there too."

Stepping onto the street, they were momentarily blinded by the bright sunlight. Sophie took his hand, leading the way.

"That was fun!" Nick said, looking at her with their fingers intertwined.

"Yes, and to be honest, I'm still a little bit high," she admitted with a shy smile. "It feels like a throwback to my university days. Only this time, you're here with me."

"It seems you really cherished that time."

"I did."

Sophie paused in front of a building they were passing, an art gallery with panoramic windows and freshly painted walls.

"This is the Gambert Gallery. We did our internship here," she reminisced with a smile. "It's strange. You see a new city, new buildings, new people. But for me, it's filled with ghosts. Everywhere I look, there are fleeting memories."

"You miss home, don't you?" Nick finally asked.

"Any immigrant misses home, no matter how they feel about it. It's natural. But I don't want to go back to London. It's not the walls I miss; it's the details, the culture, the times when I was immersed in art."

"What's stopping you from pursuing that in New York?"

"You've asked me that before."

"And you haven't answered."

"Let's not dive into heavy conversations now. We need coffee, and besides, Natalie is probably waiting for us."

"Did you set a time to meet?"

"No, but that café was always our rendezvous after parties."

They were seated in the cafe, amidst the sparse crowd of early Saturday morning patrons. Natalie arrived, appearing well-rested and in high spirits. After a quick breakfast, she reclined in her chair with a cup of coffee in hand, observing her sister and Nick as they quietly ate their breakfast across from her. Sophie made herself comfortable on the couch, crossing her legs in her usual manner when wearing jeans. Her leg brushed against Nick's knee, prompting him to rest his hand on the inside of her thigh.

"Do you two have an oxytocin addiction or something? You're practically on top of each other," Natalie teased.

Sophie chose to ignore Natalie's jibe and continued to focus on her plate, while Nick smiled, contemplating his response.

"Well, you know, when the night has gone so well, you want to extend that feeling for as long as you can," he replied.

"Ahh, I see. So, I wouldn't recommend something that wasn't good, huh?" Natalie chuckled. "I'm happy for you, especially for my little sister. Judging by the sparkle in her eyes, it seems she's in safe hands, fingers, and so forth."

"Natalie... Your baby sister is right here," Sophie snorted.

"You're an adult, yet you're acting like a child," Natalie responded, her lips curling into a half-smile as her gaze shifted to Nick. "Tell me, were you the most popular guy in high school? The star quarterback, perhaps?"

"No," Nick replied, his smile persisting despite a touch of embarrassment. "I was more into reading, wore glasses, and was pretty clueless about talking to girls."

"Interesting," Natalie mused, interlocking her fingers. "So, when did you lose your virginity?"

"Are we really discussing this over breakfast?" he laughed. "At nineteen."

"During your freshman year?"

"Yes."

"Pretty late, I'd say," Natalie teased with a playful eyebrow raise. "But I'll admit, you certainly give off a different impression now."

"I never really considered the impression I'd make. But reflecting on that day, how awful it was, made me realize I needed to change something."

"And thus began the splendid transformation," Natalie chuckled.

"Indeed."

"Sorry," Sophie interjected, placing her hand on Nick's wrist. "I've just realized that our relationship has progressed to a point where I don't want to know the details of your... transformation."

Natalie and Nick couldn't help but burst into laughter.

"And just like that, she's all grown up," Natalie observed, looking at her sister with admiration. "She used to share everything with her boyfriends, I mean every little detail," she added, batting her eyelashes for effect.

"At the beginning of our relationship, you were keen on asking about those kinds of things in detail. I never quite understood your need for it," Nick added.

"Okay, enough," Sophie cut in, clearly annoyed. "I'm ending this discussion now. No more talk about how anyone lost their virginity today," she declared.

This prompted Natalie and Nick to laugh even louder, attracting the gaze of the disinterested waitress at the bar.

"I get the feeling the guy from last night is notably absent," Nick teased, starting again.

"Why would we need him here?" Natalie responded. "By the way, he was one of Sophie's classmates."

Sophie just rolled her eyes at the mention, although she was already aware of their connection.

"What draws you to this lifestyle, if you don't mind my asking?" Nick inquired, curious.

"It's about being true to myself," Natalie replied with a shrug. "I'm not implying that everyone in long-term relationships is fooling themselves. It's just that I know it's not for me; I don't see the point in making meaningless compromises."

"It's her way of asserting her independence," Sophie interjected, lips pursed.

"Are you trying to compete with me in something that's been my livelihood?" Natalie challenged, locking eyes with her. "Then tell me, have long-term relationships brought you much happiness in your life?"

Sophie diverted her gaze in response, and Natalie, acknowledging the moment, did the same.

39

As they loaded their suitcases into the trunk of the Land Rover, Natalie quickly claimed her spot in the back seat. "Dibs on sleeping in the back!" she declared.

Sophie sighed, looking at Nick. "Guess who's driving," she said.

"Sorry, Soph, I don't think now's the best time for me to learn how to drive on the left," he replied with a chuckle.

As they merged into traffic leaving the city behind, Natalie stretched out in the back seat with a satisfied sigh. "Let's play Never Have I Ever," she suggested, laughing.

"You're falling asleep... Goodnight," Sophie said, turning up the music to drown her out.

"Good Lord, your poor parents... I can only imagine the fights you had as kids," Nick smirked and rubbed his forehead.

"Yeah, that's about right. Maybe that's why our biological father left," Natalie quipped.

Sophie often felt Natalie's sense of humor crossed lines, while her sister saw her jokes as harmless. This time, Sophie chose to focus on the road, ignoring the comment, but Nick noticed her tight grip on the steering wheel.

They faced a four-hour drive ahead. Located north of Manchester, the town of Scarborough is nestled harmoniously along the shore of the North Sea. It boasted the charm of an old English town, with its ancient, crumbling castles, inviting promenade, and cozy pubs and restaurants. Nick wasn't sure what to expect from this kind of vacation, yet he was eager to observe everything around him. Travel was a rarity for him, prompting him to wonder why. He couldn't help but question the depth of life's experience when viewed only from one's window. He knew the answer, and for someone who wrote books, it was sobering.

As they took the road running along the coast, the weather began to worsen. Dark clouds gathered on the horizon, signaling an impending storm. Soon, lightning flickered in the distance, dashing any hopes for pleasant weather. They reached their destination in the afternoon, by which time the rain was already falling, veiling the surroundings in a gray mist. Sophie parked the car in front of a tall house built from dark red brick. Perched on a hill, the house's backyard offered a view of the coastline. The driveway, paved with small, light-colored gravel, was flanked by spacious flower beds. On the eastern wall, wild green ivy climbed, lending the recently renovated house a touch of old-world grandeur.

"I feel like I've wandered into a Tolkien novel," Nick marveled, watching the heavy raindrops assault the windshield.

"The weather's definitely on par, even if the scenery might not match," Natalie added, swinging the rear door open.

"But why would anyone choose to vacation here when there are warmer spots by the ocean?" Nick pondered aloud.

"For many who were born here, this weather is part of their lives. They don't want to leave," Sophie said, her smile serene as she turned off the engine.

Upon entering the house, they placed their damp suitcases by the door. Sophie, with a practiced move, set the keys on a marble table adorned with a vase of fresh, pale purple crocuses and a stand holding the morning's newspapers, which, notably, were not damp — indicating that the morning had been clear. The hallway opened into a semicircular layout that seamlessly connected the kitchen, dining room, and living room, with a staircase facing them that led to the second floor. From the kitchen wafted the faint clinking of dishes on stone countertops and the inviting aroma of a pie, likely still baking in the oven. The muffled sound of a television came from the other wing.

"Mom?" Natalie called out, slipping off her sneakers with haste.

A woman emerged from the kitchen archway, her warm smile lighting up the room. She was dressed in an apron over light-colored trousers and a cashmere blouse.

"My girls, I'm so happy to see you," she said, enveloping each of her daughters in a warm hug, holding onto them for a moment longer than expected.

"Mom, this is Nick," Sophie said, introducing him as she shook the rain from her hair.

Before Nick could extend his hand in greeting, the woman approached and gave him a welcoming hug.

"I can already hear your 'Mrs.' coming, so just call me Margaret," she said, looking at him kindly. "Kids, dinner will be ready shortly, so you might want to get changed."

"Where's Dad?" Natalie asked.

"He's fixing the broken sprinkler in the garage. He should be back soon," Margaret answered, turning back towards the kitchen.

When Nick entered the living room, he was greeted by the spaciousness of the room, with its modern and refined interior. However, what immediately captured his attention was the fireplace. Unlike the contemporary versions often seen today — mere recesses in the wall shielded by glass, or worse, holograms — this was a true, grand fireplace made of stone masonry, complete with a wide chimney. The soft crackling of the logs within was delightful. The house seemed to belong to people who valued comfort over showing off their wealth. It was spacious, yes, but designed more for the owners' enjoyment than for impressing visitors. Nick thought about how his father always aimed to surpass others, and how his mother had a talent for transforming that ambition into elegance.

Next to the couch, he noticed a small table with a half-empty glass of red wine and an open book. Driven by curiosity, Nick picked up the book and flipped to the cover: 'A Tale of Two Cities' by Dickens.

"Great reading to clear your mind," commented a male voice.

Turning, Nick saw a man in the doorway, stepping forward to introduce himself.

"I'm Charlie, Margaret's husband. You must be Nick?" He extended his hand.

"Pleasure to meet you, Charlie," Nick replied, shaking his hand. "Thank you for the invitation."

"We're truly delighted you could visit," Charlie said, picking up a glass and standing by the fireplace. He appeared to be no older than fifty-five, in such excellent physical shape that pinning down his exact age was difficult. His dark brown hair, sprinkled with gray, lent him a somewhat youthful appearance. Nick noted that despite being at his country house on vacation, he was cleanly shaven. Tall and commanding, his whole demeanor radiated a strong-willed and masculine character. Yet, he possessed a calm confidence and composure that made him seem in control, even during pauses in their conversation.

As everyone took their seats around the table, Margaret was the last to sit down, continuing to bustle about. She lit candles and, with an inspired sigh, placed her hand on Charlie's shoulder before taking her own seat.

Nick watched the family interactions with keen interest, always fascinated by the dynamics at play, especially as the newcomer.

"How's working in Berlin, Natalie?" Charlie inquired as dinner commenced.

"It's been absolutely fantastic," she responded with confidence. "My contract is almost up, and I'm planning to defend my Ph.D. in New York before returning to London."

Margaret, beaming with pride at her daughter, added, "Charlie and I are incredibly proud of you. I must admit, I'm eagerly awaiting your return."

"But what about your discussions on joining the American Association of Psychotherapists?" Sophie chimed in.

"That would only feed my ambition. Besides, my time in Berlin made me realize how much I've missed home. The rain and the gloomy faces," Natalie added.

Nick smirked as he listened to her. Natalie's behavior within the family mirrored her typical demeanor elsewhere.

Turning to Margaret, Nick inquired, "Sophie mentioned you're a doctor too?"

"Yes, a cardiologist," Margaret confirmed, taking a sip of her wine. "And Charlie is involved in medical equipment development," she added, nodding towards her husband.

"That's quite..." Nick started, but Sophie cut in.

"The whole family's in medicine, except for me," she laughed.

"And I couldn't be happier about it. Your heart has always belonged to art... I just wish you'd return to your true talent," Margaret expressed, gazing earnestly at Sophie.

"Mom," Sophie responded softly, her gaze dropping.

"I completely agree," Nick interjected.

However, Nick couldn't help but notice a shift in Sophie's demeanor. The robust independence she typically displayed appeared diminished, replaced by a quieter, more introspective air.

"I believe Sophie knows what's best for herself," Charlie stated firmly and confidently.

Sophie offered him a grateful glance and smiled, almost shyly. Over the next few days, Nick observed her interactions with her parents, confirming his initial impression. Sophie shared a close and trusting bond with her mother. In her most challenging moments, filled with despair or in need of advice, it was to Margaret she turned. However, her relationship with her stepfather was fragile and somewhat distant. Charlie struggled to understand Sophie's vulnerability and emotional depth, treating her with a cautious tenderness akin to handling delicate glass. Sophie, in return, showed respect and kindness but remained guarded.

This contrast became stark against the backdrop of Natalie and Charlie's mutual understanding, which appeared almost telepathic, marked by their ease and directness with one another. Natalie, however, showed more reserve with her mother, hesitant to indulge in every sentimental moment. Margaret seemed to embody the role of the quintessential nurturing mother, whose instinct to care extended beyond her family to her many patients in her medical practice. Perhaps it was this constant demand on her time that ensured her children received precisely the level of independence they needed.

In the evening, as the sun set, Sophie and Nick ascended to the bedroom, their steps heavy with exhaustion. Sophie closed the door behind them and, without even looking, lit a floor lamp. Despite not having been here for three years, she knew this house inside and out. And now, it felt as if that time had simply vanished from her memory. If not for Nick, standing just a step away, she might have forgotten that she had ever left this place.

Approaching the bed, Sophie traced her fingers along its cool, thin metal bars. "This was Natalie's and my room," she reminisced, her eyes sweeping over the space. "It was the safest place in the world for us. No hardships, no harsh people, no disappointments. Outside, the world was vast and intriguing, but here, it was always safe and warm. I can't remember a time when I wasn't anxious about the past and the future, except in this room. Here, I found moments of true peace."

"Thank you for bringing me here," Nick responded softly.

"I feel like you belong here," she smiled gently. "As though we've known each other all our lives."

"You have a wonderful family, Sophie. And I think you're aware of that."

"Now, through your eyes, I see that I've never fully appreciated them," she admitted.

"I understand," he smiled, his eyes reflecting a deep-seated sadness, "We tend to appreciate things more as time begins to slip away. Perhaps it's a flaw in our nature."

Sophie felt a warmth spread within her as she listened to him. His words resonated with a beauty she hadn't encountered before. Regardless of how others saw him, to Sophie, his perspective was invaluable. At that moment, she felt as though she had found everything she'd been searching for.

"You know," Sophie moved closer, her hands resting on his broad shoulders, "I want more, too, even though it scares me."

In that instant, Nick gained a profound understanding of Sophie — her complex emotions, her inner conflicts, and her deepest fears. This moment underscored how often we presume to know what's best for others, sometimes even dictating their actions and decisions. Yet, it's in these very moments that people tend to choose paths contrary to expectations.

40

NICK AWOKE TO THE FIRST RAYS OF SUNLIGHT PIERCING THROUGH the curtains, the desire to sleep evading him, a common torment of jet lag. He walked to the window and watched as the previous day's mist, which had shrouded the horizon, now dissipated. It revealed a rocky coastline that stretched to the edge of sight before vanishing into the ether.

He approached the bed and gently kissed Sophie, careful not to wake her.

"Where are you going?" she murmured, her eyes still closed.

"I'm going for a run. Get some more sleep, baby."

After tossing and turning without success, Sophie made her way downstairs. Natalie and Margaret were already bustling about in the kitchen.

"Is the whole house awake already?" Sophie asked, taking a seat on a barstool, the weight of sleep still pressing down on her.

"I've gotten used to waking up early for work," Natalie replied. "Where's Charlie?"

"He's out on his morning bike ride," Margaret said, examining the new coffee machine. "Does Nick usually drink coffee?"

"Yes, black, but not too strong. No milk, no sugar," Sophie responded, resting her head in her hands. Natalie chuckled.

"What's so funny?"

"Nothing... It's just the sweetest thing I've heard you say. Love suits you," Natalie answered.

"What's on the agenda today?" Margaret inquired.

"Is it acceptable to do nothing at all?" Natalie asked, smiling as she joined Sophie.

"I feel like I've forgotten what a summer holiday is," Sophie lamented.

Sophie looked at Margaret, marveling at the boundless energy her mother always possessed. Even on vacation, she was up at dawn, brewing coffee for everyone. Already dressed and well-groomed, she radiated good spirits.

"You'll find something to do. You've spent every summer here since you were children," Margaret said, looking at her daughters lovingly.

"I think the best summer was when I was fifteen," Sophie recalled with a smile.

"At fifteen?" Margaret mused. "Wasn't that when you two snuck out without permission?"

"I was allowed out, and Sophie wanted to tag along. I was curious to see how it would all pan out," Natalie said, attempting to ruffle Sophie's hair, who dodged skillfully.

"That night, I had my first kiss," Sophie revealed, a hint of nostalgia in her voice.

"Was it at that beach where everyone gathered around the bonfire?" Natalie inquired.

"Yes."

"Nick is in for quite the tour," Natalie said, rising from her chair with a laugh before Sophie could retaliate.

Holding her mug, Natalie stepped out into the backyard and closed the door behind her. She inhaled the fresh, sea-infused air and, out of habit, walked barefoot on the lawn, her back to the house. Even with her eyes closed, the familiar view played vividly in her mind, down to the tiniest details. Soon, Margaret joined her.

"Darling, I've been thinking about Sophie's birthday," Margaret began, standing beside her with her own cup of coffee. "What should we do this year?"

"We usually throw a home party when we return to London," Natalie replied nonchalantly.

"That surprise party has become a tradition, hardly a surprise anymore. She mentioned we shouldn't do it this year."

"Oh, come on. She says that every year! But deep down, you know she loves those parties."

"I'm not so sure, dear. Do you think she really needs it?" Margaret glanced at her daughter with concern.

"What she really needs is therapy, especially after finally meeting and talking with her father. And you know this as much as I do," Natalie said, sadness evident in her eyes. She was referring to their biological father. Although she also called Charlie her father, there was no longer any confusion about whom she meant.

"I know," Margaret replied, gently fixing a stray lock of Natalie's hair. "Have you seen him recently?"

"About a year ago. I call him from time to time."

"How's he doing?"

"Not great, honestly. Last year, the doctors warned him about the risk of liver cirrhosis."

Margaret rarely contacted her ex-husband. He had continued his drinking habits after their divorce; especially after their divorce. Deciding to leave him to spare their children from such a future felt right, yet she harbored feelings for him during the initial years of their separation. Their common ground was minimal: she, a determined medical student; he, a musician playing in small pubs. Margaret had been captivated by his talent and charm, failing to notice as their paths diverged. Over time, his musical career was insufficient to support the family and raise their children. Reflecting on those years, she was grateful for her decision and for having met Charlie. Her anger had dissipated over time, leaving no desire for further communication.

"From the look on your face, it's obvious he's crossed a line," Natalie observed, her voice flat but her words tinged with regret.

"Darling, that's no longer my concern."

Returning from his run, Nick found Sophie in the kitchen, engrossed in her laptop.

"I thought you were the one who suggested we forget about work during the holidays," he remarked, planting a kiss on the top of her head as he caught his breath.

"I know, I just needed to check in quickly to see how things are going," she replied.

Nick glanced over her shoulder at the laptop screen, recognizing the project that had initially brought them together. She was still deeply involved in it, evidently committing far more than she had originally planned. He sensed what attracted her to this project but remained puzzled as to why she hadn't aligned her life with her true passions.

After breakfast, Margaret suggested Nick and Sophie explore the surroundings by bicycle, an offer they accepted with enthusiasm.

"Let's go to my favorite place," Sophie said, a smile brightening her face as she wheeled her bicycle out of the garage.

"I don't mind getting lost here with you," Nick responded, smiling. "It's so peaceful. I'd almost forgotten what real silence sounds like."

"No wonder, with New York's constant noise. By the way, why did you and Mike stop going to the mountains?"

"I guess all the changes over the past year might be why."

They coasted down a grassy path from the hill towards the main road, heading into the town center. Descending, they noticed more people, from large families to smaller groups, all mingling together. It was a scene repeated throughout: when people are content and serene, distinctions blur into insignificance. In moments like these, everyone is united, happy to leave behind the city's clamor, their concerns, and their troubles.

Cycling along the waterfront, Sophie glanced towards the beach, where teenagers were enjoying themselves, oblivious to the world around them.

"Just look at them. Why can't adults let loose like that, even if just for a bit?"

"That's exactly it," Nick said. "They haven't yet learned what time can take from you."

"They must be about fifteen or sixteen. At that age, the biggest concern is starting a romance that feels like it'll last forever," Sophie mused.

"Ah, you must have many memories from summers here. Any cheesy rom-com stories?"

"Maybe," she smirked. "We adored this beach. Every summer started with a bonfire party right here."

"Adorable."

"And what about you? Do you remember being that age?" Sophie asked, trying to suppress her laughter.

"Hey," he turned to her, their elbows touching, "I'm only thirty-four. But you know what we couldn't do at fifteen? Spend the whole night on the beach, drinking and having sex."

"That almost sounds like a date proposal," Sophie teased, raising an eyebrow.

"Sure."

As they pedaled away from the crowded town center, Sophie steered onto a secluded road winding up a hill. The landscape opened to expansive green meadows, and as they climbed, the horizon widened, leading their gaze to the ocean. Yet, it was the sight ahead that took their breath away: a colossal, partially ruined medieval castle, its light sand-colored bricks glowing under the sun, with the main keep towering five stories high. Surrounding it were outbuildings and a long wall, punctuated by small forts extending for miles.

"This is my favorite place in the whole world," Sophie declared, her gaze locked on the magnificent structure.

Dismounting, she breathed in deeply, the sea salt flavor mingling with the fresh air.

"When I met you, I knew instantly you were the type of girl who has her own castle," Nick remarked, his voice a mix of awe and affection as he surveyed their surroundings, feeling transported to another realm. The idea of abandoning everything else suddenly seemed incredibly enticing.

"Let's go," exclaimed Sophie, grasping his hand and leading the way with a brisk, almost playful stride.

Even though the castle appeared intact from a distance, upon entering, it became apparent that the eastern wall, leading to the coast, had crumbled. Sunlight bathed the inner surfaces of the castle walls, illuminating both the minute details of its history and the new life emerging amidst the antiquity. Green ivy trailing along the western wall seemed eager to breathe life into the grayness of the abandoned stones.

Nick and Sophie made their way further down to a sunlit meadow and settled on the grass. Sophie sprawled out, arms and legs stretched wide as though making snow angels, eager to relish the gentle touch of the soft grass on her skin for as long as she could.

"People say you only do this when you're happy," she observed, her eyes tracing the sky above.

"It seems to be true," Nick agreed, mirroring her actions.

They basked in a comfortable silence before Sophie pierced the calm.

"Do you remember when childhood ended?" She asked.

"No, do you?"

"I don't either. Sometimes, I just miss feeling unconditionally happy and free," she reflected wistfully.

"It's like we transition from being carefree to shouldering responsibilities; that's when happiness starts to come with conditions," Nick mused, his gaze drifting. "Do you think it's possible to be both free and responsible?"

"You're asking me?" She laughed softly. "You seem to have all the answers." Sophie paused, lost in thought. "I began asking questions too early, questions no child should worry about. Why did my father leave? Why doesn't he call? Why does my mom act as if everything's okay?"

"Have you considered talking to him now?" Nick's concern was evident.

"Should I really seek out someone who never showed he cared?" Sophie countered.

"I think you'll be grateful to yourself if you do, one day."

"It's been so long. I wouldn't even know where to start," Sophie said, quickly steering the conversation elsewhere. "You mentioned the other night how our lifestyle is consuming us. After your trip from LA, you said we don't talk enough about the future. It makes me wonder, did something happen there? Something you haven't shared?"

"Nothing noteworthy. I was just visiting a friend of my dad's who asked about my plans, and if I intended to leave New York. And I..." He paused, reflecting. "I've never really considered if I would stay in New York forever or move. I've always just done what was expected. But now, everything's different. Seeing Mike change his life so drastically, and seeing you not pursuing what you love," Sophie tried to interject, but he continued, "It's made me question my own choices. Besides, this trip has reminded me there's a whole world beyond New York."

"If you move somewhere like this," Sophie mused, watching the clouds, "You'd have to leave your job, appoint a CEO, and step back from the daily grind of the publishing house. You could live peacefully, away from the city's chaos, focusing on your writing."

"And you could finally work as the incredibly talented art curator you are."

Their eyes met.

"What's next for us?"

"Let's just enjoy the sky for now."

"Sophie," Nick said gently, a softness in his voice, "You know as well as I do, there's nothing worse than being stuck where you don't belong."

41

BEFORE THEY HEADED BACK INTO THE HOUSE, NICK STOPPED SOPHIE.

"Wait, there's something I need to tell you. I've been thinking about it all day."

Sophie's expression shifted to one of concern. Surprises of this nature always unsettled her. "I'm listening," she said tentatively.

"I want you to take over the Freeport project," he said, making sure to emphasize, "with full ownership rights." He released her hand, watching as confusion played across her face.

"What? Nick... Are you serious? What will the investors think? Have you seen those budgets? I don't have the experience to manage such a massive project," she protested, her voice tinged with disbelief.

Nick, settling onto the edge of a workbench in the garage, offered a reassuring smile. "We'll work through it together."

"No, I can't accept this for a multitude of reasons."

"Give me one," he smiled softly.

"The responsibility is enormous, and I'm not sure I'm prepared for it. I can't risk a project that's so important to you," she admitted.

"I'm not leaving. You won't be alone. Plus, you've been deeply involved and genuinely committed for nearly a year. I've seen your dedication, and frankly, they're not compensating you fairly," he paused, adding, "Besides, she would be overjoyed to see how everything turned out."

Sophie was at a loss for words, not wanting to escalate the conversation further. The magnitude of his proposition was still sinking in.

"Can I have some time to think it over?"

"Of course," he replied, looking at her with tenderness. "How about some wine?"

"Yes, please," Sophie responded, managing a chuckle despite the whirlwind of emotions.

Soon, everyone gathered on the back porch. Margaret lit candles on the table and in the hanging lamps near the entrance, casting a warm glow over the space. She also brought out blankets, anticipating the cool ocean breeze. Settled comfortably on the couch and chairs, Margaret and Sophie engaged in a lively conversation about the local town and its surroundings, praising the decision to build the house in such a perfect location. Charlie occasionally chimed in with his thoughts. Natalie, sitting beside Nick, spoke to him in hushed tones, careful not to attract the attention of the others.

"How's Mike doing?" She asked.

"He's doing well, actually, really great. He's going to be on the NBS channel soon with his new Late Night Show. I think he has you to thank for part of that success," Nick responded.

"That's all him. People only make big changes when they're truly ready," Natalie said, sounding very pleased.

"I also get the feeling he hasn't fully gotten over you," Nick ventured, observing Natalie for any sign of discomfort.

She sighed, brushing her hair away from her face. "Nick, I know he's your best friend, and I don't want to cause any pain."

"These are just my thoughts, Nat. I can't speak for him," Nick replied thoughtfully. "I wouldn't be okay with my girlfriend sleeping around with everyone. I doubt he would be, either."

"You're lucky with Sophie, then. She doesn't even let such thoughts enter her fantasies."

"I think you're all underestimating her. She's much more than what you see," Nick defended.

"I believe that's exactly how love should sound," Natalie said with a warm smile, placing her hand on Nick's forearm. "I'm going to take a walk for some fresh air. Enjoy the rest of the night!"

Natalie made her way toward the coastline, reflecting on Nick's words as she walked. Approaching the shore, she welcomed the wind against her skin, feeling no cold. Pulling her phone from the back pocket of her jeans, she scrolled to Mike's number in her contacts. After a brief hesitation, she opened their chat.

"Hey. Congratulations on the new job." She gazed at the horizon. A thousand miles away on another continent, a text message notification sounded.

Meanwhile, in the house, Sophie stood in the shower, her gaze lost on the droplets cascading down the fogged door. She knew the answer she wanted to give, yet she struggled to discern the right choice. The stark contrast between her desires and uncertainties left her feeling torn. She questioned the extent of the change this would bring to her life. Did she truly want these changes, or was she merely frightened, confused, and hesitant to take a step forward?

Nick entered the bedroom and began checking his travel bag, retrieving a fresh shirt. At the bottom of the bag, a book wrapped in coarse kraft paper lay alongside a small, velvet-lined case. After a brief glance at the case, he zipped the bag closed.

They enjoyed a few more carefree days on the coast. As Sophie's birthday neared, the time came to head back to London. On the eve of their departure, Sophie found herself in the basement, transferring clothes from the washing machine to the dryer, when she heard Nick's footsteps descending the stairs.

"Love, I wanted to ask…" she began, only for Nick to take the damp clothes from her hands and pull her close.

"Later," he said, sealing his words with a longing kiss. Their week had been filled with company, and he craved their solitary moments. Sophie, sitting on the washing machine, wrapped her legs around his waist.

"Shall we take a shower together?"

"Are you hinting that I need to cool down?"

"I'm hinting that I've missed you, too," she said, her hands gently at the back of his neck.

Nick embraced her, breathing in the scent of her hair. "Your birthday is coming. Are you ready?"

"No," she shook her head, laughter in her voice, "Let's just run away. Seriously."

"Is that my Sophie? Always ready for a challenge?"

"Anything as long as it doesn't involve my relatives," she sighed, drawing closer to him.

"Don't worry, everyone feels jittery before their birthday. It's normal."

Sophie exhaled deeply, locking eyes with Nick, ready to share her decision.

"I've thought about your offer, and I accept!"

Nick's smile widened; his expression was not one of surprise but filled with happiness.

"Great! If you decide to sell your business and start an art gallery, you'll have a head start."

"You do so much for me," she said, meeting his gaze.

Shaking his head with a smile, Nick almost kept silent, then added, "And you do so much for me, too. It's time you recognized that as well."

42

Sophie found solace in her favorite downtown café, usually her refuge on rainy days. Ironically, the sun blazed outside, mismatched with her introspective mood on her birthday. Claiming she needed time for errands, she sought solitude instead. Seated by the window, chin resting on her hands, she observed the bustling street, ignoring the incessant chime of text messages.

Sophie had always harbored mixed feelings about this day, viewing it as an overrated tradition. While she valued the attention of those around her, spending the day alone often left her feeling as if she were teetering on the edge of an abyss. Now, she marveled at how she had managed to reach this age without succumbing to that void.

She was certain, backed by her own experiences, that all goals were within reach and every wish could eventually come true. Given that people's desires often revolve around money and sex, these outcomes tend to materialize, sooner or later. However, she believed that the true significance lay not in the achievement itself, but in the journey to that achievement. It was all about the process. Sophie sighed, reflecting on her own path. The outcomes, thus far, weren't disappointing. Yet, with each day that passed, the joy they brought diminished, leaving a deep-seated sense of dissatisfaction that had quietly accompanied her every step of the way.

People seek various escapes from such emotions. They consult therapists, she mused, frowning at the thought. Others turn to drugs, some legally prescribed by therapists, or become engulfed in sexual experimentation. None of these were her path. A few throw themselves into excessive work. She smiled slightly; work was her chosen escape. Despite her strong will, she knew this couldn't be a long-term solution. Deep down, she was aware that true happiness had graced her life only in fleeting moments: during her college years studying art, and at the beginning of her relationship with Nick. She had left the former behind when she moved away from her hometown. As for the latter, she remained uncertain. Was it easy to acknowledge that someone had become as essential as air to her? Perhaps it would be wiser to walk away now, while she still had the strength to breathe on her own?

She was wary of promises. They are made by everyone, yet, unfortunately, often prove empty. She could still feel her mother's comforting hands and hear her assurances that her father would surely visit. She remembered Emily's words at graduation, promising to be there for her because friends are the family we choose for ourselves. The declarations of her first love, claiming he could never love another, echoed in her memory. All of them had broken their promises. Perhaps, she mused, she had brought it upon herself. As a young girl, she believed improving herself would make her father notice her and return to her life. But she didn't — couldn't — change enough. Yet, that wasn't the cruelest realization. It was her lack of emotional readiness to face such abandonment again. In moments like these, only faith in something greater provides solace. Some turn to God, others to nature, or even look within themselves. She had believed in none of these. And she didn't have much faith in herself either. Maybe that was her main problem.

A phone call interrupted Sophie's reflections. It was from Emily, whose voice came through on the voicemail: "Send me your address, I'll be there soon." Soon after, Emily entered the café.

"My baby," she exclaimed, embracing Sophie tightly. "Happy Birthday! I've missed you more than you can imagine," she said, planting a kiss on Sophie's forehead.

Emily was the same as ever: a wild mane of red hair, a sprinkle of freckles, and those mischievous green eyes, though now there was a newfound calm about her.

"Why haven't you been in touch much this year?" Sophie asked with a hint of sadness, not in the mood to play the part of the jubilant birthday girl.

"I didn't want to intrude on your new life, your relationship," Emily explained.

"That's silly; I don't just drop family... Well, except when they drop me," Sophie said, managing a half-smile.

"Looks like you're gearing up for the day," Emily remarked, diving into her bag to retrieve a small jewelry box. "I know the tradition is to wait... blah blah blah. Just open it!"

Inside the box were two heart-shaped pendants, one attached to a gold chain.

"This one's for me," Emily said, picking up one of the hearts, "and this one's for you."

Sophie smiled, feeling tears welling up.

"I haven't forgotten our promise to always be there for each other. I meant every word, even if it seemed like I had left you behind. My adventure abroad wasn't what I hoped for, but it doesn't change anything between us," she said, giving Sophie's hand a reassuring squeeze.

"Are you happy here?" Sophie asked.

"Yes, this is home," Emily replied with a shrug.

"Then, I'm happy too," Sophie responded with a warm smile. "Did they send you to distract me while they get the surprise party ready?"

Emily chuckled. "What do you need? A drink? A one-way ticket out of the country?"

"I'll take it all."

"Remember my birthday party in freshman year? I thought that hangover was the end of me," Emily laughed, running her fingers through her hair. "Yet, here we are!"

Emily had a crucial task: to keep Sophie out until at least seven o'clock. She accomplished her mission, and they spent a wonderful time together, reminiscent of old times. Yet, Sophie's anticipation of the party was overshadowed by a sense of unease. Nonetheless, upon their return, they found the house adorned beautifully, with family and friends filling the space. Amidst the sparkle and chatter, Sophie received hugs and compliments on her new dress, aided by a few glasses of champagne that helped her relax.

As conversations and laughter filled the backyard, Sophie slipped inside, hoping for a private moment with Nick.

"I've been looking for you," she murmured, wrapping her arms around his neck.

"I'm beginning to regret throwing this party. I can tell you're not entirely at ease. Just say the word, and we'll leave," he assured her, kissing her hand.

"It's alright. Have you seen the pile of gifts?" Sophie attempted to mask her emotions. "It's not so bad."

"Promise you'll open mine first."

"Does the company you've given me count as a gift?" Sophie teased.

"We will deal with it later. It's more complicated than it seems. But having some capital will ensure I'm not worried about you, no matter what the future holds."

Their eyes locked, and Sophie struggled to find words that felt trivial in comparison to her emotions.

"Whatever happens, I want to be with you."

Nick's breath caught as sudden dizziness overcame him. He forgot their surroundings, unable to tear his gaze from her. Then, a sheen of sweat broke out on his forehead. Damn it, even if it's just a corner in the kitchen, does it really matter?

"Sophie!" Kate's voice interrupted from the other room, her footsteps approaching.

"I'll be back soon," Sophie withdrew with hesitation, sensing Nick's reluctance to let her go.

Kate led Sophie back to the party in the backyard, where the guests seemed to be having a better time than the guest of honor herself.

"Dave, be honest, do you still have nightmares about that night?" Rosie chuckled, accepting a glass of champagne from him.

"I've sworn off getting into arguments with you!" he exclaimed, setting aside an empty bottle.

"I stopped arguing too, especially after Kate dared me to seduce our supervisor during our final year," Sophie added, casting a playful glance at Kate.

"But it made for a fantastic story," Kate chimed in, eliciting laughter from the group.

In the living room, Nick found Natalie carefully placing a small, elegantly wrapped gift on a table laden with boxes and bags of various sizes.

"You've brought two gifts?" Nick inquired, observing her actions.

"No, this is from our father," Natalie clarified with a shake of her head. "He sends her birthday presents every year, none of which she opens."

"There must be a whole collection of unopened gifts by now," he remarked, a hint of sorrow in his tone.

"Indeed. Can you believe the restraint your girlfriend shows? To go so many years without allowing herself even the smallest liberty. We could all learn something about self-control from her."

"Perhaps this is an odd question, but..." he began, cautiously choosing his words.

"You're curious why we respond so differently to the same situation?" she finished for him.

"Exactly."

"What might be insignificant to one person can shatter another's life. The human psyche is a complex and often underestimated entity," she explained, her voice becoming more matter-of-fact with each word.

Her attention was captured by the sound of her cell phone. Pulling it from the back pocket of her jeans, she smiled at the newly received message. Nick had been observing her like this for almost a week, ever since their conversation in Scarborough, yet he remained silent. Their attention shifted to the unusual noises coming from the street. It was too distant to discern the words, but it sounded eerily like Sophie's voice.

A latecomer made his entrance to the party, taking a back route familiar only to those well-acquainted with the house. Sophie saw him first through Kate's puzzled look, followed by Rosie's reaction.

"Hello, Dean," Rosie said quietly, inching closer to Dave.

Sophie turned, her face a mask of surprise, to see a man she hadn't laid eyes on for years.

"Hello, everyone," he greeted nonchalantly, brandishing a bouquet of roses. His attempt at looking uncomfortable didn't fool Sophie.

"What are you doing here?" Sophie's voice cut through the silence.

"I came to see you," he said, offering the flowers to her. "Happy Birthday!"

He chose the moment when Sophie was most taken aback to step closer. She accepted the bouquet only to immediately pass it to Kate without a second thought.

"Excuse us," Sophie indicated towards the gate leading to the waterfront, setting off first. With her arms crossed and a scowl on her face, she confronted him. "I highly doubt anyone invited you."

"No one did. I came last year too, but nobody was home," Dean replied casually, gauging Sophie's reaction.

"It's none of your business. You should forget the way here."

"I know how it looks, barging in uninvited. I just wanted to see you."

"I don't want to hear it. Not now, not ever," Sophie declared, turning to face the empty street. "You should leave."

"Oh come on, Soph! It's been ages. You're making too much of this," he began, trying to downplay her reaction.

In retrospect, Sophie believed she had counted to three in her head at that moment, although she wasn't certain. Something inside her snapped, echoing loudly in her ears.

"Get out of my house!" she yelled, her voice breaking free. "And take everyone with you! I don't care what you have to say. Just leave!"

Her last word was a scream. That was the scene Nick and Natalie encountered as they emerged onto the front porch. Natalie looked on, her expression tinged with sadness but not a surprise, and before stepping back inside, she offered Nick a consoling pat on the shoulder.

Draped in a trench coat over her dress, Sophie took to the streets for a walk. She knew this place intimately, allowing her to wander without distraction, lost in thought. She wanted this day to end as soon as possible, eagerly awaiting midnight when she could wash this day off and forget about it. Balancing on the curb, she walked until her phone disrupted the silence — it was Natalie. Reluctantly, Sophie answered.

"Natalie, I'll be back shortly," she said, her voice laden with fatigue.

"Wait, it's not about that, Sophie," came Natalie's voice, uncharacteristically shaky. "Dad's been hospitalized. I don't know the details. I'm heading there now. Will you come with me?"

Sophie, speechless, nodded despite knowing Natalie couldn't see her.

"Yes, I'm coming."

Upon her return, the house had transformed. The celebratory air had vanished, replaced by the confused milling of guests unsure of their next steps. Nick offered his support, but Sophie urged him to help disperse the guests instead.

"You'd be a great help by escorting everyone out," she rushed, thanking him with a quick kiss on the cheek. "Sorry for that."

Margaret, the pillar of calm in the chaos, swiftly prepared her daughters to leave. Standing at the door, she urged them to hurry. At the hospital, Margaret disappeared into a restricted area while Natalie busied herself at the reception desk, completing forms. Sophie, bewildered, watched without comprehending the details supplied by her sister.

The hospital's chaos enveloped her — crowds of people, medical staff, and the newly arrived — overwhelming her senses. It was only after a moment that the distinct hospital smell hit her: a mix of stifling air and sharp medicinal odors. The sight of the long, brightly lit corridor made her dizzy, and she gripped the counter for support, her face draining of color.

"The fifth floor, let's go," Natalie announced, after submitting the paperwork and catching her sister's distressed state.

Sophie shook her head, stepping back. "I can't, I'm sorry," she murmured.

Natalie paused at her words, then nodded and walked away.

43

THAT NIGHT, SOPHIE DIDN'T RETURN HOME. SHE EXITED THE hospital, the cold air reviving her senses and anchoring her to consciousness. Despite the chill, she found solace in the cold, sitting on a bench across from the hospital's main entrance, waiting for either her mother or sister. She didn't feel the tears running down her cheeks until she touched her wet face. Tear streaks and black mascara clung to her fingers. The one step she needed to take was unbearable, driving her to the brink. Inside, she burned with an agony that threatened to consume her, yet she remained immobile, fearing she wouldn't survive the night.

Hours later, Margaret emerged. Upon seeing Sophie, she hugged her without a word.

"He's in the ICU. We're hoping for improvement in the next few days," she said, her tone clinical yet hopeful. "Natalie's staying with him tonight."

Sophie managed only a few hours of sleep upon returning home but woke up feeling broken. Nick brought her coffee and sat next to her on the bed.

"I didn't even see him," Sophie confessed, her gaze distant.

"It's okay. You need time," Nick replied.

"I'm afraid time is what we lack," she shook her head, "Perhaps, this isn't what you expected from someone you wanted to share your life with."

Nick took a moment before responding, "Frankly, I've encountered more surprises here than I ever anticipated. You've shared so little of your past. The emotions I saw yesterday were unlike any I've witnessed in you," his voice carried a thoughtful, distant quality, as he continued to process the events of the previous night.

"Nick, listen. There are things I never really dealt with. Right now, returning home, I'm feeling this tangled knot of emotions inside me that I once sealed away behind a door marked 'do not enter,' "she said, placing her hand on her chest as if to ease her breathing. "I can't just leave now. I don't know how I'll sort this out, or if I ever will. All I know is that I love you. And I don't want to hurt you. That's why I have to stay and discover who this girl was, the one who ran away all those years ago."

Nick nodded, his expression unreadable.

"It seems like the right thing to do," he said, though his certainty waned.

His gaze was distant, and a heavy silence fell between them, filled with detachment and emptiness. That night, Nick was haunted by memories of his own family's tragedies. He recalled the day of the accident when his mother had died, followed by his little brother, who had lingered in the ICU for a week. He dreamed of having one more chance to see them, to say a few words. He felt utterly drained.

"I'll return to New York. I believe I can be of more use there. But you know I'll fly back if you need me."

"Even now?" Sophie asked, tears welling up again.

"You don't understand the most important thing. I fell in love with you the moment I saw you in that bar, even before I heard your voice."

Nick kissed her forehead and left the room. He flew back that evening, enduring six hours of sleepless introspection. Somewhere over the Atlantic, a disturbing thought struck him. Perhaps he was repeating the narrative of his first marriage, only this time, he was in his ex-wife's shoes — loving someone who could not love him back strongly enough to let it shape their future. Nausea overwhelmed him. It seemed like an ironic twist of fate, reminiscent of Diana. Did she also feel life slowly losing its meaning? He wondered. This might sound obsessive. No one intentionally makes another person the center of their life. But it's impossible to love someone your entire life without creating an indissoluble bond between love and life's purpose.

44

A WEEK HAD PASSED SINCE SOPHIE'S BIRTHDAY, AND SHE AND Natalie had been staying at their parents' house the entire time. Natalie dedicated her days to their father's care at the hospital. He had awakened but was still in a precarious state. Despite the doctors' optimistic predictions, Natalie's concern lingered. With her departure for Berlin imminent, she faced the reality of leaving her family and returning to work.

Sophie continued to avoid visiting her father, sinking deeper into depression with each passing day. Her family, choosing not to intrude, gave her space. She occasionally asked Natalie about their father's condition but otherwise remained passive. For the first time, Natalie decided to respect her sister's boundaries, not probing into what had transpired with Nick. Her only request was a ride to the airport.

They drove in silence. When it was time to part ways, Natalie hugged her sister, then paused and turned back before leaving.

"You know, it's heartbreaking to see you like this. You're beautiful, strong, smart, and talented. Despite having all that, you don't see your own worth. Maybe that's why you struggle to believe Nick truly loves you. You can't see the value you have in his eyes. Yet, you clearly recognize how people like Dean see you — as nothing."

Without waiting for a response, Natalie made her way to Heathrow Airport's main entrance. She quickly went through check-in and security, then settled in the waiting area, her mood somber. The uncertainty of her father's condition loomed large as she considered the remaining months on her contract. Lost in thought, she aimlessly scrolled through her phone, pausing at a chat with Mike and noting his silence to her last message. The impulse to call him was irresistible, and she gave in. Mike's voice, quieter and more restrained than usual, greeted her after a few rings, hinting at unspoken concerns. As Natalie broached the topic of her upcoming work trip to New York, Mike interjected.

"Natalie, what are you doing? I'm sorry, but we can't continue like this. We can't just be friends, and I can't be your fallback when you have doubts — and you are doubting. You said you were at peace with your choice, so stay true to that. Listen, I'm sure you'll find happiness, whatever that may be. You'll find someone who sees you as their world, someone ready to make the sacrifices you need. But I'm not that person. I can't change to that extent, nor do I want to change you. You taught me the importance of choosing oneself, a lesson I've come to understand deeply."

Natalie listened in silence.

"You're right. I'm sorry, I never wanted to hurt you. When I asked Nick about you, it made me realize how much I miss talking to you," her voice cracked, "But you're right. We shouldn't speak anymore."

With a brief farewell, she ended the call. The exchange felt less like an argument and more as if she'd dialed the wrong number. Natalie pondered Mike's words — was she indeed doubting her own choices? For once, she found herself at a loss for an answer. She had always championed the virtue of self-reflection to those around her, urging her sister and others to confront their deepest feelings. Yet, she had neglected to apply the same principle to herself. The realization that she might have turned away someone genuinely significant was chilling. Despite their divergent paths, the current moment brought no comfort.

Her gaze shifted to the departure board, noting a delay in her flight. Exhaling deeply, she settled back into her seat, confronting the necessity of a personal hiatus. It was time for introspection, to reevaluate her priorities and desires that may have evolved over time. She knew there was only one way to achieve this. Picking up her phone, she began by uninstalling all the dating apps and deleting meaningless contacts from her address book. The path ahead required embracing temporary solitude.

The day unfurled before them, seemingly infinite, as if time itself had paused, adding hours to the clock that ticked unnoticed. Returning home, Sophie tried to immerse herself in work but found herself only able to stare blankly at her laptop screen. Everything that had once held meaning now seemed utterly trivial. Closing the laptop, she retreated to her room. There, on a corner table, lay wrapped birthday gifts she had yet to open. Approaching them, she speculated about which might be from Nick. They hadn't communicated at all during the whole week. Each day, she faced the daunting blankness of an unsent text message, unable to muster the will to type. Her thoughts ran in circles, devoid of emotion, leaving her wondering when she'd find the strength to break this cycle of paralysis and take action.

With a sigh, Sophie reached for a flat package, its rough craft paper different from the rest. Tearing it open, she discovered a book and paused, processing what it was. A flicker of distant emotions stirred within her, like lights dimly flashing in the darkness. The inscription on the first page read, 'For Sophie, without whom this book would never have been finished.' Flipping through the pages, she struggled to believe what she saw, as memories of a night spent in an attic bedroom in London overwhelmed her. It felt like an adrenaline shock to her weary consciousness, a needed jolt to a heart that had been still for too long.

Overcome with emotion, Sophie covered her face with her hands, tears streaming uncontrollably. What happened next blurred into obscurity, her mind unable to piece together the events that followed.

45

DUSK DRAPED THE CITY AS SOPHIE MADE HER WAY TO THE HOSPITAL, knowing it was likely Margaret's break time. She purchased her favorite latte and suggested they take a walk together.

Margaret had always shown patience with her younger daughter. Whether it was through unconditional love or a spiritual bond, she never forced Sophie into anything. She shielded her from traumatic experiences and softened the impact of the inevitable ones. Even now, she didn't press Sophie to see her father for the first time in twenty-two years, for better or worse.

"Mom, I wanted to ask," Sophie hesitated, "Why didn't you ever tell us what happened between you and Dad?"

Margaret appeared taken aback. "Darling, when you were young, you didn't need to know about such things. And when you grew up, you never asked. Natalie found her own understanding. You, however, remained silent and lived life on your own terms."

"Yes, but it turned him into an enemy for me," Sophie said, with her eyes on the ground.

"Sophie, we all face various traumas, most of them from our childhood. But it's up to us to confront them, not our parents. They do what they can. You'll come to understand this in time."

Sophie nodded, yet it wasn't enough for her.

"Regardless, you've managed well," Margaret reassured her, "You've become strong and determined. Just look at you," she added, her voice laced with pride as she regarded her daughter. "Besides, you've found your person. You and Nick are a wonderful couple."

"I'm not so sure... I think it's over. It feels like I've ruined everything," Sophie confessed with a sigh.

"In what way?"

"By being myself, I guess. Besides, he would have left eventually, just like everyone else."

Margaret stopped and studied Sophie closely, her expression one of deep concern. She embraced her tightly as if comforting a small child.

"Sophie, your father left us when you were only two. It wasn't your fault. You shouldn't let your life be defined by that," she said, holding her close.

"I know. But it's hard," Sophie admitted, her voice breaking.

"You can overcome this. Only you have the power to change your path. You need to move forward and live the happy life you deserve. Do you understand? Chase what you truly desire, for your own sake," Margaret urged, gently shaking her daughter's shoulders to emphasize her point, looking into her tear-filled eyes. Sophie nodded, wiping away her tears.

Margaret returned to her evening shift, leaving Sophie in a somewhat calmer state. She found herself sitting outside the hospital's main entrance, much like she had a week earlier, unsure of how much time passed before she approached the reception desk.

"Sophie Lind. I'm here to visit Edward Lind."

"And your relationship to him?"

"His daughter."

"We have records of his daughter visiting since his admission."

"I'm his younger daughter."

Sophie made her way to the fifth floor, hesitating at the door of the right room. Unsure of what to expect, taking that final step felt immensely challenging. In that moment, the urge to turn around and leave was overpowering. She could easily muster a multitude of reasons why she shouldn't proceed, convincing herself it was a bad idea. Yet, her internal debate raged on until she chose to silence the endless weighing of pros and cons. By halting her internal dialogue, she gathered the strength for that final step.

Quietly, she opened the door and entered a small room. A man lay on the bed, surrounded by an array of tubes and wires, more than seemed to belong to his body. He was asleep, his heartbeat steady on the monitor.

Taking a seat, Sophie allowed herself a moment to take it all in. She was six years old the last time she saw her father, on her birthday, just before he left. He wasn't entirely sober then. She remembered his black leather jacket and the lines of his face, features that had blurred over the years. Now, she wondered if he had always been this frail, his hair so rapidly grayed. Before her lay a stranger, vastly different from the figure that had lingered in her memories.

His breathing was labored, passing through the tube.

"Am I not dead yet?" His voice was frail, yet carried a detectable edge of sarcasm.

"Doesn't look like it."

"I hope I don't end up back in this damn hospital after death. I didn't expect you to come."

"Miracles happen, even to us," Sophie said with a faint smile.

"Thank you."

"You're welcome."

A silence fell between them, during which it seemed he was mustering the strength to express long-held sentiments.

"Sophie, I won't have enough time to say everything I should. Even if this damn liver starts improving now, I don't have much time left. I've been absent all these years, though I should have been there. I can't imagine how hard it is to forgive a stranger, but please, forgive me."

"I'll try," her voice was soft, almost distant.

"That would make me happy."

"You know, forgiveness won't come instantly. We haven't spoken our whole lives. It's not just your apologies I need, but answers."

"Do you really think I have them?" He attempted a smile, but it barely formed.

"Answers to why you left us, why you missed our birthdays, Christmas, Easter. Why didn't you love us? Why was I insignificant in your life?"

He listened silently before responding, his voice heavy with the weight of a lifetime's regret.

"I know it's hard to believe, but you are everything to me. It took time, but I came to realize the pain I caused. And nothing can ever compensate for that. A parent should be with their child. I realized this too late, probably around the time I began to confront my addiction. I joined a support group and discovered my story wasn't unique. There were plenty of daft sods like me. Hearing their stories, I saw my own life from the outside. That's when I started to regret missing out on life's best moments with you and your sister. I tried to reconnect, but you didn't want it. I understood you had every right to your anger, and I deserved it."

He fell silent again, struggling to speak as his breath grew short, but desperately trying to gather the strength to continue.

"My entire life has been a battle with addiction. My first steps towards overcoming it were inspired by you."

Sophie raised her head, looking intently at her father. She had not anticipated such an admission and struggled to grasp its full meaning.

"You were my beacon of hope. You and Natalie. I told myself I had to be strong for you both. It should have been that way from the start. And I kept fighting, motivated by the thought of what you two were enduring. Natalie has kept me informed about your successes over the years. You can't imagine how proud I was. I lived your life, Sophie, in my own way, though you were unaware."

"I always thought you didn't care about me."

"You and your sister mean everything to me."

He quieted down, and Sophie noticed his pulse slow as he began to drift off to sleep. She stood, leaning over to whisper, "I'll come back tomorrow."

In the corner, his belongings were strewn about. She moved towards them, noticing a phone on top of his bag. Gently, she activated the screen, revealing a screensaver of her and Natalie as young children. She picked up his hoodie from the chair and left the room. Walking slowly down the corridor, she donned the hoodie and wiped the tears from her cheeks.

46

THAT NIGHT, SHE ROAMED THE CITY FOR HOURS. THE RINGING IN her ears was overwhelming, as was the realization of her own folly. She reflected on how this conversation could have happened a month, a year, or even five years earlier. Yet, she had persisted in living with a lie that slowly consumed her. Had she never taken that step, her life might have continued as a futile struggle against herself, marked by pain and attempts to improve — not out of self-love, but from a belief that she was fundamentally flawed. Over time, this belief, initially her father's internalized voice, had morphed into her own.

The truth she discovered that day was starkly different from the illusions she had harbored. It turned out that all she needed to do was to begin asking questions, a seemingly simple action that felt insurmountable to someone crippled by self-doubt. The fear of yet another disappointment could trap one in a cycle of feeling worthless, unable to see a way forward. She pondered, how much do we lose by not confronting our deepest fears? What decisions do we make while trapped in a vortex of our illusions and suffering? She didn't have all the answers, but she had uncovered a fundamental truth that shifted her entire perspective.

Returning home, Sophie found herself wide awake, her body buzzing with energy. She was eager to share her revelations with someone. Glancing at the clock, it was eleven at night in New York. She knew Nick would answer her call regardless of the hour, but she hesitated, wondering if he would even want to hear from her. The recollection of her harsh words to him tightened her chest, and tears threatened to overwhelm her. She was tormented by the thought that she might never be with the one she loved — loved with every fiber of her being. Only now did she acknowledge that throughout their relationship, she had been constantly battling the fear of disappointment. She had never let her guard down, even for a moment, and had unjustly attributed traits to him that he never exhibited. She concocted endings to their story that no one else had imagined. In the end, she realized she had fulfilled her own bleak predictions with flying colors.

After calming herself slightly, Sophie opened his book. It was a novel. Within a few pages, she recognized his distinctive style. His rich voice and compelling diction seemed to resonate in her head, no audiobook necessary. As she read, she was convinced of his incredible talent, certain that her admiration wasn't merely a result of infatuation. The novel was engrossing, keeping her hooked page after page. By the time she looked up, dawn was breaking outside.

In the evening she visited her father again. He was awake and greeted her as soon as she closed the door behind her.

"I didn't expect to see you so soon..."

Sophie sat in a chair by the bed and placed the book on her lap.

"How are you feeling?" She asked.

"When you're breathing through a tube, the main focus is just to keep breathing," he responded with sarcasm, though his tone didn't quite convey it. "What's that you've brought?" He nodded toward the book.

"It's a book written by someone I love."

"Ah, I seem to have stumbled upon a delicate subject. Is he a writer?"

"No, but he works in publishing. This is his only unpublished book. I hope that will change soon."

"I can hear the adoration in your voice, undeniable. What's his name?"

"Nick."

"I hope things are okay between you and Nick," he said, attempting to clear his throat but emitting a weak moan instead.

"Hardly. He's gone back to New York, and I don't know if we'll ever see each other again."

"What happened, if it's alright to ask?"

"I hurt him deeply, saying things he didn't deserve. He gave me everything, and all I could focus on were my fears of being rejected."

"We all fear that especially once we've experienced love."

"We were together for just a year. It might have been the best year of my life. He showed me that a relationship could be full of love and care, not mental abuse and manipulation. It was all new to me, and frankly, it scared me. I don't know how to love like a woman."

"What do you mean by that?"

"I've always approached love and relationships in what's considered a traditionally masculine way. I sought approval, planned for the future, attempted to rescue, and did everything in my power to sustain the relationship. In other words, I used to love like men do. After facing yet another disappointment and ending things with my ex, I reverted to this masculine approach, channeling my focus into business, setting goals, and pursuing financial success. I don't know how Nick managed to fall in love with me."

"I'm certain he wasn't the only one, but perhaps he was the only one brave enough to win your heart," he sighed, pausing briefly. "So, it sounds like a lot is up to you now."

"What do you mean?"

"Don't you think it's unlikely a few harsh words could completely destroy someone's feelings? I suspect he's suffering just as much as you are right now, sitting here."

Sophie reflected on his words. She had always categorized her actions as right or wrong. If she made a mistake, she believed she deserved punishment. Could it be possible to allow herself a second chance?

"Could you read to me?" he asked, his voice faint.

As Sophie read the next chapter, she couldn't help but notice how the main character reminded her of Nick's mother. Though she had never met her, from what she had heard, she was a woman with a kind heart, perceptive and wise, embodying femininity. Sophie sighed; she had always envied such women, feeling quite different from them. Yet, from all she had learned through books, films, and the experiences of others, she understood that the essence of womanhood lies in kindness — the ability to forgive. And often, that kindness starts with forgiving oneself.

Sophie paused, looking at her father. He wasn't asleep but listening with his eyes closed.

"If I leave town for a little while, do you promise to get better in the meantime?"

"I will," he answered.

"You made a promise, remember that."

"It's clever how from one of my actions, you've made it impossible for any of us to disappoint you... A true woman," he said, managing a faint smile.

"I see you're up for some humor today," she chuckled in response.

47

As Sophie packed her travel bag, her thoughts meandered through the familiar streets of New York, pondering where to begin. The vacation had turned out to be unforgettable. A smile crossed her face as she contemplated the time it would take to rebuild herself, piece by piece. Yet, what surprised her most were her feelings. The weight that had burdened her for much of her life had lifted, leaving her chest feeling lighter. Despite losing sleep, skipping meals, and enduring daily upheavals, her energy surged. Breathing felt easier, although her relentless thoughts kept her from fully grasping everything just yet.

Glancing at the calendar, she noted it was Tuesday — a fitting day for another significant encounter.

The office windows offered a view of Goldsmiths' serene inner courtyard. Behind a substantial dark wooden desk, an elderly man wearing glasses with round, thin frames was engrossed in reading and annotating handwritten sheets of paper. Beside a stack of papers sat a cup of tea on a delicate saucer, from which he occasionally sipped with his left hand.

Soft footsteps approached the door, followed by the sound of paper sliding across the floor. An envelope had been pushed halfway through under the door. The man's frown deepened the wrinkles on his forehead as he reluctantly rose, approached the door, and retrieved the envelope. His movements were labored as he unfolded the paper and quietly read a few lines: 'Professor Adams, I won't be able to attend your class today. I'll prepare an essay for the next one. Sophie'.

A smile crossed his face as he nodded in acknowledgment. Upon opening the door, he found his former student smiling back at him. Despite her attempts to mask her emotions, Sophie's feelings were evident in her expression.

"Sophie," Professor Henry Adams said, stepping aside and holding the door open. "Please, come in."

She entered the office, taking in the familiar setting.

"I knew I'd find you here, Professor… You've rearranged the desk."

"Yes, it allows more light in. I can work longer without needing the overhead lamp. Please, take a seat; I'll make us some tea."

He moved to a small table in the corner, equipped with a kettle and kitchenware, while Sophie settled into an old armchair that seemed as though it belonged to the Victorian era.

"I just love coming here. It feels like you'll always be here, no matter when I visit."

"You know that's not the case."

"I know, but I prefer not to think about it."

"So, unable to find any utopian concepts in fine art, you decided to recreate them in real life?"

"I haven't had much success with that, Professor," Sophie replied with a subdued smile. "Your lectures on the history of fine art were my utopia. I miss those days."

"I've heard you've embarked on a significant project in New York?"

"Yes, an opportunity presented itself."

"That's wonderful. I never doubted it."

"What do you mean?"

"That opportunities would find you."

"Really?"

"Absolutely. You've always been passionate about learning, driven by curiosity, and committed to seeing things through to completion."

Professor Adams set a tray with two tea cups and a small porcelain teapot filled with milk on the table. After several years abroad, Sophie had drifted away from the customs of her homeland, which now enchanted her anew.

"I wanted to ask how you've been," Sophie said, sparking a warm smile from the professor, who seemed to meld into his chair comfortably.

"I'm still doing well, though they've assigned me second-year students, for some reason," he shared, eliciting a soft, surprised murmur from Sophie. "Unfortunately, they're not particularly interested in the origins and purposes of abstractionism during wartime. They're more preoccupied with each other."

"It's amusing, I suppose. And I hope the administration realizes what a missed opportunity it is for the master's students not to learn from you. While the second-years might have heard of Malevich's 'Black Square,' their grasp of why people seek to escape the burdens of reality will probably mature much later."

"When you joined my class at twenty-two, your distinctiveness was already apparent," he said, lifting his teacup with an attentive gaze. "You were an outstanding student. I relished your presentations and essays, guiding you toward new insights. Yet, the more I engaged with you, the more concerned I became."

"Why were you concerned?" she inquired.

"You harbored deep internal conflicts," he explained with a shrug. "Such individuals often face diverse destinies. You always protected a profound pain, occasionally betrayed by your eyes," he sighed. "I awaited the emergence of your artistic passion, which never came. Eventually, I understood that your focus lay in interacting with people.

You pursued this with such dedication and passion, driven by a quest for justice," he said, shaking his head.

"You could see right through us, couldn't you?"

"Indeed. By the age of sixty-eight, I've learned to predict someone's future through their art," he chuckled.

"Perhaps that's why I've never painted. I'm scared to confront what's ahead," she said, her eyes sparkling. "I'm not prepared to embrace the life I deserve."

Sophie remembered the times when she used to come here as a student, cherishing the discussions with Professor Adams that helped her escape her troubles.

"I have something for you," Professor Adams said, reaching for a long roll of thick paper which he handed to Sophie. Unfolding it, she discovered a reproduction of a painting by Edgar Degas, part of his renowned series featuring ballet dancers.

"This is a reproduction by Edmund Laswell. Observe how exquisitely he captured the reflection of the golden hues. I thought it would appeal to you," he said.

"How could anyone not appreciate Degas? Thank you, Professor Adams," Sophie responded, her eyes wide with admiration as she studied the reproduction.

"People like you, my dear, belong in the art world," he continued, clearing his throat. "Not because of any diploma, but due to your innate connection and sensitivity to art. It transcends mere employment or financial gain; it's intrinsic to your being."

Listening, Sophie felt a pang of melancholy.

"I do love it. Perhaps I've simply grown too comfortable with my current path," she conceded.

"In the business realm, there's no shortage of talent, with or without your contribution," Professor Adams remarked. "A friend of mine, serving as a judge for your advertising competition…"

"Best Brands," Sophie chimed in, smiling, fully aware of the professor's critical view of such entities and the marketing field at large.

"Yes, exactly. He mentioned that an advertising agency founded by one of my students clinched a top award," he noted, his lips pressed together as he nodded with raised eyebrows. "I wasn't taken aback. Approaching any endeavor as an art form resonates with people. Yet, you possess all the qualities to make a significant impact in the art world," he emphasized, gesturing expressively.

Sophie looked down. "You're right, of course. I'll ponder over your advice. It's something I genuinely desire," she confessed, a shade of embarrassment in her voice.

"Are you married?" he inquired, glancing at her hands for a ring.

"No," she answered, suddenly feeling the room grow stifling.

"It doesn't matter. Let a potential spouse concern themselves with the pursuit of wealth," he suggested gruffly. "Why immerse yourself in that race?"

Sophie offered a sweet smile.

"Ah, and I've just recalled," Professor Adams said, eyeing the open notebook before him. "I'm lecturing the second-years tomorrow. Do drop by; they could benefit from your insight. I'm afraid they're growing a bit tired of me," he admitted with a chuckle, stroking his chin.

48

THE NEXT MORNING, SOPHIE MADE HER WAY BACK TO THE university to attend Professor Adams' lecture. Stepping into the familiar lecture hall, she chose a seat in the front row, basking in the fleeting return to a place she once knew well. Professor Adams was serious when he suggested the day before that she might take over his class.

"Given your somewhat weary looks, it seems the anticipation of my lecture has indeed been a source of excitement," Professor said with a chuckle, scanning the room. "Today, however, I bring a pleasant surprise. Since we are fortunate to have one of my most accomplished former students among us, I thought you might appreciate the chance to ask her a few questions. Please welcome Miss Lind," he announced, his smile widening with genuine warmth.

He then left the room, entrusting Sophie to the eager eyes of about fifty students.

"Alright, I'm not exactly sure what you'd find intriguing to discuss, so let's make this interactive," she began, perching herself on the edge of the desk and crossing her legs. "Feel free to ask anything that comes to mind."

"Do you have a boyfriend?" queried a voice from the back, eliciting laughter from the crowd.

"I'll entertain your question if you can tell me which early English painter's work was associated with the abstract expressionist movement," she countered.

"Paul Nash," came the reply.

"Paul Nash was a surrealist, not an abstract expressionist. However, Joseph Turner's 'Snowstorm' was reinterpreted in the style of abstract expressionism, a full forty years post its original creation," Sophie corrected with a smirk. "See, you're not destined to discover the truth."

As her gaze wandered over the students, a wave of nostalgia hit her. The same warm morning sunlight filtered through the western windows, casting playful shadows on the diligent note-takers on the lecture hall's left side, reminding her how little had changed.

"I'm not sure what drew you to this faculty, but you must realize that your opportunity to immerse yourself in the world of knowledge and science, as imagined by the greatest minds, is fleeting," Sophie started. "The reality is often starkly different. This discrepancy is precisely why true artists have historically been dissenters — those who challenged the prevailing order from their studios. They reimagined the world on their canvases, making it more beautiful, like the Impressionists, or highlighting its ugliness to draw attention to certain issues or express dissent, like the Expressionists. In either case, it was their form of resistance. If you share this drive, the hardest part will be... not surrendering to defeat."

She paused, reflecting. What had she accomplished in her own battle against the disagreeable aspects of the world? It seemed her efforts had mainly assisted corporations in amassing greater wealth. Even the Freeport project was just a tool for the affluent to safeguard and enhance their fortunes. She had wanted to initiate change there, and now, the chance was hers. The key was to persist.

"Perhaps you're not contemplating this deeply at the moment. Just remember, there will come a time when it's crucial for you not to surrender."

A thoughtful silence filled the room before curiosity gradually took over, leading to questions about her student days, internships, and various experiences.

Sophie stepped out of the building and paused on the broad stone steps, her gaze wandering. Dean stood before her, evidently having waited for some time. She wondered why such an unpleasant encounter had to mar such a beautiful day. Yet, surprisingly, she found herself free from the usual anxiety and fear that Dean's presence often stirred.

"Who told you I was here?" she asked, her brow furrowing.

"I called Kate."

"And here I was, ready to blame Natalie."

"Can we talk?"

Sophie hesitated, then gave a slow nod. Together, they made their way to the university's backyard, a place Sophie cherished deeply. It was here that she saw echoes of her younger self, surrounded by friends and the vibrancy of student life. Were those days truly as idyllic as she remembered? A glance at Dean reminded her that not everything had been perfect.

"I'm listening," she stated, focusing on the space before them as they settled onto a bench.

"I missed you," Dean confessed, turning to face her.

"Really?" Sophie's response was measured, her gaze fixed elsewhere. "Is that why you're here?"

"Isn't that reason enough?"

"So, you're done with whatever it was, and now you remember you haven't disrupted my life in a while?" Sophie's gaze met his briefly.

"Why do you say things like that?"

"You played a part in ruining my engagement," she exhaled deeply. "Although, you weren't the sole issue that night."

Sophie couldn't confirm if Nick had planned to propose that night, but the feeling had been unmistakable before he returned to New York.

"Do you love him?" His voice sounded quieter.

"It's none of your concern."

"Sophie, I've known you since you were eighteen. I understand you more than you think. And I can always tell when you're not being honest with yourself."

"Oh, what rot... You believe you know me? The truth is, in your world, there's no room for anyone but yourself."

"I concede I've made many mistakes," he sought her gaze. "But I'm here, ready to move forward with you. Doesn't a decade of back and forth signify that fate insists on pushing us together, no matter the nature of our bond?"

Sophie felt her head spinning, a ringing echoing in her ears as the sounds of the outside world faded into oblivion. She could sense her pulse quickening. In the past, this sensation had terrified her; now, it served as a shield, isolating her from the external chaos and giving her the space to introspect. She mulled over Dean's words repeatedly. But what if none of that mattered? It wasn't about destiny; it was about choice. The most harrowing realization hit her: she had always had the power of choice, yet she had consistently made the wrong ones. She had never truly chosen herself.

The power of choice is our most valuable asset. It shapes the trajectory of our lives. A single step in a new direction can change everything, and the opportunity for that step is always there, even when it seems invisible.

"I met with my father. Do you know what the most terrible insight from our meeting was?" Sophie continued, not waiting for his response. "I used to think that he saw me the same way you do — as just a background noise, a useless addition to his life. But I was wrong. He always loved me," her voice trembled, and tears welled up in her eyes. "It took me twenty-eight years to understand this, and for ten of those years, you made my life a living nightmare."

"Why cling to someone who abandoned you as a child? Now, you've found temporary solace in Nick. But this infatuation will pass... then what? Whereas I," he attempted to take her hand, "have always been there for you."

Sophie withdrew her hand, her mind unclouded by the doubts and anxieties that had once overwhelmed her. Suddenly, she felt lighter.

"Dean, please listen to me," she said, turning to face him. "Because these are my final words to you. I want you to erase me from your life. I wish to forget everything as if it were a bad dream. I'm happy now, regardless of what you think."

Dean hung his head, unaccustomed to such finality from Sophie. His eyes searched for some sign of the familiar.

"No matter what you say, I believe we can work through anything if you still love me..."

"I'm not sure I ever did love you. I wasn't myself with you. It was someone else who loved you, believed in you, and let you do all those awful things," she said firmly. "That girl is gone."

"I loved her."

"Well, the one you loved hated herself and thought she didn't deserve happiness. I wasn't happy with you."

"I'm sorry," he whispered.

Sophie stood, compelled by the urge to be elsewhere — anywhere she genuinely wanted to be. After all, it's never too late to find your way back to where you belong.

"Goodbye, Dean."

She exited the university's main gates without a backward glance, hailed a taxi, and quickly messaged her parents. She apologized for her abrupt departure and promised to return soon. Next, she scrolled through her contacts to find Mike's number.

"Hi, Mike. I need to talk to you."

"Hey, Sof. What's up? This is a pleasant surprise. I'm all ears."

"I'm on my way to the airport and will be in New York tomorrow morning. I need your help. Can you bring Nick to the bar tomorrow night? Say it's for a stand-up show, but don't mention me."

"Got it. Is this something urgent?"

"Extremely," she exhaled deeply.

"I'm on it. Safe travels."

"Thanks! See you tomorrow..." Her voice carried a warmth.

Everything that followed seemed to fast-forward, like pages being swiftly turned. The rush to the airport. Boarding the next flight to New York with just one bag — the same she had carried out that morning. Throughout the six-hour flight, she didn't sleep, and with the seat next to her empty, there was no one to share her story with.

49

SOPHIE FELT AN EXHILARATING RUSH OF EXCITEMENT, A SENSATION she considered unparalleled. Standing in the dimly lit ambiance of the bar where she first met Nick, she had arranged with the manager to close the establishment early. As she caught her reflection in the mirror above the bar counter, Sophie acknowledged her appearance wasn't as glamorous as usual, following the whirlwind of recent events. No elaborate hairstyle, no striking red dress, no flawless makeup adorned her tonight. Yet, those were trivial concerns now. For the first time, her eyes sparkled with a genuine brilliance.

Gathering the scattered candles around the bar, she meticulously lit each one, transforming the space. She marveled at how she and Nick had fatefully met in such a place. What was a man, known for wearing cufflinks engraved with his initials, doing in a bar like this? The realization dawned on her; this was his sanctuary, a place free from familiar faces, where he could immerse himself in writing. With a smile and a shake of her head, Sophie marveled at the serendipity.

Mike was driving, just a few blocks away from the bar, trying to keep Nick entertained with stories, though he was unclear about what was about to unfold. Nick hadn't divulged any details of what had transpired in London. Mike had fulfilled his part by bringing Nick to the bar. Upon entering, they found it empty except for Sophie. Mike gave a beaming smile, winked at Sophie, and clapped Nick on the shoulder.

"I guess you don't need me around, buddy," Mike said before stepping outside.

Nick, taken aback by the unexpected scenario, turned to Sophie. She looked slightly thinner, and the dark circles under her eyes were more noticeable. Dressed simply in jeans and a plain white T-shirt, she was a contrast to her usual self.

"What's happening? When did you get back to New York?" he asked as he moved closer to her.

"This morning," she replied, managing a weak smile.

Both were brimming with words yet remained silent, their gazes locked. Nick, who had missed her daily, was now at a loss for words upon her unexpected appearance.

"I have so much to tell you, but I'll start with this," Sophie began, stepping closer. "Years ago, I was terribly frightened and broken, masking my pain with all my strength. Trust was foreign to me. By my own actions, I crafted a hostile world around me. I'm not sure how much longer I could have endured it. Yet, it seems someone believed I deserved another chance, and that's when I met you... right here in this very spot, without any idea of the fortune that had befallen me. Incapable of love, yet what you offered was nothing but love. Love, coupled with endless patience."

As Nick took her hands, he saw the tears sparkling in her eyes, recalling the moments her eyes would change hue, mirroring fire, sunlight, or rain.

"Please, let me finish," Sophie implored, pausing to breathe deeply. "Your strength helped me face the fears that shadowed my life. I can't thank you enough for that. You've filled me with happiness, teaching me that the most beautiful aspects of this world thrive on love and kindness. As long as one person harbors this light within, everything persists. You opened your heart to me, and now, my only wish is to spend the rest of my days with you, no matter the length," she said, smiling through her tears. "Nick Davidson, will you do me the honor of becoming my husband?"

She retrieved a small box from her pocket, unveiling a delicate white gold ring that seemed modest at first glance. However, inside, there was an engraving that read, "You are my home."

Nick brushed his hand across his face, overwhelmed by a surge of emotions.

"Yes, yes," he whispered, pulling her into an embrace. "I need you more than anything in this world."

He held her tightly, a sigh of relief escaping him. In her journey of self-discovery, Sophie had unknowingly become his salvation, his very breath. Now, he could breathe freely again.

Confronted with such deep emotions, one is faced with a choice: to welcome them, letting them settle in your heart and reveal the essence of all poetry, or to let them pass, never braving that moment when breath fades. To surrender means to lose the chance to pen even a single line in one's lifetime. Nick was thankful he had chosen to embrace these feelings. Through them, he realized that poetry is what truly sustains us, reaching beyond mere words. In the end, while all else may waver, poetry remains, immortalizing our existence.

AFTERWORD

Creating a story from mere thoughts, emotions, and ideas is an immensely fulfilling experience. There is nothing quite as inspiring as bringing characters to life, characters who breathe soul into the narrative. As a debut author, I must admit that publishing my first novel has been one of the most formidable challenges I've faced.

Initially, what you possess is a rough assembly of chapters — your escape and revelation. It's difficult to imagine ever releasing it into the world, shattering the private sanctuary you've built around this narrative. Yet, when the story is complete, each thought of sharing it induces a deep, almost cleansing breath. If you're fortunate, as I have been, the first reader will be someone special. The first person to read *You Are The Journey* was my soulmate and staunchest supporter. Her profound understanding of the narrative spurred me on, providing the inspiration needed to navigate the demanding publishing process.

This journey from start to finish is both energetically and time-consuming. Now, I hold every author in heroic esteem. I extend heartfelt thanks to my family, whose boundless love and patience have been my anchor, and to my initial readers, whose insights have been invaluable.

You Are The Journey is an invitation to dialogue and reflection, a conduit for sharing my beliefs. While it is an emotionally reflective novel, none of the ideas it presents are absolute. Each thought and statement is crafted with a singular purpose: to give readers a moment to pause and reflect — to reassess personal values, accept new ideas, or discard those that no longer resonate. It is about encouraging you to let go of the unnecessary or to finally embark on long-postponed endeavors. Ultimately, this story champions self-love and self-belief. Its mission is to illuminate every soul that encounters it, aiding each reader in finding a unique form of happiness within themselves.

If you possess a printed copy of this book, I encourage you to pass it along as a gift or leave it in a coffee shop on a rainy day for someone else to discover. For those who engage with the book digitally, please respect copyright laws and use it only for personal purposes.

As an author, I am always eager to learn about my readers' thoughts through your comments and feedback.

Thank you for joining me on this journey.

ABOUT THE AUTHOR

A. R. Rêve is a writer and filmmaker based in New York City, whose early fascination with the classics shaped her artistic vision. Enraptured by the works of Charles Dickens, Jane Austen, Ray Bradbury, and F. Scott Fitzgerald, she draws upon their timeless wisdom and transformative storytelling in her own creations.

In her writing, A. R. Rêve tackles complex social issues, delves into emotional intelligence, and examines the psychological intricacies of everyday life. Her narratives are rich in character depth and reflect a profound understanding of the human condition, crafted to challenge and resonate with readers.

As a filmmaker, A. R. Rêve continues to apply her keen insights and empathetic perspective, primarily through the medium of short films. Her cinematic work is an extension of her literary endeavors, seamlessly blending visual storytelling with provocative themes. Each project aims to provoke thought, evoke emotions, and inspire change, consistently challenging the audience to engage deeply with the material.

A. R. Rêve's mission is to create art that not only questions societal norms but also boldly tells truths. Through both words and images, she seeks to ignite discussions, encourage reflection, and disrupt conventional thinking. Her art is an invitation to explore, confront, and appreciate the complex tapestry of human experience.

Printed in Poland
by Amazon Fulfillment
Poland Sp. z o.o., Wrocław

36336610R00188